The window shattered in an explosion of glass.

Through the gap, with a torrential, sliding roar, poured a foaming cataract of water. It was so powerful that it hurled the furniture about and slammed me into the doorjamb.

I kicked up from the floor, swimming hard, and managed to break out into fresh air about a foot below the ceiling. Clinging to the ceiling light for support, I realized that in a second or two the room would be flooded to the top.

I plunged downwards, heading for the shattered window that had to lead outside. *There was something following me, something big and dark and perfectly at home in the underwater grotto that had once been my home.*

I was nearly out of breath, and it was upon me.

I knew I was going to die.

# Tor books by Graham Masterton

*Charnel House*
*Condor*
*Death Dream*
*Death Trance*
*The Devils of D-Day*
*Ikon*
*Mirror*
*Night Plague**
*Night Warriors*
*The Pariah*
*Picture of Evil*
*Sacrifice*
*Scare Care* (editor)
*Solitaire*
*The Sphinx*
*Walkers*
*The Wells of Hell*

## THE MANITOU

*The Manitou*
*Revenge of the Manitou*
*The Djinn*

*forthcoming

# GRAHAM MASTERTON

# THE WELLS OF HELL

A TOM DOHERTY ASSOCIATES BOOK
NEW YORK

THE WELLS OF HELL

Copyright © 1979 by Graham Masterton

A Tor Book
Published by Tom Doherty Associates, Inc.
49 West 24th Street
New York, NY 10010

Cover art by Charles Lang

ISBN: 0-812-52211-7          Canadian ISBN: 0-812-52212-5

First Tor edition: September 1982

Printed in the United States of America

0  9  8  7  6  5  4  3  2

"I think if the Devil doesn't exist, but man has created him, he has created him in his own image and likeness."
— DOSTOYEVSKY

"From his brimstone bed, at break of day,
A walking the Devil is gone,
To look at his snug little farm of the World,
And see how his stock went on."
— SOUTHEY

# 1

It was one of those crisp, cold afternoons in Connecticut when the leaves are rusting off the trees and the sky is as clear and blue as a child's eyes. I came bouncing up the driveway of the Bodines' place in my dusty Country Squire, my eyes screwed up against the fall sunlight that sparkled through the trees, my red baseball cap firmly tugged down and my sheepskin collar firmly pulled up. In the back of the station wagon, all my wrenches and spanners and lengths of pipe banged and jangled, and my faithful cat Shelley sat beside me in the passenger seat, his paws neatly together and his ears shining bright pink.

I pulled up in front of the house and climbed out. I said to Shelley: "You coming?" But he closed his eyes as if he was feigning a headache, and that meant he considered it too damned cold out there, and he'd rather stay where he was and listen to the radio, the lazy s.o.b. I said: "Please yourself," and left him.

I walked through drifts of curled, crunchy leaves to the front verandah. The Bodine house was a big old Victorian place, set on a low hill on a curve of Route 109, between New Milford and Washington Depot. This was quiet, rural country, all trees and tiny hamlets, and now that the tourists and weekenders had all gone back to New York City, it was populated as sparsely as it had been back in colonial days, and everybody was snuggling themselves down for the winter.

Jimmy Bodine was in back, raking leaves. He was a young guy, not more than twenty-five, which made him a whole decade younger than me. He had curly blond hair and buck teeth, and in his plaid lumberjack coat he looked like somebody out of an old Norman Rockwell painting. He said: "Hi, Mason," and leaned on the handle of his rake.

"How are you doing?" I asked him.

"Okay. Pretty raw this morning, ain't it?"

I sniffed the sharp, smoky air. "You betcha. Do you want to go inside?"

"Sure. Alison's got some coffee on."

He set his rake against the back verandah rail, and we went in through the screen door to the kitchen. It was warm and fragrant in there, with copper moulds hanging on an old pine hutch and a cake cooling on every window-ledge. Alison Bodine was just taking out a tray of cinnamon and apple cookies, and I thought to myself that when I died there could be worse ways to go than choking on Alison Bodine's cookies while making love to Raquel Welch on a well-sprung mattress.

Alison Bodine looked older than Jimmy, somehow, but then she'd always been the motherly type. She had dark hair, drawn back in a bun, and a thin friendly face with wide brown eyes. She was real small, one of those tiny women you could never hold around the waist, only round the neck, not without kneeling anyway. She said: "How are you doing, Mason?" and brought down three pottery mugs and poured coffee.

We sat down at the heavy old kitchen table and ate cookies while the pale afternoon light came straining through the windows.

"You're having trouble with the well, then?" I asked them.

Jimmy just managed to catch a piece of cookie that crumbled as he bit it. "That's right," he nodded, collecting fragments. "It's pretty recent. Only about the past two or three days. But I'm worried in case we're going to have trouble with it during the winter, when the ground's hard."

"Well, you're right to call me," I told him. "What's going wrong, exactly?"

"It's not all the time, but every now and then the water's been coming out discoloured. Kind of yellow-greenish. Not a strong colour. Just a tint. And it don't taste of nothing, neither. But it don't look right."

Alison nodded. "I'm kind of hesitant to use it, you know? I've heard all that stuff about seepage and chemical fertilizers getting into the water supply."

"Does it run clear if you leave the faucets open?" I asked them.

Jimmy nodded. "If we leave it running for ten, fifteen minutes."

"And how about residue? Does it leave a ring

around your basin? Is there any sediment in it?"

"No, nothing. The water is just tinted."

I sipped at my coffee. It didn't sound like anything very important to me. There were all kinds of factors that could affect the quality of well water—soil, minerals, seepage—and the only thing that the Bodines really had to worry about was somebody's sewage leaking into the water table. We'd had a pretty wet year, on the whole, and that meant the ground was saturated. When the underground water levels were as high as they were now, they could occasionally flow into a septic system, but the chances of that happening were pretty rare. From what the Bodines were saying, it sounded to me like their water was filtering through some underground minerals or vegetable matter, and that was what was colouring it up.

"The best I can do is take a sample," I told them. "I could have it over to New Milford this evening, and if Dan Kirk does a rush job on it for me, I could let you know by this time tomorrow. It doesn't sound any too serious, though. I remember a couple of years ago, up at Kent, an old fellow turned on his faucet and the water came out the colour of blood. It was only some kind of potassium in the soil, and all we had to do was dig the well a few feet deeper."

Alison gave a vague smile. "Well, that sounds more reassuring. I was worried the water was poisoned."

"You haven't been sick, have you?" I asked her.

"Not at all. None of us have."

"Young Oliver's okay?"

"He's fine. Tough as a truckload of logs."

I finished my coffee, and stood up. "Do you want to lend me a glass jelly jar, something of that kind, so that I can take a sample?"

"Sure thing," said Alison, and brought me one from her cupboard. I stole another cinnamon and apple cookie from the plate and stuffed it into my mouth as I followed her into the scullery. No wonder I was having trouble with my waistline. A fellow could jog three miles before he'd burn off one of those cookies.

"At first I thought it was rust from the pipes," said Jimmy, as we gathered around the sink.

"Oh, did you?" I answered, showering out cookie crumbs.

"It seemed the natural answer," he nodded. "But when it came out the same colour from every faucet, I guessed it was probably something else. And like I said, there's no deposit, no flakes of rust."

I turned on the kitchen faucet and let it run. At first, it came out clear, but after a little while I began to notice a distinct coloration. Nothing startling, not like the blood-coloured water up at Kent, but a pale, unpleasant kind of yellow. Crudely speaking, it looked like piss. I solemnly took a sample in the jelly jar and held it up to the light.

"What do you think?" asked Jimmy.

I shrugged. "Almost nothing right now, except that it looks as if it's some kind of mineral. It's clear enough."

I smelled the water, but it didn't seem to have any particular odour. I passed it around for Alison and Jimmy to smell, too. Jimmy just shrugged, but Alison sniffed it once, and then sniffed it again, and said: "Fish."

"Pardon me?" I asked her.

"Well, maybe I'm crazy," she said, "but it smells to me like fish."

I held it under my nose again and inhaled. "Not that I can detect," I told her. "How about you, Jimmy?"

Jimmy tried again, but he shook his head, too. "I think it's just your imagination, honey. In any case, there ain't going to be any *fish* down our well, now are there?"

I screwed the lid on the jar and tucked it in the pocket of my sheepskin coat. "Whatever it is, Dan Kirk will find it. He once found insecticide that was seeping through eight layers of limestone into a subterranean stream and ending up in someone's drinking water seven miles away. I mean, he's the Sherlock Holmes of $H_2O$."

"And who are you?" asked Alison. "The Scarlet Pimpernel of plumbing?"

I grinned. "Just because I'm difficult to get hold of, that doesn't mean I'm *impossible* to get hold of. I have to work hard, okay? Right now I'm supposed to be putting in new radiators round at the Harrison place. Did you know they're having new radiators?"

"Sarah told me," nodded Alison. "Don't you have any fresh gossip?"

"The Katz boy got kicked out of college, if that's of any interest."

Jimmy raised his eyebrows. "Really? David Katz?"

"I knew that already," said Alison. "Wendy Pitman told me down at the Northville Store."

"The Northville Store," I remarked, as we walked back through the kitchen and out on to the back porch. "That's where they say that if they don't have it, you don't need it, and believe me that's true. Including all the gossip that's fit to whisper."

It was real sharp outside, and I pulled on my baseball cap. The sun had already sunk beyond the rim of the woods, and the tops of the trees were irradiated with orange light. Our breath smoked in the cold, and we rubbed our hands briskly to keep warm. A dog was barking over at the next house.

"I'll call you tomorrow as soon as I know," I told Jimmy. "But from what I can see here, you don't have anything to worry about. You've all drunk the water and you're still walking about and eating cookies, so whatever it is, it can't be that serious."

"Do you want a bag to take home?" asked Alison.

"No, really. I don't want to put on any more weight. I had to crawl along a warm-air duct a couple of weeks ago, and I can tell you that I only just made it. What a way to die, huh? Ducted to death."

Jimmy and Alison walked around the side of the house with me. "At least that's better than drowning," Alison remarked.

"Drowning?" I asked her. "Who said anything about drowning?"

"Ask Jimmy," said Alison. "He's been dreaming about drowning for the past week."

"Maybe you shouldn't fill your bathtub so full,"

I told him.

Jimmy looked embarrassed. "It's nothing. It's just one of those dreams."

"One of what dreams?"

Jimmy turned on Alison. "Why'd you have to go tell him that?" he asked her. "It's a stupid dream, that's all."

"I'm an expert on water dreams," I told him. "Come on, I'm a plumber and I've got myself half a degree in psychology. Who else could interpret a dream about drowning better than me? I'll tell you what your problem is: you have a repressed urge to go down with the *Titanic*, thwarted by the fact that it sank over sixty-five years ago. Or maybe your mother put too much water in your Kool-Aid when you were a kid, and you're suffering from dilution phobia."

Jimmy stuck his hands in the pockets of his lumberjack coat and shrugged. "It's just one of those stupid dreams, that's all. I dream I'm underwater, under some kind of dark water, and I want to get out but I can't."

"Is it a long dream?"

"I don't know. Maybe just a few seconds. But I wake up and I'm cold and sweating. I mean, really cold. And I always have this feeling that I've swallowed gallons and gallons of freezing water."

I walked around the front of my Country Squire and opened the door. Shelley was still sitting there, listening to Dolly Parton, and he gave me a haughty wink. I could have kicked that cat's ass sometimes, the arrogant way he behaved. Sometimes I wondered who was running Mason Perkins, Plumbers & Heating Contractors, me or that goddamned Shelley. I could have kicked his ass.

Jimmy wiped his nose with the back of his hand, and said: "The thing that always gets me is the feeling that the water has no surface. I mean, it isn't the water that scares me so much, it's the fact that it's under the ground, underneath tons and tons of solid rock. So even if I did reach the surface, I couldn't breathe."

I gave him a sympathetic pat on the shoulder. "It looks like you and water ain't been getting along lately. Maybe you've been worried about the well."

"That's what I told him," said Alison.

I climbed into my car and put the window down. "If that's what's worrying you," I told Jimmy, "then I'll make sure I get you these test results just as soon as humanly possible."

"He needs to stop working so hard, that's my opinion," put in Alison. "It could be one of those struggling-to-succeed dreams, couldn't it?"

"Listen," I told him, "I did almost all of an advanced course in psychoanalysis, and we had dreams from ordinary people that would have made your hair go white. What you've been dreaming about is nothing. It's just an anxiety dream. Take a couple of sleeping tablets before you go to bed and you won't ever dream it again."

Jimmy smiled. "Do you charge for medical advice, as well as for plumbing?"

"I charge for everything. How do you think I got so rich?"

I left the Bodine place and gave them a last toot on the horn and a wave when I reached the letter-box. Then I turned west on 109 towards New Milford, switching on the lights to see my way through the clinging dusk. I drove up and down the winding hills and valleys, my Country Squire whirling up leaves behind me as I went.

I was interested in Jimmy Bodine's dream, but I was always suspicious of analysis. That was one of the reasons (apart from a pregnant sophomore) that my college course in Freud and Jung and Est had come to a premature conclusion. Maybe I didn't take life seriously enough. Maybe I wasn't cut out for the couch and the collective unconscious and the role-playing routine. Maybe I was too selfish and didn't particularly want to rescue the world from its phobias and its complexes. Whatever it was, I had quit college halfway through an encounter session, numbed by the self-indulgent dumbness of it, and I had taken a bus home and shaved off my beard, in that order. My mother, a short and kind lady with a strong line in flower-print housecoats, had cried; my father, a taller person but no less kind, had shaken my hand and told me it was about time I got on with something useful. That's when I took up plumbing, and that's what I've been ever since, Mason Perkins, plumber.

I think, to tell you the truth, that I look more like a plumber than a psychiatrist. I'm six-one, with dark wavy hair, and a long thin face, and one of those expressions of constant bafflement that plumbers always have. If I'd taken up psychiatry, I think my patients would have spent most of their time wondering when I was going to bring out my wrench and screw their heads on straight by force.

My manner has always been more bathside than bedside, if you get my drift.

I have been married. It didn't last very long, although she was pretty nice in her way. Her name was Jane and she wanted a neat, neat house in the suburbs, and a television set, and a polished Pinto, and I guess whatever it was that I wanted and *still* want, it wasn't quite that. We sat in silence for three years staring at the wallpaper and then she went home to Duluth. I guess one shouldn't really try to marry people from Duluth.

But, anyway, here I was, with my plumbing business in Connecticut, and Shelley, and I was trying very hard with the waitress from The Cattle Yard restaurant down on the Danbury road, although I hadn't gotten much further than unbuttoning her chaps. Life was okay, and not too hostile, and I felt that I could cope, even if I was ultimately copping out.

I drove into the outskirts of New Milford. It's a sleepy, pretty little town on the Housatonic, with dozens of picturesque colonial houses, and a main street with a wide grass mall and a bandstand. I parked outside of the New Milford Savings Bank and switched off the engine. Shelley, who had been sleeping soundly, stretched himself and yawned.

I took the jar of water out of my pocket and checked that it wasn't leaking. It could have been the deepening dusk, but the water looked more darkly tinted than it had before. I unscrewed the lid and sniffed at it.

It was then that Shelley stiffened, and bristled, and let out a spitting hiss that made *my* hair stand on end, too. He was arched up so much that he was almost bent double, and his tail was bushed out. His eyes were wide with something that was either fear or hatred.

"Shelley, for Christ's sake—" I told him.

He stayed where he was, his claws scraping at the vinyl seat, snarling like I'd never heard him snarl before. I made a move towards him, but he only spat harder, and let out one of those tortured yowls that have people throwing their left boot out of the window in the middle of the night.

I screwed the lid back on the jar. Almost at once, Shelley's fur subsided, and he began to relax. He still looked at me suspiciously, but then cats are experts at making humans feel guilty for upsetting or discomfiting them. I looked back at him with a frown, and then I looked at the jar again. It was only water; why should it make him go so crazy?

Maybe Alison had been right, and the water did smell of fish, or something like fish. After all, both Jimmy and I liked to smoke an occasional cigar, and perhaps our sense of smell wasn't as keen as hers. But then, Shelley didn't go berserk, even for fish. As a matter of fact, he preferred left-over pizza to almost any food you could name. He could possibly go berserk for a pepperoni, but I doubted it.

I climbed out of the car, locked it, and then I took the lid off the jar of water and sniffed it. There was some faint trace of odour, I had to admit. Some chilly, lingering smell that was more metallic than fishy. It gave me an odd sensation for some reason, like I'd smelled something that was very strange and hostile, and I stood there in the dusk of New Milford feeling unusually lonesome. Beyond the bandstand, three or four children were playing ball in the gloom. Their laughing was like the cries of birds.

Crossing the green, I mounted the steps of the New Milford Health Department. There were still lights in the upstairs window, and I guessed that Dan Kirk and his associates were working late. I walked inside through the tall black-painted doors, and went up the broad colonial staircase until I reached the first landing. The building was brightly lit with fluorescent tubes, and painted a dull Adam green. I went up to the door marked Health Department, Private, and walked in. Mrs. Wardell was sitting at her desk in the front office, all upswept glasses and red lipstick, and she said: "Hi, Mason. What brings you down here?"

I raised the jelly jar of water. "They're poisoning the wells," I said, melodramatically. "Is Dan there, or did he duck out early?"

"Did Dan duck out early? Is that a joke? Dan thinks going home at dawn is ducking out early. They have a swine disease crisis over at Sherman."

"Can I go straight in?" I asked her.

I knocked, and went through into Dan Kirk's laboratory. Dan was there, sitting at the end of a long varnished workbench, peering into a microscope. He was young, but very bald, and in his white laboratory coat he looked like a mad professor, or at the very worst a boiled egg. I noticed Rheta Warren there, too, and that was always good news. She was Dan's assistant researcher, on her first job since she graduated from Princeton

Biological college, and compared with most of the quail around New Milford she was most provocative. She had long muddy-blonde hair, wide hazel eyes, and a figure that obviously wasn't meant to be hidden by a starched white overall. I gave her a more-than-friendly wave as I crossed the laboratory to have a word with Dan.

"The plumber cometh," I said, and set down the jelly jar. Dan looked up from his microscope and blinked at it balefully. Then he blinked at me.

"My stars said this was going to be a silly week," he told me.

"What's silly? This is coloured water, possibly contaminated. I'd like you to test it for me."

He picked up the jar and peered at it with bulging, short-sighted eyes. "Where'd you get this?" he asked.

"Out at Jimmy Bodine's house. He says he's had discoloured water for two to three days. Alison Bodine swears it smells of fish, and Shelley seems to think the same way."

"Shelley? Your *cat* Shelley?"

"That's right. When I took the lid off the jar he went crazy. When I put it back on again, he returned to his normal condition of utter indolence."

Dan switched off the bright light over his microscope and rubbed his eyes. "Do you think Shelley would like a job here?" he asked. "I have a vacancy for a lab assistant with a good nose."

"I'm serious, Dan. All I'm asking is that you test it."

Dan Kirk smiled tiredly, and nodded. "You know that I have to anyway. If you like, we'll run through it now. I think I've had a bellyfull of swine fever for one day."

"Is it bad?"

"About as bad as it can get. Poor old Ken Follard had to slaughter every damn pig on the farm. You can smell burning bacon as far away as Roxbury."

I took out my handkerchief and blew my nose. It was the effect of walking into an overheated laboratory from a freezing street. I looked at Rheta over the handkerchief as Dan led the way to the centrifuge, and winked. I guess it wasn't very romantic, but I believe in taking every chance you can get.

"You want to tell me something about this sample?" asked Dan, switching on the lights around the grey-painted centrifuge. "Which faucet did it come from? Any other details?"

"Poured straight from the kitchen faucet. Jimmy says it's the same out of every faucet in the house."

Dan took the lid off the jar and sniffed. He paused, considered what he had smelled, and then sniffed again.

"Maybe Shelley was right," he told me.

"You think you smell fish?"

"That's one way of describing it."

"What's another way? Turtle soup?"

Dan dipped his finger in the water and licked it. He frowned, and then licked again. "There's definitely some kind of unusual taste and smell associated with this water. But it's pretty hard to define. It doesn't taste like any of the usual salts or minerals we get around here. It's not like manganese or potassium."

He tore off a piece of litmus paper and dipped it into the water. As the water soaked into it, the paper gradually turned from pale purple to a reddish colour.

"Well," said Dan, "that indicates the presence of acids."

"What kind of acids?"

"I don't know. We're going to have to make all the proper tests. We're going to start by putting a sample into the centrifuge, and seeing if we can separate any solids out of it. Did you see if it left any deposits on the Bodine's kitchen sink, or maybe their tub?"

"Not a trace. Mind you, it's only been troubling them for a couple of days, and that's hardly long enough to leave a stain."

Dan switched on the centrifuge and we waited while it whirled the Bodines' water around and around. Dan said: "Did you see the Hartford game Thursday?"

"I missed it. Mrs. Huntley had a burst pipe."

Dan wearily rubbed the back of his neck. "I missed it, too. I was up half the damn night analysing fertiliser."

Rheta came across the laboratory with an armful of files and reports. Close to, she was very pretty, in an odd kind of way. Her nose was a little too short, and her lips were a little too wide, but what she lacked in symmetry she made up for with an infectious smile. "I like men who put their work first," she said, in a mock-serious voice, as if she was presenting us each with a medal. "It shows a responsible, moral character."

"That's me," I told her. "Pipes before pleasure."

Dan finished his centrifuge test, and then he took the water over to the spectroscope. He was a slow, meticulous worker, and I knew that it was going to be three or four hours before he'd completed his analysis. As the electric clock on the laboratory wall crept past seven, my initial enthusiasm began to pall, and I began to feel bored and hungry, and very much in need of a beer. It was so dark outside now that I could see my weary reflection, sitting on a laboratory stool with my chin in my hand. Rheta had almost finished tidying up the rows of test tubes and pipettes and assorted laboratory junk, and I guessed she was getting ready to quit for the day.

"Is this really a job for a girl like you?" I asked her, as she put away her Bunsen burner hose. "Why didn't you take up something interesting, like go-go dancing? Or you could have been a Playboy bunny with your looks."

"Believe me," said Rheta, closing the cupboard door, "analysing swine fever samples is a hell of a lot more interesting than serving cocktails to lecherous people like you."

"Who's lecherous? Just because I have this mental picture of you in one of those tight satin outfits, with a cotton puff on your backside, that doesn't mean anything. Anyway, how about dinner tonight?"

"How *about* dinner tonight?" she asked, unbuttoning her lab coat.

I shrugged. "We could do anything you like. We could go up to Gaylordsville and have bluefish and white wine at the Fritz & Fox. Or we could go to Conn's Dairy Bar and have milk shakes and hamburgers.''

"You really know how to live, don't you?" she asked me, with good-humoured sarcasm. "Well, thanks, but no thanks. I have a date with Kenny Packer at nine.''

"Kenney Packer the football player? Pigskin Packer?''

"That's him.''

"He's like the Incredible Hulk, only pink.''

Dan said: "Hold on a minute, you two," and without taking his eyes away from his microscope, he beckoned us over. "Come and take a look at this.''

We came over, and Dan shifted his stool back so that we could take a look into the binocular lenses. I took a squint first, and all I could see was blurry shapes swimming around in a sea of dazzling light. But then Rheta took her turn, and she spent two or three minutes frowning at the slide in silence, occasionally adjusting the focus or moving the slide from side to side.

Eventually, she stood straight, and looked at Dan with a questioning, concerned expression. Dan looked back at her, and shook his head like he didn't know what to say, or what to do.

I said, impatiently: "Do you mind letting me in on this? All I saw were curly little squiggles.''

Dan nodded. "There are always curly little squiggles, even in the clearest water. Micro-organisms which filtration and purification never remove. They're quite harmless, on the whole. You drink millions of them every day.''

"What are you trying to do?" I asked him. "Put me off dinner?''

"Not at all. But those things you can see in this particular sample of water ought to put the Bodines off *their* dinner."

"What are they? Anything serious?"

Dan smoothed the palm of his hand over his bald head. "It's hard to say. From a cursory look at them, they appear to be nothing more than un-usually developed microscopic organisms. But when you look at them more closely you can see that they're much more sophisticated than the usual run-of-the-mill organisms and microbes you find in water supplies. They seem to have a rudi-mentary respiratory system, and they also seem to be exuding some kind of substance which is min-gling with the water."

I sat astride one of the stools. "Is that what's making the water discoloured?"

"I would guess so. Yes, it almost certainly is."

"So what are these things? You ever seen them before?" I asked him.

Dan glanced at Rheta. "Have you?" he asked her. She shook her head, and said nothing.

Dan said: "They're not in any way familiar to me, either. They're not the kind of bug you'd normally expect to find in water, and from what little I've seen of them so far, without having had the chance to study their full life cycle, I'd say that they lead a most unusual existence. This yellow or green stuff they keep producing is coming out of them in enormous quantities, comparatively speaking. You take a look at them again. If you or I excreted any kind of substance at that rate, we'd be pushing out twenty gallons an hour."

I pushed a disgusted face, but Dan said: "Go

ahead. Take another look," and so I bent over the microscope and peered intently at the sample of water.

Now I knew what I was looking for, I could identify the organisms that Dan was talking about. They were transparent and shadowy, but they had a distinctive shape, like sea-horses, and I could even see where their respiratory systems were. They seemed to take in water through gills around their necks and let it flow through their transparent bodies. When it was excreted at the other end, it came out tinted yellow. Perhaps when I'd compared the water with piss, up at the Bodines' place, I hadn't been too far wrong.

It was the shape of these organisms that disturbed me, though. If you forgot they were so goddamned small that you couldn't see them with the naked eye, they were monstrous. They had projections like twisted horns on the part of them which I took to be their heads, and crusty-looking bodies. And all the time I was watching them, they were jerking and swimming and writhing about. I suddenly remembered that I'd tasted some of the water on the end of my finger, and I began to feel distinctly nauseous. I stood straight again and looked from Dan to Rheta and back again.

"Can you find out what they are?" I asked them. "I mean—is there a way you can identify these things?"

"We're not sure until we try," said Rheta. "There are thousands and thousands of different types of micro-organisms, and it's going to take quite a while to check through all the identifying data. But this is my specialty, you know, and I follow most of the latest discoveries, and I don't ever recall anyone reporting anything like this before."

I took a cigarillo out of my coat pocket and clenched the plastic tip between my teeth. "Don't you have any ideas at all?"

Dan bent over the microscope again for a fresh look. He focused and refocused, but then he sat up and shook his head. "I don't have any useful suggestions right now. If it wasn't patently ridiculous, I'd say they most closely resemble some kind of marine life."

"That's what I thought," I put in. "They look like some kind of sea-horse."

"You mustn't be misled by superficial appearances," said Rheta. "They may *look* like sea-horses, but they came out of a dug well miles away from the ocean. They're probably nothing like sea-horses at all, biologically."

"Are they safe to drink?" I asked Dan. "I mean, what shall I tell the Bodines?"

Dan let out a long breath. "To be on the safe side, I'd say they shouldn't drink the well water until we've investigated these organisms further. I've managed to isolate a certain amount of nitric acid, and there's some sulphurous substance in there, too, but it's very hard to say whether they're connected with these organisms or not. Whatever's floating in that water, it's very complex and most unusual."

I stood up. "Okay. I'll give the Bodines a call and tell them to lay off. How long do you think it's going to take to track these things down? They'll want to know."

"It's impossible to say. Sometimes these analyses take months. Occasionally, years."

I took out a book of matches and lit my cigarillo. "What if I tell them a week or two? I don't want to scare them."

Dan nodded. "That's probably the best idea. I'm going to have to go up there and take some more samples for myself, though. Perhaps you could warn Jimmy to expect me sometime tomorrow."

"Okay. Now—are you going to join me for a beer?"

Dan glanced up at the clock. "All right. Maybe I'll have a sandwich, too. I don't think I've eaten since breakfast. But I'm going to have to come back here later and finish off my swine fever samples."

I buttoned up my coat. "You can do what you like later. Right now, I need to feel a cold Schaefer on the back of my throat."

We all left the laboratory together, and Dan locked the door behind us. Mrs. Wardell was going home too, putting the grey plastic cover over her typewriter and tidying her desk. The lights were being switched off all through the building. Outside, we could hear cars starting up and people calling good night.

"Good night, Gina," said Dan to Mrs. Wardell.

"Good night, Dr. Kirk. Did you remember to set the mousetraps?"

"I'll do it later. I'm coming back up to check on my swine fever samples on the way home." He turned to me, and said: "Never work in an old colonial building. They're always alive with mice. Rheta caught a mouse eating her lunch last week.

The damn thing had eaten its way right through the plastic bag."

We left the building and walked across the darkened grassy mall, our breath smoking in the cold evening air. The stars were bright and sharp, and that meant a hard frost in the morning. Still, frosts were always good for business. I knew that I'd be spending most of the morning thawing out faucets and repairing bursts.

Dan said: "What's hard to understand is what the organism is *doing* in that water. There doesn't seem to be any purpose behind its life style. It takes in water, it pours out yellow fluid. What's the point of it all?"

"What's the point of anything?" I asked him. "Human beings take in water and pour out yellow fluid, and nobody goes around saying that *they're* lacking in purpose."

Dan shook his head. "You misunderstand me. If this fluid was simply excreted water, then that would account for a lot of things. But from what I've seen so far, it seems as if the discoloration is a substance that's being *added* to the water as it flows through the organism's body, perhaps by some internal gland, if that's not too grand a word for one of the parts of a microscopic creature's physiology. And the creature is quite obviously expending an enormous amount of time and energy exuding this substance—in fact, so *much* time and energy that it seems to be the main purpose of its whole existence."

We were walking along by the old railroad yard now. Rheta said good night, and went off to collect her Volkswagen from the parking lot across the street, and I blew her a cold and breathy kiss as she went off. Then Dan and I walked a little further along to Stanley's Hotel & Dining Rooms, a green-and-red painted flat-fronted building where you could usually get a decent steak and a passable whiskey sour. We pushed our way in through the front door, and walked along a musty carpeted corridor to the dimly-lit back room. It was a small bar, smoky but almost empty, and a television flickered silently above the shelves.

"Good evening, Henry," I said to the dapper little man behind the black vinyl counter. "The Professor and I want two big ones, quick as you can pour them."

"Pretty damned frosty out there tonight, huh?" said Henry, pumping up two draft Schaefers. "Do you want a shot to go along with these?"

"I'm working," said Dan. "I want to keep a clear head, thanks all the same."

"I'm relaxing," I said. "Give me a Jack Daniel's."

"Did you hear about the Denton kid?" asked Henry, pouring out bourbon.

I shook my head. "What's he done now?"

"It's not what he's done, it's where he's gone. He's been missing since this morning. The police are looking all over."

"That's too bad," I said. I knew the Dentons. They were a quiet, poor family who lived not far away from the Bodines. Their son Sam was always walking around with patches in the knees of his jeans, but he was one of the nicest and politest kids you could meet. He was only nine, and I hoped that nothing had happened to him. It was too goddamned cold to go missing at this time of year.

"He went out on his bicycle, and that was the last they saw of him," said Henry. "They found his bike about a mile up the road, in the trees, but there was no sign of Sam. I guess his folks must be pretty distracted by now."

I drank my beer, subdued. Dan said quietly: "Let's drink to them finding him, shall we?"

We talked a while more with Henry, and then we got back to the subject of the Bodines' water and its organisms. Dan was clearly irritated by the mystery of the creatures' greeny-yellow excretion, and he struck off on his fingers a whole list of purposes it couldn't possibly have, and a whole list of purposes that it *could* have, but that still didn't make any sense.

I said: "I don't know why you're so worried about it. You know damned well that you'll get to find out in the end. A few months of patient research, and you'll probably discover that it's making itself mid-morning coffee. The first microscopic organism to provide its own refreshments."

"Are you *ever* serious?" Dan asked me. "This organism could be one of the most fascinating discoveries for years. I could make my name with this."

"I didn't think you were that kind of a scientist," I told him. "The next thing, you'll be telling me you have dreams of winning the Nobel Prize for analysing fertilizer."

Dan went slightly pink. "Everybody has ambitions," he said, evidently embarrassed.

"*I* don't," I said, bluntly. "I used to, when I was younger. But I'll tell you something for nothing. Ambitions don't get you anywhere. When you have ambitions, you spend your whole life trying to reach some place only to find out that you didn't particularly want to be there anyway."

"Is that how a half-trained psychiatrist justifies being a plumber?" he asked me.

I looked away. "Maybe it's the way a fully-trained human being justifies a peaceful and happy life."

"Are you really peaceful and happy?" he wanted to know.

"Are you really sure you want to have your name up in lights at the Smithsonian?" I retaliated.

"I think you need to fall in love," he declared, and took a long drink of beer.

We had one more beer each, and watched a few minutes of the basketball on the television over the bar. Then I put a dollar on the counter for Henry and we went back out into the night again. I walked back as far as the mall with Dan, and we stood for a while on the corner, talking about the water problem. Finally, Dan said: "Listen—I have to go check those samples. I'll probably call you tomorrow when I've been up to Jimmy's place."

I reached into my pocket for a cigarillo. To my annoyance, the goddamn pack wasn't there. I must have left it in Stanley's, or maybe up at the laboratory. I said to Dan: "Do you remember if I left my cigarillos on your desk?"

"You can come up and take a look if you want to."

He unlocked the office doors with a pass key. Inside the building, it was gloomy and echoing now, and there was nobody else around. We climbed the stairs and walked along the landing towards the health department door.

"Doesn't this place give you the creeps when you work late?" I asked Dan.

"Not as much as my apartment," he replied. "I have a landlady who looks through the keyhole to see if I have ladies in my rooms."

"And do you?"

"That's a trade secret, Mason."

"Oh. I thought, being a smart scientist, you would have brewed yourself up some potion to make yourself irresistible to women."

Dan unlocked the door of the outer office, and we crossed past Mrs. Wardell's empty desk to the inner laboratory door. He unlocked that, too, and we went in. The fluorescent lights flickered two or three times, and then went on.

"I think you left your cigarillos over there someplace by the microscope," said Dan. "I'm just going to the icebox next door to get out my swine fever slides if you want me."

I looked along the varnished laboratory benches, and there, under a sheaf of loose data paper, were my cigarillos. I took one out, and lit it, and waited for Dan to come back so that I could tell him good night. The laboratory was silent, except for the faint buzzing of the neon tubes. I coughed, and watched myself smoking in the dark window. I wondered if I was going to be too late to pick up a steak before I went home. I needed some roughage to soak up two beers and two Jack Daniel's.

It was then that I heard the rustling noise. I didn't take any notice at first. I thought it was just the sheets of data paper, shifting from where I had moved them aside. But then I heard it again, more distinctly, and even though it *was* coming from the paper, it certainly wasn't the settling of the paper itself. It was too quick, too scrabbly. There was something under there, and it sounded like a mouse.

"Dan!" I called out.

"I'm coming!" he told me.

"I think I've caught the lunch break bandit!" I said.

I saw the paper stirring, and I tippy-toed nearer and cupped my hands over the place where the rustling was coming from. There was a pause, but then the creature squeaked, and I flung aside that data paper like a blizzard and caught its wriggling body right between my palms. It squeaked again like crazy, and even tried to nip me with its teeth, but I had it trapped in there good and tight.

Dan came in with a tray of samples and laid them on the bench.

"Here he is," I announced. "The sandwich nibbler himself."

"You caught him? That's a neat trick. Now what are you going to do with him?"

I looked down at my cupped hands. "I don't know. Squash him to death, I guess."

Dan blinked at me. "Could you really do that?" he asked.

I shook my head. "I guess not."

"Well, why don't you just let him go? The traps are going to catch him sooner or later."

"Maybe I ought to drive him up to Canada and release him at the border."

Dan laughed. "Go on, just let him go."

I hunkered down, and gradually opened up my cupped hands. I saw a tiny pink nose, brown whiskers, pink ears, and a furry back. And then I saw something else that made me whip my hands away from that mouse so fast that I lost my balance, and fell with my shoulder against the cupboards under the bench.

I said: "Dan! For Christ's sake!"

Dan turned and looked down at the floor where I had dropped the mouse. He didn't realize that anything was wrong at first, but then he stared in horror and fascination at the creature that stood shaking and trembling on the polished parquet, unwilling or unable to move.

"What in hell happened to *him?*" he asked, under his breath. He knelt down beside the mouse and peered at it even closer. The mouse squeaked a little but didn't try to run away.

It couldn't, of course. From the middle of its back towards its hindquarters, it was covered in some kind of dark, horny excrescence that gave it the appearance of a huge black beetle. Even its rear legs and its feet had been affected, and they were claw-like and scabrous. Its back and sides had a dull greeny-black sheen, with ragged edges.

I got to my feet, my knees weak with disgust and fright, and I went and washed my hands in the laboratory sink. I had felt the shell when I had caught the mouse, but I had imagined I was being prickled by nothing but sharp claws. My last beer rose in the back of my throat, and it was only by taking a deep breath that I persuaded it to go down again.

Dan was on all fours now, with a transparent plastic foot-rule, and he was gently prodding the mouse with it.

"Did you ever see anything like this before?" he asked me.

I shook my head. "I hope I never see anything like it again."

He turned the mouse over on to its back, and it lay there squeaking with its feet waving in the air. Its abdomen was even worse than its back. Below its ribcage, its body went into insect-like folds, like a pale caterpillar or a wood-louse. Its hind claws had saw-tooth edges, and moved with a repulsive jerking motion.

"Well," said Dan, "what the hell do we make of you, little fellow?"

The mouse squeaked again, and twisted its head from side to side.

"Would you go get me that wire cage over by the window-ledge?" asked Dan. "I'll keep an eye on our friend here and make sure he doesn't make a run for it."

"He's no friend of mine," I said, crossing the laboratory.

It was only when I was on my way back with the cage that I glanced at the culture dish in which Dan had left a sizable sample of the Bodlnes' water. There were a couple of mouse droppings beside it, and it was almost empty.

I handed Dan the cage. I didn't know what to say. But when he'd carefully lifted the mouse in through the wire door, balanced almost lifeless on the end of the plastic ruler, I cleared my throat and said: "Dan . . ."

## 2

I dialed the Bodines' house four times, but the phone rang and rang and there was no reply. I checked the clock on the wall. It was way after nine now, and there should have been somebody there. After all, it was Oliver's bedtime, and even if Jimmy and Alison weren't at home, they would have had to bring in a babysitter. I waited and waited, but at last I had to put down the phone and shake my head.

"They're not in, or they're not answering."

Dan was still inspecting the chitinous mouse in the wire cage, watching it intently as it tried to pull itself from one side of its prison to the other. It was so grotesque that I had to look away, but I could still hear its shell and its insect-like claws scraping on the wire.

"In that case," said Dan, "I guess we'd better get out there and warn them in person. I can't tell for certain if the water's done this, not until I've made some tests. Maybe it has nothing to do with it at

all. But we don't want to take the slightest risk.
Not where people's lives are concerned."

"I'll drive you," I told him.

We took a last queasy look at the mouse and
then we locked the laboratory and went downstairs. We crossed the mall at a fast walk, breaking into a trot as we neared the station wagon. It
was so cold now that the windshield was iced over
with white stars and fingers of frost, and the hood
shone a dull misted green in the light from the
streetlamps. I unlocked the doors and we climbed
in. Shelley, looking very haughty and put out,
climbed over on to the back seat.

"It smells like cats and putty in here," said Dan,
as I started up the engine. "I don't know how you
can stand it."

"At least they're honest smells," I told him,
backing up and then pulling out into the main
street.

"What's a dishonest smell?" asked Dan.

I drove up to the top of the mall, turned right,
and then joined Route 202 at the sloping corner by
the cemetery. The gravestones looked whiter and
colder than ever as I took a left and headed north.
Dan took a notepad out of his coat pocket and
started to jot down incomprehensible hieroglyphs
with a blunt chewed pencil.

"Supposing it *was* the water?" I asked him.

He looked at me, his face patterned with
shadows. "Supposing it was?"

"Well—if it does that to a mouse—what's it
going to do to a human being?"

"I don't have any idea. Sometimes small creatures like mice and rats are affected by chemicals

or organisms when humans aren't. Look at the whole saccharin affair. Saccharin was found to cause cancer when given to laboratory rats in fairly heavy doses, but that's not indisputable proof that it has the same effect on humans. The same goes for many micro-organisms, which can maim or kill rodents, but don't harm people at all."

I turned off right on to Route 109. The road was dark and strewn with dead leaves, and already coated with a white frosting of sugary-looking ice.

"I just wish they'd answered the phone," I said. "Then I would have been sure they were still okay. I mean, they *should* have answered the phone."

It took five or ten minutes of driving through the dark and the cold to reach the Bodine house. I blew my horn a couple of times as we turned up the driveway, but the old, square house seemed to be deserted. There were no lights at any of the windows, only an outside light on the verandah, and none of the living-room drapes had been drawn. I pulled the station wagon to a halt, and we climbed out. Shelley gratefully returned to his front seat, revelling in the warmth left by Dan's backside.

"Jimmy!" I called. "Alison!"

There was no reply. The house and its grounds were silent, except for the occasional scuttling of dry leaves. I walked around the side to the back yard, but that, too, was deserted. Jimmy's rake rested where he had left it that afternoon, against the brown-painted weatherboarding. The screen door creaked and banged, creaked and banged.

"They could have gone out for the evening," suggested Dan. "Maybe they're staying overnight some place."

"They didn't mention it to me."

"People don't have to ask your permission to go out for the evening, you know. You're only the plumber."

I wasn't in the mood for humour. There was something unnaturally creepy about finding the Bodine house empty. The windows were as dark as old men's eyes, and the wind hummed in the telephone wires. Behind me, Dan coughed and shuffled his feet in the leaves.

I went up the back steps to the kitchen door. I held back the screen and tried the main door handle, and to my surprise I found that was unlocked, too. I opened it a little way, and called: "Jimmy? Alison?" into the chilly gloom of the kitchen.

Dan said: "You're wasting your time, Mason. They're just not here. Maybe they went over to the Clarks' place at Washington."

I strained my eyes to see through the shadows. I could see the edge of the kitchen table, and the corner of the pine hutch, but it didn't look like there was anybody there. I called: "Jimmy?" louder, but still there was no reply.

"It's unlike Jimmy to leave the place unlocked," I remarked.

Dan shrugged. "Maybe he forgot. Maybe he thought he'd locked up and he hadn't."

"I don't know," I said slowly. "That doesn't seem like Jimmy at all."

I opened the kitchen door wider and stepped inside. The kitchen was very dark, and odd shadows clung in every corner. I heard something squeak and I froze for a moment, wondering if it was one of those hideous little mice, but then it squeaked again and I realized it was only a floorboard. One of the faucets in the kitchen sink was dripping steadily, making a flat plip-plapping noise. I went on tippy-toes across the room, bumping into the corner of the table as I passed, and turned the faucet off. There's one sound a plumber can't stand to hear, and that's the sound of dripping.

I paused for a moment, listening and looking. Dan came in through the kitchen door, banging the screen behind him, and I said: "Ssshh."

"What is it?" he whispered, hoarsely.

"I'm not sure. Do you hear anything?"

"I don't think so. Why don't you turn on the light? Do you enjoy being scared?"

I turned and frowned at him. "Who's scared?"

We waited in silence for almost a whole minute, and if you've ever waited in silence for a whole minute, then you'll know how long that is. I was sure, somewhere in the house, I could still hear dripping.

I said to Dan: "Do you hear water?"

"Water?" he queried. "What do you mean, water?"

"Listen."

We strained our ears again, and this time we both heard it clearly. It was the steady, distinctive sound of water, pattering on to a carpeted floor. It had a splashy quality to it that told me the carpet was already soaked through.

"What do you make of that?" I asked Dan.

"I don't know. You're the plumbing expert.

Burst pipe, maybe?"

I crossed the kitchen again and found the light-switch. I flicked it down, but all that happened was that the lights shone dimly for a moment, and then fizzled out. A small shower of blue sparks danced from the switch and there was a smell of burned plastic. The water must have short-circuited the wires.

"I have a flashlight in the glove box of my car," I whispered to Dan. "Why don't you go get it, while I see if I can find where this water's coming from?"

"Sure. But take care. It sounds like the whole place is leaking."

Dan went out of the back door, and the screen banged again. Myself, I waited in the darkness of the kitchen for a moment, and then I ventured out into the hallway.

The hall was almost totally dark. Only a thin blue reflected light from the frosty ground outside filtered in through the crescent-shaped window over the front door. An antique warming-pan gleamed copper-and-blue in the shadows, and on the opposite wall there was a dim painting of Lake Candlewood. I touched a potful of feathery pampas grass as I crept along towards the stairs, and I practically suffered a heart attack where I stood. But at last I reached the foot of the stained oak staircase, and looked up to the landing above.

Less bravely, I called: "Jimmy? Are you up there?" knowing damned well that he wasn't. I think I just wanted to hear the sound of my own voice. Out of the darkness, however, there were no answers, no whispers, no reassuring hellos. Only the dripping and trickling of water, and the spongy noise of rugs soaking it up.

I placed my foot on the first stair, and it made a squelching noise. I reached down and the stair carpet was sodden. It seemed as if the water was trickling down the stairs in a slow cataract, and that meant the whole of the landing must be flooded.

Right then, Dan came through from the kitchen with the flashlight.

"Will you look at this place?" I told him. "It's almost afloat."

He shone the flashlight onto the red-patterned stair carpet. It was glistening and dark with wet, and the stain was already spreading across the hall.

"This isn't a burst pipe," he said. "This is more like Niagara Falls."

I looked around. It wouldn't be long before the water poured out of the hallway and into the living-room, and that would mean that the Bodines' furniture and carpets and drapes would be ruined. "What I want to know is where are Jimmy and Alison?" I said. "If this *is* a burst pipe, it's been leaking like this for hours. You can't tell me they went out for the evening and left their house full of water. It just doesn't make any sense."

Dan glanced apprehensively up the stairs. "I guess we'd better go see what's happening up there."

We hesitated for a moment, not sure who was going to go first. "You're the plumber," said Dan, handing over the flashlight, and that's how I volunteered. I led the way cautiously up the soaking stair carpet, my feet squeezing out water with every step, and by the time I reached the darkened landing at the top of the stairs, my shoes were letting in the wet.

"Is there anybody there?" asked Dan, in a heavy whisper.

"Maybe a killer whale or two," I told him. "There's enough water for them."

I flicked the flashlight beam around, at the panelled walls, at the oil paintings of Connecticut scenery, at the small semi-circular table at the far end of the hall with its copper vase of dried flowers. There were five doors leading off the landing—three to the left and two to the right, and the two on the right were both ajar. Everything looked quite normal. It was only when I shone the light downwards at the dark reflecting lake of water that covered the whole floor that I saw how strange this whole situation was. My flashlight was mirrored in the slowly-moving surface, and I could see myself, hanging upside-down from the soles of my shoes, drowned like a mariner in the blackness of an indoor pool.

"Where's the water coming from?" asked Dan. "It looks like the walls are quite dry."

I shone the flashlight at each of the doors. As far as I could make out the water was swirling out of the end door on the right, which was slightly open. There was a noticeable pattern of ripples, and I could hear a dripping, splattering noise from inside.

"Maybe the tank cracked," I said, splashing across the landing. The water was at least an inch deep, but my shoes were so wet by now that I didn't bother. That was the last time I was going to spend thirty-one bucks on a pair of fashion shoes with a fancy gold chain across the front. I'd rather be unfashionable in leather than fashionable in cardboard.

I reached the end door. It had a small ceramic plaque on it with a painting of an antique car, and it said "Oliver's Room." I shone the flashlight on the plaque for Dan's benefit, and he read it and pulled a face.

Carefully, shining the flashlight ahead of me, I pushed open the bedroom door. Again, my own light was reflected back at me out of the glittering darkness. The dripping noise was louder, and there was another sound as well, a sound that made me stay still, right where I was, and gave me a freezing, tightening feeling all around my scalp.

It was the sound of somebody, or something, gurgling.

"Dan," I hissed. "Dan, there's someone in there."

"You're kidding," he said. His face was rigid with tension.

"I can *hear* something. Listen, for Christ's sake. Can't you hear that?"

He listened. There was nothing, except for the incessant dripping and splashing of water.

"You must have imagined it," he said, with a nervous smile that showed he didn't believe for one moment that I had.

I took a breath, and pushed the door wider. The room was alive with reflections and shadows. I shone the flashlight across to the far wall, where the bed was, but there was nobody lying there. I shone it along the skirting board, across to the closet, and back to the bed again.

"What did I tell you?" said Dan. "It was just the water."

I waded farther into the room. It was still impossible to say where the water was actually coming from. The only difference between this room and the landing outside was that, in this room, the walls were wet almost up to the ceiling. The crisscross patterned wallpaper was damp and wrinkled, and there was a clear tide-mark right up by the picture rail. Impossible as it might have been, it looked as if the entire room had been filled with water.

Dan said: "Mason."

I turned. His face looked distinctly odd. He pointed at the floor behind me, and said again: "Mason. Look down there."

I shone the flashlight downwards. The bed itself may have been empty, but I hadn't looked *under* the bed. And in the pale oval beam of the flashlight, I could see something stirring there, something white and strange. I bent down closer, my hand shaking with nerves, and tried to make out what it was.

"Jesus wept," said Dan. "It's a foot."

Together, splashing in the water, we took hold of the foot and the leg that went with it and dragged it out from under the bed. I dropped the flashlight once, but it still worked when I picked it up, and I directed it downwards on to the face of a young boy, his cheeks pale and his lips blue, and his eyes staring sightlessly upwards. Dan pressed down on his chest, in a hopeless attempt to see if there was any life left in him, but the boy's mouth and nose gushed water, and it was plain that he was dead. I recognized him, of course, even though I hadn't seen him in a while. He was Oliver Bodine, Jimmy and Alison's son, and he was drowned.

"We'd better call for Carter," said Dan. "This is police business now."

I stood up. The feel of Oliver's cool, soft flesh still haunted my fingertips. The water seemed to stir, and Oliver's body stirred too, still dressed in his Six-Million-Dollar Man pyjamas.

"Oh, Christ," I said. "This is too much for one day. This is all too goddamned much. Look at this poor kid."

Dan stood up too, and nodded. "I don't know what happened here. It sure looks like he drowned. Although how in hell anybody managed to fill up the whole bedroom with water, I don't have any idea. It couldn't have been done slowly, either. The window isn't sealed, and neither is the door."

"We'd better check the other rooms," I said, un-enthusiastically. "Supposing Jimmy and Alison are—well, supposing something's happened to them, too?"

"Okay," said Dan. He looked about as keen to go searching for more bodies as I was. "I guess you'd better bring the flashlight."

We left poor young Oliver Bodine's body where it was, and splashed back on to the landing. We tried the master bedroom first, but apart from water stains on the rug where the wet had crept in from outside, it was quite dry, and empty. The brass colonial bed with the pink bedspread was neatly made, and nobody had slept in it. On the dark pine dressing-table, Alison's hairbrush and hand-mirror and bottles of perfume remained undisturbed, and on the wall by the carved pine closet was a colour photograph of Jimmy and Oliver on the beach at Cape Cod. I shone the flashlight on it, and then looked at Dan, and shrugged.

We tried the next two bedrooms. They were both empty, both reasonably dry, both untouched. We gave them a nervous once-over, opening the cupboard doors as if we expected to find monsters lurking in them, and then retreated to the sodden landing. The water was slowly beginning to subside, and it was clear that it hadn't come from a burst pipe at all.

"It seems to me that Oliver's room was filled up with water somehow, but that was all the flooding there was," I said. "Now his room's emptied out, that's it. There's no leak, no fractured tank, no damaged faucet, nothing."

Dan turned towards me with an expression on his face that made him look like an anxious Humpty Dumpty. "Who did it, though?" he asked me. "And what's even more pertinent, how did they manage it? I just don't see how anybody could physically fill up a room with water. It's impossible."

"We haven't looked at the bathroom yet," I reminded him. "Maybe there was some kind of freak back-up in the pipes."

"You don't believe that any more than I do."

I took out my cigarillos and offered one to Dan. He shook his head. "I have to start rationalizing sometime," I told him, taking out a book of matches from The Cattle Yard. "I might as well start now."

We opened the bathroom door. It was noticeably cold in there, not just ordinary winter-evening cold, but a damp and clammy cold. I sniffed, and even though I was smoking a cigarillo, I was sure that I could detect that odd, unpleasant odour of metallic fish, the same smell as the sample of water that I had brought out from the house only this afternoon.

"Do you smell that?" I asked Dan.

He nodded.

"What does it remind you of?" I said.

He had a long think. Then he said: "Fisherman's Wharf, San Francisco, on my last vacation. Shellfish and diesel fuel, all mixed up."

"Me too," I told him.

The shower curtain was drawn across the tub. It was misty plastic, with pictures of turquoise fish swimming across it. I shone the flashlight that way, but there didn't appear to be anybody in there. I stepped across the cork floor and pulled the shower curtain back.

Lying in the bath was something that looked like a thin, bony helmet. It was larger than a helmet—in fact, you would have needed a head that was twice the normal size to wear it. But it had that kind of dull, tough shine and that kind of curved, nutlike shape that put you in mind of a helmet.

"Dan," I said cautiously. "What do you think it is?"

He leaned forward and peered into the tub. He stared at the "helmet" for a while, and then he reached in and lifted it out.

"It's light," he said. "It's some kind of shell, or bone. But look."

He held it up in front of the flashlight beam and showed me. It was formed out of two halves, like the halves of a clam or a mussel shell, and it was hinged down the center by some tough but flexible material like celluloid. All down the hinge were black hairy spines, short and bristly and sharp.

"Is it real?" I asked him.

"Real? You mean, does it come from a real creature?"

"I guess so, if you have to put it that way."

Dan tapped it, and looked it over as best he could in the dim light. Then he said: "It looks real. It looks like the discarded carapace of some pretty big kind of armoured insect."

I didn't know whether I wanted to burst out laughing or run out of that house as fast as inhumanly impossible. I looked at that bony piece of creature and I felt as if I was right in the middle of one of those nightmares that doesn't frighten you until you wake up and see how gloomy it is in your bedroom, and hear those noises and whispers that shouldn't be there, and see shapes that can't exist.

"That's all—an insect?" I asked Dan, "That was actually part of something that walked around?"

"It could be. It could be a clever hoax. But I don't think the kind of creature who could drown a boy in his bedroom would have much of a sense of humour, do you?"

I stared at the carapace in dread. "You mean that could be a lobster shell, a crab shell, something like that? Do you know what you're *saying*?"

Dan laid the shell back in the tub. It rolled over with an unpleasant clattering sound, backwards and forwards, until it settled.

"I don't know what to say, to tell you the truth," he said, unhappily. "It looks like the shell of a lobster, or an insect, but the size is insane. I don't think I understand any of this at all."

I heard more dripping noises from outside the bathroom. I felt nervous enough without standing around in that house debating whether Oliver could have been attacked by some horrific insect. I said: "Maybe let's go call Carter. At least the police have a procedure for dealing with weird things. I can't solve a problem unless I can solder it, or lag it, or tighten it up with a wrench."

Dan smoothed his hand over his bald head. His eyes were uneasy. He said: "None of this makes any sense. Look at that thing. It's a carapace, or a clever copy of a carapace, but the nightmarish *size* of it, Mason . . ."

"Let's go call Carter, huh?" I repeated. "You know what happens when people have to fight giant lobsters in the movies. They send for the police, and the police send for the National Guard, and the National Guard drop atomic bombs on them. Well, let's go do that."

"For God's sake don't joke about it," Dan snapped. "There's a boy dead in there."

"I'm not joking," I insisted. "I'm just tense. I'd just rather be out of this place. Now, shall we go?"

He took another long look at the carapace, and then nodded. "All right. But I want to ask Carter to let me have some photographs of that thing."

We left the bathroom and squelched back out on

to the landing. We paused there for a moment, and listened, but all we could hear was the constant drip-dripping of water. Stepping carefully on the wet carpet, we went back downstairs again, and into the living-room. There was a telephone there, and I was hoping that the water hadn't fused that out, too. I picked it up and listened. It was crackling a little, but I had a tone.

Carter Wilkes took a long time to answer. When he did, he said tiredly, "Sheriff's office, Carter Wilkes, hold on, will you?"

"Carter," I said quickly, "it's me, Mason Perkins."

"Oh, how are you doing, Mason? Can you hold? I'm right in the middle of a briefing on the Denton boy."

"Carter, this is worse than the Denton boy."

"What are you talking about?"

"I'm up at the Bodines' place on Route 109," I said. "There's been an accident or something. Young Oliver Bodine's been drowned."

"Drowned? Where?"

"In the house. In his bedroom, as a matter of fact."

"In his *bedroom?*" asked Carter, with hoarse incredulity. "Are you sure you didn't stop by the Northville Liquor Store on your way home? Are you quite sure you're sober there, Mason?"

"Carter, it's true. And there's something else, too. But you'll have to come up and take a look for yourself."

Carter put his hand over the receiver, and I could hear him talking in a muffled voice to some of his deputies. Then he came back on the line again, and said: "Do you have Jimmy and Alison up there with you, Mason? Are they okay?"

"They're missing. We've been here for a good half-hour, and we haven't seen any sign of them."

"Okay," said Carter. "I'm coming out straight away. You just stay there and wait for me, and you make damn sure you don't touch anything."

He banged the phone down. I held my own receiver in my hand for a moment, and Dan turned towards me and said: "Well?"

"Carter's coming right out. It shouldn't take him more than ten minutes. Not the way he drives."

"What did he say?"

I shrugged. "He thought I was drunk at first. I'm beginning to wish I was."

"Did he say wait?"

I nodded. "Let's go do it outside, shall we? This place is giving me the creeps. I don't fancy meeting up with one of those giant-sized crustaceans, for starters. And I always did believe in ghosts."

"You believe in ghosts?" asked Dan, interested, as we made our way cautiously across the wet hallway and out through the kitchen.

"Sure. Don't you?"

"I guess not. I never saw one. My mother used to swear by ouija boards, but I never actually saw a ghost walking about. Did you?"

"I used to have an apartment on Tenth Street, in the village," I said. "I was sure I could hear people whispering in my bedroom in the night."

Dan opened the screen door, and we stepped out into the frosty night air. "What did they say?" he asked me.

"I don't know. I was always taught it was impolite to listen to other people's conversations. But seriously, it went on for months. Later on, the janitor told me that two girls had been murdered in that room by some schizo rapist."

We walked around the house to where my station wagon was parked, with its sidelights on. I climbed into the driver's seat and Dan considerately got into the back, so that he wouldn't disturb Shelley. I started up the engine so that we could have some heat.

"At least a schizo rapist is a schizo rapist," remarked Dan. "But don't ask me what the shell-thing in the bath is, or where it came from."

"Something just occurred to me," I said. "When I was out here this afternoon, talking to Jimmy, he mentioned that he'd been having dreams about drowning."

"He did? Was that all he said?"

I thought for a moment. Hadn't Jimmy said something about being underground, in a subterranean pool? *The thing that always gets me is the feeling that the water is underneath tons and tons of solid rock, so even if I did reach the surface, I couldn't breathe."*

I said: "He seemed to think he was drowning under the ground. Maybe in a flooded mineshaft or something like that."

"Under the ground? That doesn't make too much sense."

I nodded towards the Bodine house, dark and silent in the freezing night. "What happened to young Oliver doesn't make too much sense, either. But it still happened."

"It could have been some kind of premonition,

Jimmy's dream," suggested Dan. "I don't believe in ghosts, but there are several recorded cases of genuine clairvoyance."

"And what about the insect shell, or lobster shell, or whatever it is?" I asked him.

"There's something about that which worries me more than anything," said Dan. His face was illuminated pale green by the lights from the station wagon's instruments. "It reminded me too much of our shell-backed little mouse. It's hard to say without having the mouse right here to make comparisons, but there seemed to me to be some similarity between the shell on that mouse's lower body and that big shell upstairs."

I switched off the Country Squire's engine so that we wouldn't all die of carbon monoxide poisoning. It was warm enough now to last us until Sheriff Wilkes arrived. Shelley yawned and stretched and curled himself up into a hairy, tabby ball. It really needed talent to be as lazy as that.

I took out a cigarillo. It was my last. I stuck it between my teeth and said: "You think some bigger animal could have drunk the well water, just like the mouse, and had the same thing happen to it?"

"If the water was to blame, then the odds are in favour of it, I'd say," said Dan. "It could have been a dog, maybe. The Bodines do have a dog, don't they, and we haven't seen any sign of that."

"We haven't seen any sign of the Bodines, either," I reminded him.

He looked away. "That's been on my mind, too. But until we know if it is the water for sure, and until we know if those organisms affect humans, then that's the kind of conjecture I don't think I want to make."

I took out my matches. "At least it didn't affect Oliver. I mean, he drowned, but he must have drunk the well water just as much as Jimmy and Alison, and there weren't any signs of changes on him."

Dan rubbed his eyes. "I don't seriously think that Jimmy and Alison are walking around looking like some kind of advertisement for Schwom's Sea-food Shanty, do you?"

I struck a match, and at that moment I thought I saw somebody crossing the front lawn of the house. The flaring orange reflection of the match on the inside of the windshield made it difficult to make sure, and so I quickly blew out the match and stared into the darkness again.

"What's the matter?" asked Dan.

"I don't know. It looks like there's someone out there. Hold on a minute."

I opened the station wagon door and got out. For a brief split-second, I thought I saw a man walking away from me, over by the far fence. It was too dark to see very clearly, but he appeared to be hunched and bulky, and moving with an odd kind of swaying step. I called: "Jimmy? Is that Jimmy?" and the man appeared to turn towards me, but so quickly that I couldn't see who it was before he vanished into the grainy shadows. I called out: "Jimmy!" once more, and then I started to run across the grass towards the fence. Behind me, I heard Dan open his door and come loping in hot pursuit. My breath froze in the cold air, and the sound of my heartbeat and my rustling clothes seemed to be the loudest noises in the whole world.

I reached the rail. Beyond it, there was a thick hedge of thorn bushes, impossible for a man to penetrate without scratching himself to hamburger meat. I stopped, panting, and Dan came gasping and wheezing after me, and we both stood there and looked at the hedge in bewilderment.

"Did you see who it was?" asked Dan.

"I don't know. It could have been anybody. Maybe it was just the shadows. I don't see how anyone could have gotten through those bushes."

We walked a little way along the rail in each direction, but there didn't appear to be any gaps in the hedge at all. If there had been somebody there, he must have cleared the hedge with one tremendous bionic leap, or else he'd simply run the length of it under the cover of the shadows. I didn't think he could have done that, though, without my seeing him. When I started running, he couldn't have been much farther than one hundred and fifty feet away. Only an Olympic-class athlete could have run right down to the road and out of sight before I got there; and from what I'd seen of this fellow, he was heavy and gimpy and slow.

We listened. The wind blew soft and cold through the hedge, and the dead leaves curled among the thorns crackled with a sound that was too much like cracking lobster claws for comfort.

"I don't know what we're being so damned nervous about," said Dan, cross with himself, and equally irritated with me. "We don't have any evidence of anything, and yet we're jumping around like a couple of college students in a haunted house."

I started to walk back towards the station wagon, and Dan followed me. I didn't know whether I was over-reacting or not. I knew that a certain amount of the adrenalin that was rushing around my bloodstream had been evoked by imagination. Under the circumstances, it was pretty difficult not to have horrible images of Jimmy and Alison Bodine being slowly overtaken by some kind of chitinous growth. But I knew I had seen something, or somebody, and considering young Oliver had been drowned only a few hours earlier, I think I could be forgiven for feeling edgy. I'm not a coward. I'll bend a pipe-wrench over anybody's head without a qualm, if it's necessary. But I'm not so sure about things that whisper in the dark, or creep about gardens at midnight, and I'm certainly not sure about bedrooms that can be unnaturally flooded in deserted houses.

We had almost reached the station wagon when there was a single whoop of a siren, and Sheriff Wilkes' car came around the curve in the road with its red light flashing. It pulled up right behind my Country Squire and Sheriff Wilkes got out, accompanied by three of his deputies.

"The coroner's on his way, too," called Carter. "Can you tell me where the body is?"

"Upstairs, second bedroom on the right."

Carter Wilkes was a big man, almost six-four, with a belly to match. His face was coarse and broad, with intent, crow's-footed eyes, and shaggy eyebrows. His uniforms were always immaculately laundered, and his shoes always sparkled, and he was a lifelong devotee of dental floss. He had a pretty Chinese wife and a son who played basketball for Hartford.

"You guys want to come up with me, show me what you found?" asked Carter.

"If you think it's absolutely necessary," I said. "It isn't very pleasant in there."

"Sudden death doesn't often improve a home too much," countered Carter.

"I guess not," I told him.

We showed Carter and his deputies the way through the kitchen to the sodden-carpeted hallway. He wanted to know when we'd arrived, and what we were doing there, and what had first made us suspicious. Had we seen any footprints on the wet staircarpet? Had we heard any suspicious noises? Where did I think the water had come from? Why hadn't I turned it off at the main stopcock straight away?

All six of us squelched upstairs, and I pointed to young Oliver's bedroom. Two of the deputies carried heavy-duty flashlights, and they lit the place up in all its damp, clammy sadness. Oliver was still lying where we had left him, his face blue and his eyes wide open. Sheriff Wilkes squatted down beside him and stared at him for a long time. He didn't touch him. Then he looked up and all around the room, taking in the peeling wallpaper, the dripping furniture, the tidemark around the picture-rail.

"You're the plumber," he said, turning to me. "What do you think could have caused all this?"

"I don't know," I admitted. "The room wasn't even sealed up, so it must have been some kind of freak flash flood. But I don't know where the water came from, or how it could have filled up the place so fast. A room this size would take anything up to five thousand gallons."

"As much as that, huh?" asked Carter.

"Easily. Maybe more."

Carter stood up and hitched his gunbelt over his hips. "It doesn't look like there's five thousand gallons out in that hallway, though, does it? Five thousand gallons would have washed the whole place out, wouldn't you say?"

"Yes. I guess it would. I didn't think of that."

"So the water came in, filled the place up, and then disappeared, mostly?" asked Carter.

"I suppose so. I don't know how."

"I'm not asking you how. What I'm asking is, do you think that's what happened?"

I nodded. "That's what happened, all right."

"Okay, we agree with each other," said Carter. He stepped across Oliver's body to the other side of the room. "The room was filled up with five thousand gallons of water. Then the water was emptied out again, almost as quick. Now, what kind of equipment could do something like that? Something like a pump, maybe, or a special kind of hose?"

I thought about it. There were some firehoses that could deliver water at a rate of several thousand gallons a minute, but they were equipped with tremendously powerful and noisy pumps, and the idea of a would-be murderer driving something like that up to the side of the Bodines' house in the early evening, rigging it all up and switching it on, was totally out of the question. Apart from that, how had all these thousands of gallons been removed, almost straight afterwards? I didn't know of any portable pump that could suck up five thousand gallons in a matter of seconds.

Oliver's drowning seemed to be pointless, purposeless, and to have been achieved by means that were quite impossible.

I said to Sheriff Wilkes: "I'm sorry. I can't even begin to guess how this was done. I would have said it couldn't have been done at all, if I hadn't seen it with my own eyes."

Carter rubbed his chin. Outside, we heard the warble of the coroner's siren, and the sound of his car tires as they squealed to a halt on the driveway. Doors slammed, and there were footsteps and voices.

"There's one more thing," Dan told Carter. "We found something strange in the bathroom."

"You don't think *this* is strange?" asked Carter.

"Yes. But what we found was stranger."

Carter glanced at one of his deputies, and then said: "All right. You'd better lead the way."

We trooped along the landing to the bathroom. Dan pulled back the shower curtain, and said: "There, what do you make of that?"

Carter frowned, and peered into the bath. His deputy leaned over too. Then he stood straight, and looked from Dan to me and back again. "It's a bathtub," he said suspiciously.

"Not the tub," I said, pushing my way forward. "The—"

The bathtub was empty. There was no sign of

the carapace at all. I pulled the shower curtain aside even further, but it wasn't hidden anywhere there. I looked behind the toilet, but it wasn't there either.

"Do you want to tell me what you're looking for?" demanded Carter. "Or was it so strange you don't even know what it is?"

"It was a carapace," explained Dan, trying to describe it by drawing shapes in the air with his hands.

"A what?"

"An insect's breastplate, in simple language. Horny and tough, and hinged along the spine."

Sheriff Wilkes watched Dan's attempts to outline the carapace, and then raised his finger and thumb and held them just a few millimeters apart.

"When you say an insect's breastplate, you mean it was round about this size, don't you? You don't really mean it was *that* big."

Dan looked down at his hands, almost two feet apart. Then he looked back at the sheriff. There was a moment when I wondered what he was going to say but then he lowered his arms and gave a resigned, surrendering grimace.

"Yes," he said, in a tired voice. "I don't suppose I really meant that big."

"So what was strange about it?" Carter asked him. "You said it was stranger than five thousand gallons of water in an upstairs bedroom, didn't you?"

"Did I?"

I laid my hand on Carter's broad, flesh-padded shoulder. "I think that Dan's suffering from shock, Carter. Maybe it was just an illusion."

"Maybe *what* was just an illusion?"

"This thing he thought he saw. This carapace."

"I thought you said you saw it, too."

I smiled weakly. "We all make mistakes, Carter. We've both had a difficult day."

Carter rested his hands on his bulky hips and stared at us silently for almost half a minute. Then he said: "Okay. I'll let it go this time. But if there's any suggestion that anybody's concealing any material evidence, then it's going to be trouble time. You get me?"

"Nobody's concealing anything, Carter," I assured him. "We're just as anxious to find out what happened here as you are."

"Okay. But remember what the penalty for concealing material evidence is. It's jail. Okay?"

We all left the bathroom and crossed the landing again. The deputy coroner, Lawrence Dunn, a thin, bespectacled, grey faced man in a shiny tan suit, was coming up the stairs with his old brown leather bag.

"How are you doing, Larry?" asked Carter. "Are you ready for a second-floor drowning?"

Lawrence Dunn sniffed, and blinked. "Whatever it is, Carter, I'm ready for it. Hi there, Dan. Hi there, Mason. I gather you were the two unlucky finders. Poor young Oliver Bodine, huh?"

"That's right," said Carter. "I've just had Erroll put out an APB for Jimmy and Alison."

"They're missing?"

Carter led Lawrence to the drowned boy's bedroom. "They weren't here when Mason and Dan arrived, and that was a good hour ago by all accounts."

Lawrence knelt down on the wet carpet beside Oliver's body, and opened up his bag. First of all he flashed a penlight into the boy's eyes, and then he checked for other vital signs—pulse, respiration, reflexes. It was all a formality. There was no question that Oliver was dead.

"I'm going to have to take his body temperature now," said Lawrence. "Would one of you people give me a hand just to turn him over?"

Sheriff Wilkes bent down, and between them, Lawrence and he carefully turned Oliver on to his face. As the boy rolled over, water ran out of the side of his mouth and out of his nostrils. The sheriff stood up quickly and gave the coroner an unhappy kind of a frown.

"If there's one thing that scares people more than finding out that someone who was once alive is now dead, it's finding out that someone who was once dead is now alive," said Lawrence. He cut open Oliver's Six-Million-Dollar Man pyjamas at the back and rummaged in his bag for his rectal thermometer.

Sheriff Wilkes said: "Larry?"

"Umh-humh? That damn thermometer's here someplace."

"Larry," repeated Sheriff Wilkes. "What's the matter with the kid's back? Is that bruising, or what?"

Lawrence Dunn adjusted his spectacles and looked down at Oliver's exposed back and buttocks. He squinted closer, and then he touched the boy's skin, very gently, with his fingertips. "Hand me a flashlight," he said.

Dan and I both stepped nearer as one of the

deputies gave Lawrence his light. Sheriff Wilkes
said: "Don't crowd him, huh?" but he pushed forward himself and bent down so that he could see
what Lawrence was doing.

The deputy coroner pulled Oliver's pyjamas
open even further, and what he revealed in the
bright, theatrical light of the torch made my
stomach rise and tighten. One of the deputies
whispered: "Jesus—what in hell's name is that?"

Around the small of Oliver's back, and around
his buttocks and upper thighs, his skin had taken
on a hard, shell-like appearance. Each buttock,
instead of being round and soft, was now a plate of
greenish-grey shell, and dark lumps were forming
along the spine. Where his thighs met his buttocks
there was a gristly, lobster-like joint. Lawrence,
his hands shaking, turned the boy's body back
over again, and we could see that where his sexual
organs had once been, there was instead a spiny
array of blue and green crustaceous filaments.

We were all silent. We stood around Oliver's
body in the light of those police torches, gathered
together in that dark, sodden house, and none of
us knew what to do or what to say. Lawrence at
last stood up, tugging the wet cloth of his pants
away from his knees, and taking off his spectacles.

Outside, the wind blew sadly; and inside, the
rugs and the carpets sponged up the water with a
slow ticking sound. Sheriff Wilkes cleared his
throat.

"I think we have an idea what may have happened here," said Dan, in a low, almost inaudible
voice.

Lawrence Dunn looked at him, but Carter

couldn't take his eyes off the dull sheen of the shell on Oliver's body.

"If you think you have an idea, you'd better spit it out," said Carter.

"It's the whole reason we came up here," Dan explained. "The Bodines were complaining about discoloration in their water supply, and Mason here brought me a sample to test. I found some kind of organism in it, a microscopic creature that kept giving off a yellowy-green fluid."

"Did you identify it?" asked Lawrence.

Dan shook his head. "I didn't have time. One of the mice in my laboratory drank some of it by accident while Mason and I were out, and when we came back—well, the same thing had happened to the mouse that's happened to poor young Oliver here."

"So you think he's been drinking the water and it's made him turn all shell-backed like this?" asked Carter.

"There's no definitive proof, not yet."

"Do you think it might affect anybody else's water supply?" Lawrence wanted to know.

"I haven't any idea," said Dan. "But just to be safe, I'd try to put out a warning if I were you, telling the local folks to stick to bottled water for the time being. Until I find out what these organisms are, and why they affect people this way, then I think we have to assume that the whole community's in danger."

Carter looked down at Oliver's jointed thighs, and slowly shook his head. "I'll be damned if I've ever seen anything like that before."

One of the deputies, Erroll, a young sandy man

with a ginger moustache, came up from downstairs with a radio message from the volunteers
out looking for the Denton boy. As soon as he
walked into the room, he said: "My God, what's
that smell?"

"Smell?" asked Carter.

"That smell of bad fish. Hasn't it hit you?"

# 3

I was living, temporarily, in a stone-and-weatherboard weekend house just outside of New Milford, on the back road to New Preston. The house belonged to my lawyer, the same lawyer who had handled my divorce for me, but he rarely came up from the city these days, not since he'd broken up with his mistress. I used to live over a macrame and pottery store just across from the Foodliner store in the center of New Milford, but the lease had expired and the landlord had wanted the place for his aged sister. Shelley and I, rather than argue, had packed our bags and our ballcocks and our lengths of piping, and moved out.

Still, Shelley liked it out at New Preston. There was a small farm right opposite, where black-and-white cows grazed in the foggy fall mists and that meant there were plenty of mice to be played with. And the place was quiet, too. So quiet that you could step out of the back door at night and take a deep breath of that chilly Connecticut air, and hear nothing at all but scurrying leaves.

I didn't get back to the house until it was almost dawn. I parked the Country Squire on the sloping driveway, and climbed tiredly out. Shelley stretched himself out like a watchspring, and climbed after me. I'd named him Shelley after the poet Shelley, who had written: "How wonderful is Death, Death and his brother Sleep!" It never took a genius to figure out why.

It was cold in the hallway when I opened the front door. The log fire had long since died away, and there was nothing in the hearth but a pile of grey ashes. I kept on my red baseball cap and my sheepskin coat while I shovelled the ashes away, and stacked fresh logs on the firedogs. I crumpled up a copy of the New Milford paper and put a match to it. Shelley watched me from the sofa with an expression of haughty impatience.

Next, I went into the kitchen, which looked out over the sloping back yard, and put on the kettle. I needed a cup of coffee and a dose of Jack Daniel's. I stood by the window staring out at the grey and unwelcoming dawn, and thought about poor young Oliver Bodine and his missing parents.

Carter Wilkes had put out an alert for Jimmy and Alison, and he had distributed their description to the volunteers who were already searching for Paul Denton. He had also sent his deputies around, knocking on doors and instructing people around the New Milford and Washington Depot area not to drink their own well water. There were going to be radio and television bulletins, too, although all that Carter had told the news services so far was that the danger came from a possible sewerage leak. As for Oliver's death and Jimmy and Alison's disappearance, he had played those completely straight. Oliver had died "in a domestic accident," and Jimmy and Alison were being sought "in order to aid police inquiries."

Carter had made no public mention of the crustaceous growth on Oliver's back and thighs, neither had he given the Press any leads on Dan's investigations of the mouse and the Bodine well water. "The last thing I want around here is a goddamned flying-saucer panic," he had remarked.

The coroner's office, who were going to perform a full-scale autopsy on young Oliver's body, were also keeping tight-lipped. The medical investigator there was a quiet, grey-haired man called Jack Newsom, and he had always expressed a distaste for publicity and pyrotechnics. Lawrence Dunn felt the same way, and that meant Oliver's death would remain confidential until Sheriff Wilkes wanted to make a full-scale announcement.

It was just as well. It was going to shake New Milford rigid, knowing that their drinking water might turn them crusty as lobsters. It was as much as I could do to believe it myself, and I'd stood right there and seen young Oliver's body.

The kettle boiled and I made myself a jug of coffee. When it had brewed I took down a bottle of Jack Daniel's from the kitchen cupboard and poured a couple of fingers into the bottom of a mug. Then I topped it up with coffee, gave it a stir, and went through into the living-room to sit down beside Shelley and watch the log fire burn up. I felt chilled and exhausted and just about ready to join Shelley in a long sleep.

I was almost dozing off when the telephone rang. I yawned, stretched my face, and got up to answer it. I said: "Who is it?" and took a hefty mouthful of coffee and whisky.

"It's Dan," said Dan. "I'm back at the laboratory. I've been running some more tests on that water."

"Have you had any sleep yet?"

"Who needs sleep? This is important."

I yawned again. "Okay, it's important. What have you found out?"

Dan said: "I ran some dating tests on the water and the organisms in it. I got Rheta in to help me, and we must have gone through twenty or thirty tests, just to make absolutely sure."

"So? What does that do?"

"A dating test tells me the age of the organic material in the water, and that gives me a pretty clear idea about the depth from which it's risen out of the ground. If, for instance, the organic material is seven to eight thousand years old, then it probably originates from the deciduous forest layer which you can find about twenty feet under the surface. See what I mean?"

"Sure," I said. "The older it is, the deeper down it originates. So how old is the stuff in the Bodines' water?"

Dan paused. "Would you believe two million years? Or thereabouts, anyway."

"Two million years? You mean the organic stuff in that water is prehistoric?"

"That's right. We've checked, and there's no mistake. That water must have come up from subterranean sources more than a mile and a half under the surface."

I finished my coffee and whisky, and coughed. "That's ridiculous. Their well isn't more than a hundred feet deep, if that."

"The tests are conclusive."

"Okay, they're conclusive. But what do they prove? So the Bodines drank some very old water. Where does that leave us?"

Dan said patiently: "I don't think you're following me. The organisms in that water are also two million years old."

"I beg your pardon?"

"The little squiggly creatures. I've tested the fluid that comes out of them, and I've tested their own organic fabric. The results are always the same. I'm sending a small sample over to the radio-carbon laboratory at White Plains, just to make doubly sure, but I don't think there's any room for doubt. They're two million years old."

I closed my eyes. It was all getting too much for me. "Listen, Dan," I said tiredly, "how can anything be two million years old and still be living? Those organisms don't even have beards."

"All the same, it's true. They're living fossils. Rheta's checking up now, to see if we can relate them to any known prehistoric species."

I was silent for a long time. Standing there listening to Dan on the telephone, I suddenly felt tired and lonesome and mystified by everything that had happened in the past twelve hours. I was frightened, too, to tell you the God's-honest truth. I kept thinking about Oliver's terrible skin and the bony carapace in the bathtub, and the shuffling hulking figure I had seen disappearing over by the Bodines' fence.

Dan said: "I think we're going to have to make

some more tests, Mason, and maybe dig down into the well itself. That water's coming up from someplace, and for the public's protection I need to know where. Maybe you'd like to come out with us later this afternoon and give us some help. I've already advised Carter, and he's going to give us all the cooperation we need."

"What time would you like me to be there?" I asked him.

"Get some sleep first. I'm going to, just as soon as I've finished up here. Make it two-thirty, up at the house."

"All right," I said, and put the phone down. I looked across at Shelley and he squeezed his eyes closed, as if he was bored with the whole business.

"It's no good looking like that," I said, walking through to the bedroom. "There's a whole gang of two-million-year-old fossils in this town's drinking water, and so far it looks like they're giving people lobster shells. Do you want to wind up with a lobster shell? You, a cat?"

I undressed, straightened the bed out of the rumpled condition in which I had left it the morning before, and climbed between the sheets. I was so exhausted that it couldn't have been longer than four or five minutes before I was asleep.

While I slept, I had the weirdest dream, or dreams. I felt I was standing by the seashore, at night, and the moon was shining its shattered light across the surface of the ocean. Then, I was swimming, carried up and down on the waves, and I could feel the chill of the briny water. The moon appeared and disappeared like a remote and alien signal lamp.

Before long, I was plunging beneath the surface of the ocean itself. I wasn't afraid, and for some reason I felt no need to breathe. The water itself seemed to be breathable, and I could feel the cold, refreshing flow of brine through my lungs. It was almost impossible to see anything, though. The water was very dark, and I could only feel my way through the currents and undertows, and through the icy glittering schools of herring and bass. But what made this dream seem especially strange was that *I knew where I was going*, with great sureness and certainty. I knew that if I continued to swim in a wide leftward curve, I would soon reach a jutting headland of dark submarine rocks, and that once I reached those rocks I would only be a mile's hard swimming away from my destination.

Already ahead of me I could see dim shafts of moonlight playing down through the waters. Then the dark shape of the rocks began to appear out of the murk, and I swam faster and more urgently. It was dangerous to swim in the sea at night, and I knew it. The ocean was alive with slithery predators.

I had almost made the peak of the rocks when I sensed a vibration through the water. I took a deep gulp, and began to push myself forwards as hard and as fast as I could. Something had sensed that I was there, and was already coming after me. Something vicious and evil that was out to destroy me. I tried to dive deeper, twisting around in the water to evade capture, but I felt something seize my ankle, something as crushing and painful as a steel mantrap.

I woke up. For a while I couldn't work out where I was. I couldn't understand that I was on dry land, and that I was breathing air instead of water. I sat up, and I was chilled with sweat. Outside, it was a cold, pale morning, and the cows were munching peaceably on the rocky slopes of the farm. I left the bedroom and went back through to the living-room, where the fire was crackling and spluttering and burning up well. I stood naked in the middle of the room and swallowed down another Jack Daniel's.

Coughing, I returned to the bedroom. But the bed didn't look so appetizing any more. I was still tired, but the twisted sheets looked too much like the surface of an unpleasant and nightmarish ocean.

I called Rheta at the laboratory. Dan had left to get some sleep, but she was still there working on the water samples. She seemed surprised that I wasn't sleeping, too.

"I sleep very badly when I'm by myself," I told her. "You wouldn't consider coming out here and assisting me to rest, would you? Purely in the interests of public safety, of course."

She laughed softly. She might have been cool and independent and three times more brainy than Shelley and me put together, but she wasn't above responding to an improper suggestion or two. I like that in a girl. Especially when a girl takes me up on it.

But Rheta, of course, didn't. She was too busy saving the world from the prehistoric lobster people. She said: "Dan's really worried about what's happening here. He thinks it could be some kind of disease that's been lying dormant for centuries. Like when they dug up an old mass burial pit from the Black Death in London, three hundred years later, and two of the construction workers went down with a plague."

"He really believes that?" I asked her.

"He doesn't know for sure. We still have more tests to run on the mouse but there's no question that it's a pretty sick little animal."

I rubbed my eyes. "Is it a disease that anyone's heard of before?"

Rheta said: "I've been doing some checking, but it's real hard to come up with anything conclusive. I found out a couple of things."

"Such as?"

She riffled through her notepad. "Well, for instance, I called a paleontologist I know this morning. He said that the Currie expedition of 1954 to the Central Rift Valley of Africa found seven or eight fossilized creatures, and that two of them, even though they were early mammals, a species of deer, had skulls and front limbs like crustaceans. They looked as if they were gradually turning from endomorphs into ectomorphs. Or, of course, the other way around."

"Was anything proved?" I asked.

"Not a thing. There was a minor ruckus about them at the Wendell Institute, but in the end they were shelved as hoaxes, or completely atypical oddities. The truth was they didn't fit into any of the established theories of mammal development, and it was easier to discredit them and forget them."

I sipped some more whisky. "Is that all?" I wanted to know.

"There's only one thing more," said Rheta. "There was an outbreak of what was thought to be leprosy in Cuttack, in India, 1925, but the British doctor who treated most of the patients, a man called Austin, wrote a long report saying that it certainly *wasn't* leprosy. He said it was a form of ossification—you know, a sort of bony growth. He tried to pinpoint what caused it, and in the end he decided the disease had stemmed from the local drinking water. There was a very heavy monsoon that year, and the rivers had overflowed into the irrigation ditches and the dug wells."

"Did he describe this ossification?" I asked her. "Did he say what form it took?"

Rheta said: "He did better than that. He put together a beautiful descriptive addendum to his report, all in copperplate handwriting, with drawings."

"He did *drawings*?"

"He sure did," she said. "And the terrible thing is that his report was lost, about twenty years ago. It was borrowed from the Harvard University Library and never returned."

I reached for a cigarillo and lit it. "That's a goddamned shame. I'd like to have seen those drawings, even if they proved that what young Oliver Bodine went down with was something else altogether."

"Well, me too," said Rheta. "But I managed second best. I called my old professor of specialist medicine. He lives in Miami now, in retirement. But he remembers looking through the Austin report when he was a student. He thought Austin must have been off his head, and so he didn't take much serious notice of it. But he does recall one phrase in particular."

"What was that?" I asked.

"He said it came at the point where Austin was describing a patient he had visited in a village on the River Mahdnadi, in September of 1925. Apparently Austin had to drive fifty miles through heavy rain and thick mud before he found this village, and he was exhausted when he got there, and so he says himself that his impressions might have been distorted by tiredness. But he was taken to an isolated hut on the outskirts of the village, and led inside by an old woman. The hut was almost totally dark inside, with drapes over the windows and a blanket screening the door. There was somebody lying on a bed in there, but Austin could scarcely make him out, and the old woman insisted that he stood at least five or six feet away, and shouldn't make any attempt to examine the patient. But Austin wrote that he'd made out a heavy and bone-laden head, and an arm that was strangely oval in section, with the shine of dull leather. He also said that the patient's voice was hoarse and difficult to understand."

"Go on," I told her. Austin's evocation of his crustaceous patient was making me feel distinctly uneasy. I only had to half-close my eyes and I could imagine young Oliver Bodine's shell-plated thighs and buttocks, and that hideous spiny bone in the bath.

"There wasn't much more to tell," said Rheta. "Except that Austin was nauseated by what he called 'a stench of decaying fish so strong that I thought I must stifle.'"

"That's it," I said quietly. "That's exactly what Alison Bodine said about the water I took from their well, and that's exactly what Carter's deputy noticed in the Bodines' house. And I've smelled it myself now. A strong, overpowering stench of fish."

Rheta said: "I know. And I think there could be a connection. But we mustn't leap to instant conclusions. Just because Austin smelled fish in 1925, and Alison Bodine smelled fish yesterday, that doesn't mean we've established a scientific connection beyond reasonable doubt. There are plenty of things that smell like fish apart from fish. Have you ever smelled an overheating electric plug?"

"I know there weren't any overheating plugs at the Bodines' house," I said. "And I don't suppose Austin's patient on the banks of the River Mahdnadi had an overheating plug, either. Not unless a fuse was going in his hair rollers."

Rheta didn't laugh. Instead, she said: "I know it's tempting to come to snap conclusions, but we mustn't do it. This is too serious a situation to make mistakes. We're going to have to go through dozens more tests before we have any clear idea of what's happening."

I said: "How about Austin's drawing? Did your old professor remember what any of those looked like?"

"Not really. They were just sketches of hands and joints. Very detailed and accurate, but not very memorable."

"It's a goddamned shame that report's lost," I repeated.

"I know," said Rheta. "I even called the library

and had them look back over their records to see who had taken it out. Their records don't go back that far. They've just had to write it off as pilfered.''

I finished my drink. ''I guess that's as far as we can go, then, until we get the coroner's post-mortem report, and until we see what's down that well. Do you fancy some lunch?''

''Aren't you going to sleep?''

''Unh-hunh. I keep having bad dreams. And, like I told you, I hate to sleep by myself. How about the Iron Kettle at one o' clock? I could use one of their steak brochettes.''

''All right,'' agreed Rheta. ''As long as you don't let me drink too much wine.''

''Of course I won't,'' I told her. ''I don't need to make a lady drunk to impress her.''

''I wasn't thinking about that,'' Rheta retorted. ''It's just that I find it difficult to perform accurate scientific tests when I'm under the influence of alcohol.''

''Trust me to go for a bluestocking,'' I said. ''I'll see you later.''

The Iron Kettle is a colonial-style restaurant In an elegant white-painted house a few miles north of New Milford. It's the kind of place where you can sit at lunch for hours, surrounded by elderly Connecticut matrons with elastic support stockings and fraying white hair, while plates of tidily-arranged salads and neatly-prepared avocadoes are carried to and fro in an atmosphere of quiet gentility. Rheta and I sat at a table by the window drinking a plain white wine and looking out over the russet slopes of a fall garden.

Rheta was looking more attractive than ever. In the grey light from the window, her hazel eyes took on a translucent look, and her off-blonde hair shone with an appealing softness.

I said: "I can't imagine you dating Pigskin Packer."

"Are you jealous?"

"Why not?"

"Well," she said, with a gentle smile, "jealousy is the most destructive of all feelings. Jealousy destroys the people who feel it, as well as those for whom it's felt."

"I'm not *consumingly* jealous," I told her, looking at her over the rim of my glass as I drank. "I'm just *ordinary* jealous. And surprised, too. I don't know what a big lunk like that could possibly give you that I couldn't. Apart from fifty pounds of extraneous muscle, of course."

She smiled again, and looked away. "Maybe I'm just responsive to extraneous muscle," she said. "After all, there are plenty of men who are responsive to extraneous breast tissue."

"What's extraneous about breast tissue?" I demanded, a little too loudly. An old woman in a purple hat turned in her wheelback chair to stare at me through her half-glasses. I grinned at her reassuringly, and then hissed at Rheta: "Packer is such a dumb-bell. He has no class at all. His conversation comes right out of *Raggedy Ann*. An exclamation point after every sentence."

Rheta shrugged. "At least he's safe."

"Safe? What does that mean?"

The waitress arrived with my brochette of steak

tips and with Rhetta's grilled fish. I couldn't have eaten fish right then, but I guess scientists are less squeamish than the rest of us. I ground some black pepper over my rice, and then took a mouthful of steak and tomato. But I was still waiting for Rheta to answer me.

"Well," said Rheta, reaching for another breadstick, "I guess he's safe as opposed to unsafe."

"And I'm unsafe?"

She nodded. "I think you would be for me."

"What's unsafe about me? I'm the safest guy in the universe."

She squeezed lemon on her fish, and then started to eat. "I think you're attractive," she said, without looking up. "But I also think that you're too wound up in your own life. You're too wound up in yourself. You could hurt someone like me, hurt them bad, and never even realize you'd done it."

I didn't answer for a while, as I finished my mouthful of steak. But then I drank some more wine, and said quietly: "I wouldn't hurt you for anything."

"You may not *want* to hurt me, Mason, but you would. I know the kind of man you are. It's like the way you can never take anything seriously. That's okay, for a while. Every girl likes to laugh. But then the time comes when she needs to know that, even if you don't take the world seriously, you take *her* seriously. You see what I'm getting at?"

I reached across the table and laid my hand on hers. "I can take you seriously," I said simply. "What sort of proof do you need?"

"I don't know. What sort of proof are you prepared to give me?"

The old woman in the purple hat was eavesdropping on our conversation with increasing interest. I sat up and stared at her coldly, and she bent herself over her plate with exaggerated absorption, and applied herself to her breadcrumbed veal.

"Finish your lunch," I told Rheta. "Then come back to the house. I've built up the fire, and there's a bottle of Chablis in the icebox. The only thing I haven't done is tidy the bed."

She stared at me for a long time. The light brightened a little, as the grey clouds broke, and the sun shone down through the flaking leaves of the birch trees. She was wearing Gucci perfume, and she was so warm and delicious that I could have leaned across the table and kissed her right then.

She said: "You're supposed to be meeting Dan at two-thirty."

"So? I can still make it. It's only up the road a ways."

She licked her lips with the tip of her tongue. "I have to be back at the laboratory to finish those tests. Dan will skin me if I don't."

"Why don't you let me square it with Dan?" I asked her. "This thing is bigger than testing water."

She laid down her fork. "Aren't you too tired?" she inquired.

"Are you trying to talk yourself out of it?"

"No," she said, "I don't think I am."

"Well, then," I told her. "Finish your lunch, and then we'll go."

We didn't say very much more as we ate our fish

and our steak, and drank our wine. We looked into each other's eyes a lot, weighing-up, calculating, checking, prying. Then, when the meal was over, and I had paid at the desk and collected a book of matches and a mouthful of peppermints, we left the restaurant and walked across to our cars like two lovers in a European art movie, testing the wind and the weather and each other's feelings with every step.

Rheta had brought her Volkswagen. It was beige, and very battered. I said: "Why don't you come with me? I'll bring you back here later, and you can drive straight back into town."

"Okay," she nodded. I don't think she wanted to break the spell any more than I did. We both knew that she was going to have to go back to the laboratory this afternoon, and that when she left the laboratory in the evening she was going to meet up with Pigskin Packer; but right now we were living in our own magic time loop, where anything at all was possible, and where there were no rules.

Shelley grudgingly moved over for Rheta, and I started the Mercury's engine and drove out of the Iron Kettle parking lot. I turned on the radio to fill in the silent moments. We glanced at each other from time to time, and smiled, but I think we were both aware how fragile this interlude was, and how little it would take to finish it before it had even really begun. On the radio, Nils Lofgren was singing *Slow Dancing*.

The minutes to New Preston passed like a projector slide show. A view of Northville fire station. Trees, rocks, and white weatherboard houses. A steep-sloping side-road through the showering leaves. My front driveway. My front door. My living-room.

By the fire, I unbuttoned her russet wool coat for her. I kissed her forehead, the tip of her nose, her lips. She hesitated momentarily, and then kissed me back., Her coat fell to the floor.

I looked at her, and said softly: "This is one of those moments that I've been waiting for."

She looked back at me. The fire crackled brightly in the hearth, and the whole room was filled with the warmth of our suddenly-flowering affection. I twisted the top button of her blouse free, and glimpsed a bare-look nylon bra.

Then a voice said: "Mr. Perkins?"

I jerked up my head in shock. Rheta pulled away from me, and buttoned up that one vital button again. Standing in the open kitchen doorway, in a torn plaid shirt and jeans, his face scratched and bruised and his hair tousled, was young Paul Denton, the nine-year-old boy Carter had been looking for with a whole posse of deputies since late yesterday. He was pale and shaking, and it looked as if he hadn't eaten or drunk anything since he had vanished. He blinked at us, and swayed, and then he fell against my drinks trolley and sent glasses and bottles and cocktail sticks cascading on to the rug

I knelt down beside him and lifted his head. He was still conscious, although his breathing was laboured, and his eyes flickered as if he was concussed. I said: "Paul? What's the matter, Paul? Where have you been?"

"Mr. Perkins," he whispered.

"Rheta," I said, "go call Carter. Tell him he's

going to need an ambulance, too. This kid looks terrible."

"Mr. Perkins," repeated Paul. "Mr. Perkins."

"Just stay quiet," I told him. "Rheta's gone to call the police."

Paul shook his head desperately. "No police, please. No police, Mr. Perkins, not yet. Please."

Rheta was already dialing. I said: "Everybody's been worried sick about you, Paul. We have to tell the police."

*"No!"* he shouted. *"I promised I wouldn't!"*

I raised my hand to Rheta. "Hold it a moment, Rheta. Don't call them yet. Paul—what do you mean you promised you wouldn't? Who did you promise?"

Paul was trembling now. Every muscle in his body was tense and quivering and he had to speak between clenched lips. He reminded me of a woman I had taken to the hospital after a bad road accident on the Danbury road. Shocked, almost incapable of speech, and yet determined to tell me what had happened.

I said: "*Who* did you promise, Paul? Who said you mustn't call the police?"

He stared at me with a wild expression. "No police, Mr. Perkins, please, no police. I promised."

"I'm not going to call the police, Paul. But you have to tell me what's happened. Where have you been? Have you been with someone?"

He nodded. "I saw them—both of them."

"Who? Who did you see?"

"They were hiding in the woods. It was dark. I didn't know what I was doing there."

Rheta brought over a cushion and I lifted Paul's

head so that she could tuck it under him. As I laid him back, I asked him gently: "Tell me who it was, Paul. I need to know. *Who* was hiding in the woods?"

"They asked for you, Mr. Perkins," he said, as if he hadn't heard me. "I heard them calling, and I went to see what they wanted. I couldn't believe it when I saw them. I didn't understand at all. But they talked to me, and they said they had to see you. They said it was life or death. That was what they said. Life or death."

"Paul," I insisted, "who was it? Who said it was life or death? I can't help if I don't know who it was."

Paul's eyes rolled up into his head so that only the whites were exposed. In a shaking whisper, he said: "It was Jimmy and Alison Bodine. They said they were Jimmy and Alison Bodine."

"They *said* they were?" asked Rheta. "Surely you know them well enough to know for sure?"

"It was dark," Paul said huskily. His eyes flickered again, and the pupils reappeared. "I don't know what I was doing there, but it was so dark."

I sat up straight, biting at my thumbnail. Paul lay there among the broken glasses and scattered cocktail sticks, still shaking, and I said to Rheta: "I think you'd better call Carter. Whatever he promised, he needs medical help."

Rheta nodded, and went to the phone. I heard her talking to Phil More, one of Carter's deputies, and then she came back and told me that a police car and an ambulance were on their way. Paul was shuddering more feebly now, his eyes opening and closing and turning around as if they were com-

pletely uncontrolled, and it seemed to me that he
was in a heavy state of shock.

"Don't try to talk," I said quietly. "You'll be
okay in a little while."

Paul muttered for a while, and then he said, in
quite a clear voice, but with a curiously detached
kind of intonation: "I was lost, you see. I was on
my bicycle and I knew that I had to go into the
woods. But once I was there I didn't know where I
was."

"It's all right, Paul," I comforted him. "You
don't have to talk. Just rest easy and we'll have
some people around to help you in a while."

But Paul was unstoppable. He spoke as if he was
under hypnosis, as if every word had been taught
to him while he was in a trance. In his high,
childish voice, he said: "I felt I was close to the
place. I didn't know for sure. But I had a feeling I
was. It was the great place that you read about in
books. I was frightened, but not too much. I could
hear things I never heard before. Loud noises,
loud shouts."

"Did you hear what was being shouted?" I asked
him. But again he ignored me, and whispered: "I
knew what was going to happen. I would have to
wait. It was almost dark then I waited and waited,
and then I knew that I had to walk as far as the
Coleman house. It was very dark, and I fell over
four or five times. I scratched my face on the
trees."

"Was that when you saw Jimmy and Alison?"

Paul nodded. "They called to me, from the
bushes. They said I mustn't come close. They said
I had to go find you, and bring you out to the

woods. They made me promise no police. If you go with police, or anybody else, you won't ever find them."

"Did you see them?" asked Rheta.

Paul shook his head. "It was too dark. They looked like they were wearing blankets over their heads. I didn't understand why."

I bent forward again. "Their voices," I asked Paul. "Did you hear their voices clearly?"

"They weren't clear," he said. "They must have been talking with their blankets over their mouths. They weren't clear. They were kind of growling. I didn't like it."

"Do you know where they were—where I can go to find them?" I asked.

Paul said feebly: "No police. They won't come out if you bring the police."

"I promise no police."

"All right. They'll be waiting for you when it's dark. They're in back of the old barn on the Pascoe place, maybe three minutes' walk straight into the woods. They told me to say that. In back of the old barn on the Pascoe place. But only when it's dark."

Rheta felt Paul's pulse. She said: "He's very weak. I hope that ambulance doesn't take too long. He could use some oxygen."

I stood up and went to the window. Very faintly in the distance, I could hear the whoop-whoop scribble-scribble sound of the ambulance siren and I knew that they wouldn't take longer than a couple of minutes. There was only one more question I wanted to ask Paul.

"Paul," I said softly, kneeling down beside him again.

Rheta frowned at me, but it was something I had to know.

"Paul did you *smell* anything in the woods? Was there a smell you remember?"

Paul trembled and twitched, and didn't answer.

I hesitated for a moment, and then I went into the kitchen, opened the food cupboard, and rummaged quickly through for a can of tuna. I had one small size Chicken-of-the-Sea left, and I took it across to the can opener and lifted off the lid.

Rheta said: "What are you doing?" as I came back through the dining-room with the can opened up.

"You'll see," I told her. "I don't like to do it, but it could make all the difference. Both for Jimmy and Alison, and for me, too."

I raised the can of tuna and wafted it under Paul's nose. Then I withdrew it, and waited. He stopped shaking for a moment, his hands drawn up to his chest in a weak but self-protective gesture. Then suddenly his eyes opened wide and they were nothing but naked white eyeballs, and he screamed a long, throat-scratching scream of terror and agony. He twisted and writhed on the rug, and I had to throw the tuna aside and hold him down. It was all I could do to keep him still, even though he was only a nine-year-old boy, and it wasn't until Rheta shushed him and calmed him that he began to stop jerking and shaking and settle down again.

There was the falling drone of a siren outside. I sat up, feeling shaken, and I looked at Rheta as if the moment that had brought us back here in the first place had passed more than a hundred years ago.

She said: "It's true, then. What's happened to that mouse, what happened to those people in India. It's happened again."

I stood up. There were hurried footsteps outside, and a ring at the doorbell. All I could say was: "I don't know. I guess we're going to have to wait until we see Jimmy and Alison for ourselves. Meanwhile—for Paul's sake—I don't think we ought to tell Carter where they are."

Rheta thought for a moment, and then nodded. I went to the door and opened it up for the medics, who came briskly into the living-room with a stretcher and an oxygen bottle. One of them said: "Is this your son?"

I shook my head. "No. I guess he's just a lost boy."

Dan had been waiting for me for fifteen minutes when I arrived at the Bodine house. He was sitting on the rail of the front verandah reading a copy of *Scientific American.* He wore a fawn-and-blue plaid coat and a matching cap to cover his bald head, and if I'd been a plain twenty-five-year-old girl from just outside of Brainerd, Minnesota, I think I might even have taken a fancy to him.

I said: "Hi. I'm sorry I'm late. Something interesting came up."

"Oh, yes?" said Dan, a little tartly. He was a dedicated man, and he didn't like his time to be wasted.

"We found the Denton boy. He was in my house, looking for me. He just showed up, looking like he'd been dragged through a venetian blind backwards. He's in the hospital now, having treatment for shock and exhaustion."

"What happened to him?" asked Dan, folding up his magazine and tucking it into his coat pocket. He was just the kind of guy who would carry around a magazine in his coat pocket.

"He, er, well he's all right. He got lost, that was all."

We walked around to the back of the house, where the wellhead was. Dan said: "He got *lost?*"

"Maybe he fell off his bicycle, something like that. Knocked his head. You know, amnesia."

Dan held my arm. "Now, wait a minute, Mason. I know when you're telling the truth and I also know when you're spinning me a story. I've known you long enough for that."

"Dan," I told him, "I'm just a simple plumber, plying my trade the best way I know how."

"You're a goddamned smartass plumber. Now what's up with Paul?"

I sighed. I looked away across the distant hills. Towards the west, the sky was a threatening metallic grey, and it looked as if it might rain in an hour or two. The rust-coloured trees swayed and champed in the wind.

"Paul's found Jimmy and Alison Bodine," I said.

Dan blinked. "He's found them? What do you mean? Where are they?"

"He says they're hiding in the woods in back of old man Pascoe's place. He says he came across them by accident. There's something badly wrong with them, Dan. They're keeping themselves covered with blankets, and they won't let anyone come close."

Dan looked at me, wide-eyed.

"There's something else," I told him. "It may be nothing more than a wrong guess, but I tried waving an open can of tuna under Paul's nose. He went crazy. He screamed like all the devils in hell were after him. So my guess is that whatever's happened to Jimmy and Alison, it has a lot to do with the smell of fish."

Dan coughed. He said, in a thick voice: "I think I believe you. If you can tell me something like that without making a joke of it, then I think I believe you."

"You sound like Rheta," I told him. But he didn't understand that at all and he continued to frown in concentrated thought.

"Rheta told you about Austin?" he asked. "The 1925 outbreak?"

"Sure. And the Currie expedition."

Dan nodded. "She was able to track those down in a single morning. If you ask me, a good search through the medical history files would turn up a whole lot more. It would take time, though. And I'm not too sure how much time we've got."

"What's that supposed to mean?" I asked him.

"Just think about it," he replied. "Jimmy and Alison complained about their water Tuesday morning. By the same evening, they were infected by whatever their water contained. So was Oliver. I don't know what time of the evening young Oliver was drowned, not until the police pathology people give us some kind of report, and so I don't know how quickly that shell started to overtake his body. But I do know this. It happened damned fast. Now, if this thing is spreading, if all the wells around here are infected, then we don't have any

time at all. We're going to find that the whole
damn town of New Milford is turning crustaceous,
and once that happens—"

There was a grumbling of far-away thunder.
Lightning stalked behind the hills.

"More rain," said Dan. "We've had more rain
this year than we have for a half-century. The
water-table is so damned high we're practically
paddling in it."

I said: "Don't you think we'd better take a look
at the well, now we're here? Take a couple more
samples, just to make sure?"

Dan paused for a moment, and then nodded. We
stepped down from the verandah and walked
around the side of the house. The thunder
rumbled again, and, for an odd moment, I felt as if
the earth itself was stirring under my feet. I
looked at Dan and said: "Did you feel that?"

"A kind of a tremor? Like an earthquake?"

"That's right."

He stood still, and lifted his head to the breeze.
At the far end of the Bodines' yard, their barn was
illuminated with unnatural brightness by a wash
of sunlight from behind the clouds. I felt as if I had
stepped into an Andrew Wyeth painting, where the
colours were all pale and sharp and life was
threatened by its very ordinariness.

"I don't know," he said. "I guess it was thunder,
that's all."

We waited a little longer, but there were no
more tremors, and so we continued around to the
back yard. The screen door trembled and rattled
in the threatening wind, and there was an air of
desolation around that made me feel unaccount-

ably depressed.

We paused again. I was sure I could hear something. A crackling, or a bubbling sound. I wasn't quite certain which. Dan was about to mount the steps to the kitchen door but I held his arm and said: "Sssh. Listen to that."

He listened. Then he said: "It sounds like water. Now, where the hell could that be coming from?"

We skirted the back of the house. It was even darker here, because of the overhanging trees, and crisp fall leaves whirled all around us. The first heavy rain-drops began to plop against the roof of the rear porch and rattle through the trees. But the bubbling sound was louder now, and distinctly water, and we followed it across the sloping lawn to the old garden hand-pump, a rusted Victorian relic painted with red lead.

"Look at that," said Dan. "That water's bursting out all over."

From the foot of the pump, out of an inch-wide fissure in the dirt, a torrent of well-water was jumping and bubbling. Already it had washed itself a water course across towards the ditch which bordered the Bodines' property to the east, and its pressure was so high that it was detaching chunks of soil and stones and widening its outlet all the time.

Dan knelt down on the wet grass and took out a sample bottle. He filled it with water directly from the fissure, and then he stood up and corked it.

"What causes an outbreak like that?" he asked me. "These wells aren't usually under that much pressure, are they?"

"No, sir," I told him. I hunkered down, too, and

felt the force of the water against the palm of my hand. It was icy cold, and seemed to be growing in strength with every moment.

"Do you have any ideas about it?" Dan asked me.

I shrugged. "This sort of pressure could be caused by any one of a whole lot of different factors, or even two or three different factors combined. One underground water system could have filled up so much that it's poured through into another. Or there could even have been some kind of mild volcanic activity."

"That tremor we felt?"

"Maybe. I don't know."

I was still thinking about it when I saw a man come around the side of the house and walk slowly towards us. He looked like a neighbour, a red-faced man in faded dungarees and a soiled fawn hat. He was stocky, and he walked with his hands in his pockets. When he came within a few feet of us, he stood still and looked at us like a farmer who finds a courting couple in his wheatfield.

"I saw your cars outside, reckoned I'd drop by and see what was up," the man remarked.

"Glad to see the Bodines have a neighbour who takes an interest," I said, standing up and wiping my wet hand with my handkerchief. "I'm Mason Perkins, the plumber, and this is Dan Kirk, from the county medical department."

"I've seen you around New Milford," nodded the neighbour. "My name's Greg McAllister. I just moved into the house next door a few weeks back."

"Greg McAllister?" asked Dan. "Aren't you

William McAllister's son? Used to live in the same house?"

"That's right. The house has always been in the family, only I left it when pa died, and went to farm in Iowa. Now I've sold out my farm and come home to Connecticut. Getting too old for the outdoor life, you understand."

Dan said: "Have you heard the warnings about the well water around here? You haven't been drinking it, have you?"

"No, sir," said Greg McAllister. "I've never drunk the well water in my whole life, not me nor my father in front of me, nor his father."

"You haven't? But why ever not?" asked Dan.

Greg, with his hands till firmly in his pockets, gave us a noncommittal shrug. "Maybe it was stupid," he told us, "but the belief in my family always was that the wells around here were cursed. My grandpa used to call them the wells of Hell."

# 4

From the hills over by Kent, there was a long rumble of thunder like a dinosaur with chronic gas. Greg McAllister looked up and said: "That rain's going to come down like all Moses in a moment."

I said: "We'd better take shelter on the porch. Do you have all the samples you need, Dan?"

Dan nodded, and so we left the garden pump and walked quickly back to the house. Just as we reached the porch, the rain came down in torrential sheets, drumming on the tarpaper roof over our heads, gurgling in the gutters, and drifting across the lawns in ghosts of spray.

"Sure been a wet one this year," said Greg McAllister, taking out a pack of Camels and lighting up. "The back end of my four-acre field is just awash."

"You still farm?" asked Dan.

"I keep a couple of cows, but that's about it. And they're just for scenery."

I leaned against the wooden planking of the house and took off my baseball cap. "I never heard any stories about any curse," I told him.

"On the wells you mean?" asked McAllister, blowing out twin streams of smoke from his hairy nostrils. "Well, it was a pretty old story, one of those real old folk stories that died out, you know? Some of the people round here have heard about it, the geriatrics, but most of them haven't. New Milford ain't the same place it was when I was a boy."

"What kind of a curse was it?" asked Dan.

Greg McAllister sniffed, "Well, it was a kind of a rhyme, that was all I ever knew. My pa used to tell it to me when I was going to sleep, when I was real small boy. He said nobody round these parts ever drank the local well water, they always went across to Squantz Pond. But they never drank from their own wells, only used it for washing or irrigation or watering the beasts."

I took out a cigarillo and lit it. I was feeling slightly nauseous, and I wondered if maybe I'd eaten my steak brochette too quickly. I had been in a nervy sort of condition, after all. I could have done with a pint and a half of Pepto-Bismol, and a couple of packs of Rol-Aids.

"You smoke those things with the plastic tips?" asked Greg McAllister. "I heard those plastic tips could give you cancer of the teeth."

"Cancer of the *teeth?*" asked Dan.

"That's right. Plastic's supposed to be the biggest cause of cancer, bar cheese."

I glanced at Dan. It seemed like Greg McAllister was slightly less than a reliable witness on the subject of health. But Dan pulled a face as if to say, well, he's the only witness we've got. Out loud, he said to Greg: "Tell us about this rhyme, then, Greg. Can you remember how it ran?"

Greg smiled, a crinkly smile that folded his mouth like a used tissue. "I sure can. My pa told me that rhyme over and over, every night of my boyhood, and I guess I won't forget how it ran until I'm stiff as a board and ready to meet my Lord."

He took a deep drag at his cigarette, blew out smoke, and then said: "The way it went was this:

'Don't drink thee water,
Drink thee wine,
Lest old Pontanpo's curse
Be thine.

'We sup us not
From Preston's well,
And so we keep
Our skin from shell.'"

Dan raised his eyebrows. He said to Greg McAllister: "Your father told you that rhyme? How long ago was that?"

Greg rubbed his chin and thought. "I'm sixty-one come February, so I guess that was all of fifty years ago."

"Did he ever say what the words meant?" I asked him.

Greg looked puzzled. "What they *meant?*"

"That's right. Did he say what old Pontanpo's curse was, for instance? Or what keeping your skin from shell meant?"

The rain spattered on to the boards of the porch. Greg shook his head slowly from side to side, and said: "I don't reckon he did. He may have done, when I was real young. But I sure don't remember any meaning. It never did occur to me to look for a meaning. The words mean what the words mean, and that's all."

"Can you *guess* what they mean?" I persisted.

"Well, sure," he told me. "When it says 'drink thee wine', it means you have to stay off the well water, and I guess old Pontanpo was some kind of a Red Indian. It sounds like a Red Indian name, don't it? Maybe the Red Indians put some curse on the well water, one of them old-time Algonquians, you know? Or maybe he didn't, who's to know? But anyway the second verse says that we don't drink well water from around New Preston on account of it keeps our skin from shell."

"Do you know what that means? Can you guess? Did anyone ever tell you?"

Greg drew hard at his cigarette, and the tip of it glowed bright orange. When he'd considered a while, and scratched the back of his leathery neck, criss-crossed with wrinkles and deep red from years of farming, he shook his head in resignation.

"I think I asked my pa once," he said "And my pa said it was something to do with the knee people."

"The *knee* people. You mean, knee like in halfway down your leg?"

"I guess so. He didn't know any more. He just said the rhyme was to warn folks about the knee people, and that was it. He didn't know no more.

Some of the older residents did, but not him, and he wasn't particularly minded to ask. He said it was one of those things it was best not to know of anyway."

Dan took out his sample of water and held it up to the grey light of the rainy afternoon. Even from where I was standing, I could see that it had the same yellowish tint as before, although that might have been partly due to the dirt which the bubbling well water had stirred up as it came gushing out of the ground. Only a full analysis would tell us.

He said to Greg McAllister: "Did you ever see the well water? Did you ever see it yellowy-green, like this?"

Greg squinted at the sample, and then shook his head again. "I don't remember the well water ever being anything at all but clear. That's full of mud, ain't it, that water?"

Dan said: "No. If it were, the lower part of the water would be tinted more darkly by now, as the suspension settled. But it's still the same tint of yellow all the way up."

"Is that poison?" asked Greg.

"It's possible," said Dan. "That's what I'm trying to find out."

I puffed at my cancerous cigarillo and put in: "That's why we wanted to know about the rhyme. There might be some kind of clue in one of the old stories."

Greg looked from Dan to me, and then back again. "You're really interested in all them old tales? All them old rhymes?"

"Sure. Do you know any more?"

"Not myself. But my grandpa kept a book in the house in which he said were old stories of New Milford and Washington and all around. *Legends of Litchfield*, that was the name of it."

I checked my watch. It was still raining, and it was already a few minutes after three. I began to think about Jimmy and Alison Bodine, hiding out in this downpour, waiting for dark, and the thoughts that I had were less than reassuring. They were frightening, even. Something was terribly wrong with Jimmy and Alison. The shell had overtaken their skin, and for some reason they wanted me to help them. I guess I was the only person they felt they could trust. I guess I was the only person who wouldn't shoot first and worry about what to do with lead-and-lobster Newburg afterwards.

Dan asked Greg McAllister: "Do you still have that old book? I'd really like to take a look at it."

"It's in store now. Everything went into store when pa died, and we rented the house out. It's all down at the Candlewood Furnishers. If you want to see it real bad, I could always give you a letter for old man Martin. He'd let you lend a borrow of it for a while."

"That would be real neighbourly," said Dan. "Whatever happened to Jimmy and Alison, this water and all the old stories about it could help us to get them out of a real fix."

Greg tossed his cigarette butt out into the rain. There was a bright wash of sunshine appearing from the west now, and the rain began to glitter as it drifted across the grass. Greg said, in a low voice: "I heard they killed young Oliver. Drowned him in the bathtub, something like that. Is that the truth?"

I said: "No. We don't know what happened yet. We haven't even found Jimmy and Alison. Carter Wilkes says the case is still wide open."

"I'm only repeating what I heard tell," said Greg McAllister. "I didn't mean to cause any mischief."

"I know that," I told him. "But you can tell whoever told you that it's not true, and you can make sure they spread the right story just as fast as they managed to spread the wrong one."

"Well, I sure will. Do you want that letter now, for old man Martin? If you want to give me a ride back to my property, I could set it down for you straight away."

"Thanks. That would help."

Greg McAllister gave another of his crumpled, wrinkly smiles. "I'm real glad of that. I'm a neighbour, see, and I can tell you straight that I'd do anything in the world to be of help. Anything at all, bar nothing."

Dan sighed. "Thank you, Mr. McAllister. Now let's go, shall we, while the rain's still easy?"

By the time we returned to Dan's laboratory in New Milford, the sky was almost black, and there was a smell of more rain in the air. Mrs. Wardell had gone home with a migraine, but Rheta was still there, working at the binocular microscope on sections of skin taken from the body of the crustaceous mouse. She sat alone in a bright ellipse of lamplight.

The mouse itself was lying on a pad of cotton at the bottom of its cage, panting. It was still as shell-backed as ever, although its encrustations didn't seem to have spread any further along its body. I took a quick look at it and then turned away. It reminded me too much of poor young Oliver Bodine, and of what I might have to face when I went out to meet his parents. Shells, and gristly joints, and bony carapaces.

Dan hung up his wet raincoat, and said: "How's it going? Any luck with the Hersman tests?"

Rheta sat up straight on her lab stool and rubbed her eyes. Dan leaned forward and peered into the microscope himself.

"That looks like a regular crustaceous structure," he said.

Rheta nodded. "There really isn't anything unusual about the cell formations at all. The chitinous parts of the mouse have a type of cell structure similar to a crab shell, and the mousey parts of the mouse are absolutely normal and unremarkable."

"Have you tried giving the mouse more of the Bodines' water?"

"No. I haven't gotten around to that yet. And I'm not sure that we have the equipment or the expertise to handle an experiment of that magnitude. At the very least, we'd need a Morton refractor."

Dan smoothed the top of his bald head thoughtfully. "You think we ought to pass this on to Hartford?"

She climbed off the stool and walked across to the mouse's cage. She stared at the tiny monster through the bars for a moment, and then she said: "The change is so sophisticated. Ordinary soft mouse flesh has metamorphosed into something like crab shell, and the whole process has happened without killing the mouse or thirty even interfering with its bodily functions. I made twenty or thirty X-rays, and they all show that, internally, the mouse is still functioning properly. Let me show you."

We gathered around the fluorescent light table at the end of the room, and Rheta opened an envelope of X-ray photographs. She clipped them on to the light table, and we examined them with care.

"This is one of the clearest," said Rheta, pointing. "You can see that the mouse's internal bone structure seems to have dissolved, and that all its bodily calcium has gravitated somehow to its outer skin layer. What we're actually seeing is a creature that has turned itself inside out, and developed bones on the surface instead of inside."

I peered at the X-rays cautiously. "Is there any indication that the water was responsible for it?" I asked her.

She shrugged. "There's nothing conclusive. I can't say one hundred per cent. But from all the studies I've made today, I'd say that those squiggly bugs in the water are giving off some kind of enzyme which catalyzes this whole process."

"I see. So you think it's definitely the water?"

"Eighty-eight per cent certain."

Dan flicked through the rest of the X-ray photographs, and then switched off the light table. He was silent for a moment, but then he said: "The thing that still irks me is *why*."

"Why what?" I asked him.

He looked up. "Why these two-million-year-old microscopic creatures are still living, and why

they affect people and animals in such an extraordinary way. I thought at first they were some
kind of disease virus, but they don't behave like
viruses, and what that mouse is suffering from
isn't a disease in my understanding of the word. It
has a *condition*, that mouse, and I know what that
condition is, but I can't see why. I can't see where
it fits into the life cycle of the bugs, or into the life
cycle of *anything*."

Rheta said: "You must admit that we haven't yet
seen a complete cycle. This mouse is only half
ossified, just like young Oliver Bodine was. We
don't know what happens when the shell over-
takes the whole body."

I coughed. "Maybe we'll find out tonight, when
we go see Jimmy and Alison."

Rheta gave me an uneasy smile. "I hope you
won't, quite honestly. For their sakes."

I said: "Suppose these squiggly bugs are like
mosquitoes. Supposing they're just carrying this
enzyme from one host to another."

"That's a theoretical possibility," said Dan.
"But what host could there possibly be below the
Litchfield Hills, a mile and a half down? Where
could they have picked up the condition in the
first place?"

I shrugged. "Maybe there's a prehistoric carcass
down there. A dead caveman, something like
that."

Dan raised an eyebrow.

"I know it's wild," I told him, "but the whole
situation's pretty wild, and maybe we need to go
looking for wild answers."

Dan looked across at Rheta, who gave us both a

sympathetic, encouraging smile. I wished I'd been able to spend just a few more minutes with her back at the house, but I guess that was destiny. We might meet again in another existence, or even next Friday if I could persuade her to stand up Pigskin Packer.

Dan said: "Okay. Let's think of some wild answers. Got any more?"

I sat down on the edge of the laboratory bench. "I'm not sure. But I get the feeling there's some kind of *purpose* behind all this. Look at the way Oliver Bodine drowned. Whatever did that, whatever actually engineered a drowning in a second-floor bedroom, well, that being wasn't weak and it wasn't stupid. It could have been a man. If you gave me a week or two, and a handbook on hydro-engineering, I could probably fathom out how to do it. But the thinking behind it doesn't seem to be human. I mean, a human uses the easiest and most effective means available to dispose of his victims. Why drown the boy by filling the whole room up with water when he could have been drowned just as effectively in a china basin? Why drown the boy at all when you could have more easily stabbed him? Why stab him when you could have shot him? It just doesn't make any kind of sense for a human being to kill a small boy by flooding his entire upstairs bedroom."

Rheta ran her hand through her hair. "So what are you saying? That whatever did it *wasn't* human?"

I held out my hands. "If you apply the psychological law that all creatures use the simplest means available to them for doing anything, then you have to deduce that flooding that bedroom was the simplest means of killing Oliver that his murderer could draw on."

Dan sighed. "What the hell kind of a creature finds flooding a bedroom simple? A whale?"

"I don't know. I'm only speculating."

"I see. So you think that Oliver was killed by a whale. And what about the bugs in the water? Where do they fit in?"

"I'm not sure," I told him.

"I'm glad there's something you're not sure of," he answered, sarcastically. "I'd hate to think I'd be left without *any* scientific research to do."

I took out a cigarillo and lit it. I puffed out a whole cloud of smoke and then I said: "All right, it sounds weird. But what other explanation is there? An explanation that fits the facts, and the circumstances, and the psychology."

"I don't know. But you're presupposing there's some kind of creature that's capable of transporting five thousand gallons of water up to the Bodine place, and back again. You're presupposing there's some kind of creature that would actually *want* to."

"Well, somebody or something wanted to," I retorted, "because somebody or something did it."

Dan didn't answer for a while. But then he said: "Okay, let's leave that question for the moment. Maybe Carter will come up with some more details. What about the bugs? What's your theory on those?"

Rheta said: "Maybe they were put into the water supply deliberately. Maybe they're some kind of germ warfare."

"I hardly think so," said Dan, shaking his head.

"Why not?" asked Rheta. "The Soviets have nerve gas, and dirty hydrogen bombs, and viruses. Why shouldn't they have squiggly bugs that turn people into shell-backed monsters?"

"Because it doesn't make sense," snapped Dan. "The Soviets would want to kill people, not turn them into monsters. And apart from that, New Milford is hardly the most strategically sensitive spot in the United Sates."

"I think the drowning and the bugs in the water are both manifestations of the same problem," I put in. "We have to think of them as clues that are going to lead us to the same source."

"I know," said Dan. "I know. A giant whale with homicidal tendencies."

I looked outside at the thundery sky. It was almost dark now, and that meant a rendezvous with Jimmy and Alison in back of old man Pascoe's place. I had an odd jingly, jittery feeling in the palms of my hands, and I suddenly realized I had almost chewed my way through my plastic cigar-holder.

Rheta said: "One thing's plain, anyway. We don't have enough evidence yet to draw any sensible conclusions. We're going to have to wait until Jack Newsom comes up with his medical report on Oliver, and all the tests are completed on this mouse."

I asked Dan: "Are you going to come with me down to the Pascoe place? I may need some help."

"Sure, if you don't think I'll scare them off."

I gave him a wry smile. "I think they're more likely to scare us off. Do you have a flashlight

here? I think I left mine at home. And how about a
camera? Even if we don't get to see them too well,
we might be able to catch a couple of pictures."

"I have an infra-red camera downstairs. Rheta—
is there any film in the icebox?"

Rheta went to the icebox to check. Because
infra-red film is sensitive to heat, and not to light,
it has to be kept cool. While she sorted through
the trays of cultures and glass slides on the icebox
shelves, Dan and I looked soberly down at the
panting mouse and wondered what the hell we
were letting ourselves in for.

Outside, there was an ear-splitting crack of
thunder, and the rain began to pound on the roof
of the laboratory as if it was determined to break
through and drown us all.

"Do you have a Bible here?" I asked Dan. "Just
in case we need the dimensions for building an
ark."

It wasn't a long drive to old man Pascoe's place,
but the road wound through the hills and the
woods towards Sherman, and the rain turned my
windshield into a dancing, reflecting kaleidoscope
of blurry lights and shadowy trees. Shelley had
decided that he was too cold on the back seat, so
he dropped over on to Dan's lap, and sat there
looking uncomfortable, digging his claws into
Dan's thighs every time we swayed around a
corner.

We didn't talk much on the way. Dan wasn't feeling in a particularly speculative mood, and I was
too nervous. Maybe Dan was nervous, too. I think
anybody would have been at the prospect of meet-

ing two human beings who by all accounts had been turned into grotesque crustaceans. But it surprised me that we were able to accept the situation with such relative calmness. What was happening was frightening and logically impossible, and yet we were facing it without too much panic and in a pretty practical way. Mind you, a lot of our courage came from plain ignorance. We didn't know what we were up against, and what we didn't know didn't frighten us.

Old man Pascoe's place was always closed up for the winter. He used to be one of the leading dairymen around Sherman, but after his wife had died and his sons had grown up and left him, he had gradually declined into benevolent senility. He still came up to Connecticut in the summer, and sat on his porch under his proudly-waving Stars and Stripes, waving and calling to anyone who walked or bicycled past; but in the winter, when the cold was too much for his bones, he flew south to Miami, and stayed in a tacky condominium with his younger son Wilf, who sold insurance.

We reached the mailbox with the reflective letters PASCOE on it, and *New Milford Tribune* in Gothic letters beneath. Then I turned the Country Squire right through a screen of ash and birch trees, down the bumpy darkness of a cinder driveway, towards the ghostly white Colonial house with its green-painted verandahs. I pulled up outside and switched off the engine, but not the lights. The rain drummed and swept on the windshield and the roof, and we felt as if we were sitting in a lifeboat at sea.

"The barn's about seventy or eighty yards out in back, if I remember," I told Dan. "I guess what I'd better do is check everything out first, and then give you a shout."

"Do you want to take the camera?" asked Dan.

"I couldn't take a photograph in a passport-picture booth," I told him. "Wait until I call you, and then come out ready to take some shots."

"Okay. But go carefully. And if I don't hear you call in five minutes, I'm coming after you."

I held his arm. "Dan," I said, pained. "This isn't a Western. These people are friends."

Dan looked away. "Maybe they *were* your friends," he said quietly. "But before you do anything rash, just check up on what they are now."

I kept hold of his arm for a moment. Then I said: "Okay. Make it five minutes. And there's a long pipe-wrench in the back if you feel you ought to bring it."

I reached for my soiled and crumpled raincoat which I kept on the back seat. Then I opened the door of the wagon, and lunged out into the rain and the wind. I tugged on my coat as quickly as I could, and pulled up the collar, but I still got soaked. I had to plink the water away from my lashes, and wipe the drops off my nose, and then I shouted through the wagon window to Dan: "Flashlight! Pass me the flashlight!"

He quickly opened the door and passed it out to me. I looked down at it. It was a kid's flashlight with Mickey Mouse ears on it, and it gave out about as much light as a birthday-cake candle. I frowned at Dan through the rain-streaked window, but all he could do was shrug and pull a face. A Mickey Mouse flashlight was just about his level.

Clutching my raincoat collar tight around my neck, and hunching my shoulders against the rain, I crossed the cinder driveway and made my way cautiously around the side of the house and out towards the back yard. From what I could see through the rain, the barn was three or four hundred feet away across a sodden patch of worn grass, right up against a dark and wildly-waving stand of fir trees. I wiped the rain from my face with my hand, and trudged across the back yard, holding the feeble flashlight out in front of me. I stumbled once, against a rusty and abandoned plough blade, and snagged my sock. I lifted my head and listened for a moment or two, but all I could hear was the seething trees and the persistent lashing of the rain. Up above me, in the early darkness, the clouds hurried like black phantoms on their way to a ghosts' gathering. I listened a second more, and then I went on walking towards the Pascoe barn.

Soon I was standing right by the barn doors. They were old and rotted and slick with wet. I raised the Mickey Mouse flashlight and cautiously investigated the rest of the building. Old man Pascoe had obviously left it derelict for years. The shing roof was sagging and overgrown with moss, and several of the panes in the fan-shaped windows were broken. It smelled of dust and damp and neglect.

I cleared my throat and called softly: "Jimmy? Alison?"

There was no answer. About a mile away, across

in New York state, the thunder grumbled again, and I saw lightning. The rain beat down and plastered my face and my hair, and I felt like a sickly kitten that some farmer had thrown out to die of exposure.

I heard a creak within the barn, and my nerves tightened. I waited a few seconds, and then I called again: "Jimmy? Alison? Are you there? It's me, Mason!"

I waited some more, and the rain dripped off my earlobes like diamond earrings. The Mickey Mouse flashlight began to falter and dim, and I only hoped it was going to last out long enough. I didn't relish meeting up with any kind of creature in the pitch dark and the rain, no matter how friendly we used to be. A rat or a mouse scurried along the length of the barn, and made me jump with nerves.

It didn't seem like Jimmy and Alison were here. But then, young Paul Denton had said they were in back of the barn, and not actually inside it. Three or four minutes walk into the woods, he had said. I guess because it was pouring with rain, I had automatically jumped to the conclusion that they would have gone to the barn to seek shelter.

But —supposing they didn't need shelter? Supposing they were dead? Or supposing they felt quite at home in the wet?

I shook a little more life into the flashlight, and then I tossed my head to hurl off most of the drops. The woods were less than welcoming on a night like this. Close to, they made a sound like gnashing monsters, and under their branches it was as dark and baffling as the inside of a conjuror's cloak.

I took a deep breath, and started to walk away from the barn and into the trees. The ground was matted with wet leaves and fallen twigs, and knobbly with fir cones. There was a strong scent of conifers, mingled with the fresh metallic smell of the rain.

It was quieter here, and the rain was far less torrential, although it fell on the branches above me like the pattering of invisible feet on an upstairs floor. I kept both hands out in front of me, to protect my face from projecting branches, and I shuffled slowly along as if I was a blind man.

After a minute or two, I paused, and called: "Jimmy? Alison? I'm here. Can you hear me?"

There was no reply. I waited a little longer, and while I waited I made up my mind that I was going to keep walking ahead for just one minute more and if I didn't come across them by then, I was going to turn around and get my ass out of those woods as fast as conveniently possible. In spite of everything, I was scared now, and I was alone, and every drop of rain that fell on the floor of the woods sounded like beasts approaching. My heart was tumbling and beating in great aerobatic loops.

I started to walk, deeper in to the woods. The branches crackled beneath my feet, like the crackling of lobster shells. I gave a cough that was far too forced, far too loud. I didn't really need to cough at all.

A minute had passed. I stopped again, and listened. Half-heartedly, I called: "Jimmy? Alison? Are you there?"

I stood there, breathing quick and shallow with fright, and hoping to God that nobody would answer. I knew that Jimmy and Alison had been my friends. I knew that I owed it to them to try to help. But I knew, too, that I was in the middle of a dark and rustling wood in an electric storm faced with the prospect of meeting two hideous and inexplicable creatures and I wasn't at all sure that my nerve was up to it.

I called once more, just to make sure that they really weren't there. There was still no answer, so I turned around and started making my way back towards the barn. The Mickey Mouse flashlight even obliged by waxing a little brighter, as if it dimmed and brightened in response to the level of fear.

I was almost at the outskirts of the wood, when I thought I heard something. It was a low, hoarse sound, like an animal grunting. A chilly spasm went down the back of my neck, and I froze, listening. I heard the sound again, and this time it was more distinct.

It was low, thick, and guttural. It was hardly human. But it had to belong to a human mind, because it twice repeated, with painful slurriness, the single word: *'Mason. Muu.ɜɜooonnn,"*

I stood there rigid. I was so shit-scared I didn't know whether to run or stay where I was. I couldn't see anything or anybody through the darkness and the waving trees, but I thought I heard something. It might have been my imagination, fired up by fear, but it was too distinct, too plangent, too unusual. *It was the sound of rain spattering on to a hard, hollow shell.*

"Jimmy?" I asked, in a thin voice. "Jimmy? Is that you?"

"Mmaasssooonnn," repeated the sound. "Hhelllpp mmeee . . ."

"Jimmy?" I called. "Jimmy, where are you? I can't see you!"

There was a short silence. Then the thick sound came again. "Don't—come—any—nearer. Stay—right—where—you—are."

I frowned into the rainy shadows. "Jimmy, if I don't see you, I can't help you. Is that you? Is Alison there?"

"Something's — happened — something — we can't—"

"Jimmy! Where are you? I have to see you!"

There was another silence, and then I heard a heavy stumbling sound by a cluster of holly bushes, quite close to the edge of the woods. I stepped gingerly towards it, holding up my flashlight, trying to penetrate the dark-green glossy leaves.

"Are you there, Jimmy? Can you see my light?"

Pause. And then: "Yess, Massoonn. I—see—it. Don't—come—nearer."

"Jimmy, what's happened to you? We found Oliver. We came out to warn you about the water, and we found Oliver."

"We—know—about—Oliver. He—was—too—slow."

"Too slow for what? What happened out there, Jimmy? How did Oliver drown?"

"He — was — too — slow. He — didn't — drink —soon — enough. There — was — no —time — for — him — to —"

"No time for what, Jimmy? No time for him to grow a shell? No time to get away from the water?

How did the water get there, Jimmy? How did they fill up his room?"

All the time, while Jimmy spoke in that grating, guttural voice, I was slowly circling around the side of the holly bushes, to see if I could penetrate them. They were so damned thick and prickly it seemed almost impossible for anyone to have found their way inside without scratching themselves to shreds, but Jimmy must have found a gap someplace. At least, he *may* have found a gap someplace. If he was already covered in shell, then he could have forced his way right through the densest bush and not suffered a single laceration. I was praying and hoping that he hadn't. I was praying and hoping that something human had survived.

"Where's Alison?" I called. "Is she in there with you?"

"I—cannot—say—"

"Do you mean you don't know, or you won't tell me?"

"She—has—gone—"

"Gone? What do you mean, gone? Gone where?"

"I—cannot—say—"

"Well, what did you want me for?" I asked. "Young Paul Denton came up to the house half scared to death and said you needed my help. Well, I'm here. I want to know how I can help you."

There was a further silence. I sniffed the rainy air, and I was sure I could detect the lingering odour of decaying fish. I took a few more steps around the holly bushes, but with each step I took it was becoming increasingly obvious that they were quite impenetrable. At least to a soft skinned endomorph like me.

"It — happened — so — quick—" said Jimmy, harshly.

I stopped my circling. "What did? What happened so quick?"

"The—change—it—happened—so—quick—"

"Jimmy," I insisted, "I have to see you if I'm going to help you. Whatever that water's done to you, I have to see."

"We—are—so—much—stronger—"

"Stronger? What does being stronger have to do with it?"

"It—is—the—way—we—were—always— meant to—be—"

I lifted my flashlight again, and I was sure that I could see something dark and shiny stirring in the bushes. I peered forward, but it was difficult to make it out. I wiped rain from my eyes and my hair, and leaned as close to the prickles as I could.

"We—never—knew — until—now—where — the strength—really—lay—" said Jimmy. "We—never knew—how—long—it—had—been—sleeping—"

"Jimmy, I don't know what you're talking about," I said impatiently. "I can't do anything for you unless you come out of there and show me what's happened. It's no big mystery. I saw Oliver and the shell on his back and on his legs. I know what's happened. I just have to see how bad it is."

"You—don't—understand—at—all—you—could —never—understand—the greatness—of—the—ancient—world—"

I coughed. Nerves. I said carefully: "Jimmy, I want you to do something for me. I know you're in those bushes, Jimmy, and I guess I know how you managed to get inside there without hurting yourself, but I can't get in there to see you, do you understand that? Well, what I want you to do is put your arm out through the bush, do you get me? I want you to put your arm out through the bush and show me what your arm looks like. Do you think you could do me that one favour?"

The rain rattled on the holly leaves and made me jerk back in fright. I took a deep lungful of air and steadied myself, but I can tell you without a shadow of a lie that I was almost ready to turn around and run out of the woods as fast as humanly or even inhumanly possible.

"You—don't—understand—" grated Jimmy. "You—don't—understand—at all—"

"Jimmy," I begged him. "I can't stay out here for ever, and before long Carter Wilkes is going to come looking for you. If you don't come out of your own free will, he's going to flush you out with guns. I mean that. You're both suspects in Oliver's death, and they'll get you any way they have to. You can't hide in a wood for the rest of your life."

Jimmy ignored me. In his blurry, hideous voice, he said: "The—day—has— been— promised—for— thousands —and—thousands—of—years —the— day —has —been— promised."

I was getting very wet and panicky now. I said: "Jimmy, will you stop saying things like that and just listen to me? I mean, will you just listen? I want you to come out of there, because if you don't they'll kill you."

There was a threshing noise inside the holly bushes, and I stepped back anxiously. If there was going to be anything worse than Jimmy ignoring my pleas to come out, it was going to be Jimmy actually deciding I was right and showing himself. I could hear by his harsh, awkward voice that there was something terribly wrong with him, and there was something indescribably terrifying in the heavy, lurching sounds he was making in the bushes. I took one pace backwards, two, three, and then stood at a respectful distance waiting for my one-time friend to emerge.

I didn't hear the creaking of gristle behind me, or the rustling of branches. I didn't even hear the spidery sound of feet on the leafy ground. I took one more step back and then all hell grabbed me round the neck, the hard bony hell of a huge claw. It was ridged and muscular and as long as a man's forearm, and three times as thick. It crushed into my throat and my shoulder and twisted me clear off my feet, so powerfully and painfully that I didn't even have time to yell out. As my legs thrashed for the ground, I was convinced for a split-second that my head was going to be torn off, and that I was a dead man.

I was flung from side to side, choking and bruised, and the vice-like claw forced its way deeper and deeper into my windpipe. I reached up with both hands, and tried to prise it away from me, but even when I was gripping it tight and pulling it with all my strength, it wouldn't come loose, wouldn't relent.

I tried to drag air into my lungs, but my throat was too constricted. The dark woods turned darker. I saw stars exploding in front of me. I think I managed to grunt *"Dan!"* just once, but in a voice so faint that he couldn't possibly have heard me. The claw hurled me against the rough trunk of a fir tree, as if it was trying to beat me to death, and I felt the sharp projection of what seemed to be another, smaller, claw, digging into my back in search of my softer and more vulnerable organs.

There was a moment of utter pain, of utter blackness, in which I was sure I was dead. I couldn't say how long it lasted. It was probably only a fraction of a second. But then there was a harsh cry, and a smashing noise, and then the claw suddenly relaxed from my neck, and I took in a cold agonized breath of oxygen that was foetid with fish. There was another thumping, smashing sound, and a shriek that scared me so much I rolled free across the wet leaves and got myself clear. It was a shriek of cold-blooded insect rage and pain, a completely inhuman shriek, as if it came from a gristly throat lined with black hairs.

It was so dark that I could scarcely see. But I could make out Dan, his bald head shining in what little light there was, and I could make out my largest pipe-wrench held over his head. He was shouting. "Yaaahh! Yaaahh!" in a voice that was supposed to be threatening but which was almost falsetto with fear.

Behind him, in the shadows, I saw something else. Something bulky and heavy, with arms that waved with the slow-motion of things that usually dwell beneath the sea. The movement reminded me more than anything of the laboured pointless, painful jerking of live lobsters in a supermarket tray. Only this creature was scores of times larger, scores of times more powerful, and it moved away into the woods with a shuffling scuttle and a rustle of leaves that betrayed something the size and weight of a human being.

I felt dizzy and hurt, and I sat down on the ground again, rubbing my bruised throat and gasping for air. Dan came over and put down the pipe-wrench.

"Are you okay?" he asked me. "I thought that damn thing was going to tear you to pieces."

"You weren't the only one. Did you get a good look at it?"

He shook his head. "All I saw was a claw and a big boney head. I didn't even see its face. I just lashed out with the wrench and hoped it would let go."

"Thank Christ you did. It almost got me."

Dan strained his eyes through the gloom to see how badly I was injured. "Can you feel any blood?" he asked me. I shook my head. "Okay, then," he said, "let's get you back to the car. I don't fancy the idea of sticking around these woods longer than we have to."

He helped me get to my feet. I felt shocked and unsteady, but at least I could walk. I said: "Don't forget the pipe-wrench. Those things cost an arm and a leg."

We stumbled out of the woods and back across old man Pascoe's yard. The rain lashed in our faces as we came out of the shelter of the trees, and by the time we had walked around the house and back to my wagon, we were both dripping. I climbed in behind the wheel and slammed the door.

"Are you sure you can drive?" asked Dan.

I rubbed my neck. "I'm fine. At least, I'm semi-fine. That thing didn't do much more than throttle me."

"Was it one of them? Jimmy or Alison?"

I cleared my throat. "I think so. Alison, probably. I was talking to Jimmy when it happened."

"You were *talking* to Jimmy? Did you see him?"

"Not a thing. He was hiding right in the thick of a whole mess of holly bushes. I couldn't even get a glimpse."

Dan wiped condensation from the wagon's window and stared out into the dark and the rain. "You know something," he said. "Hitting that creature was like hitting a pie-crust. When I swung the second time, it *crunched.*"

"It sounds like you've injured it," I told him.

"If I'd known it was Alison—"

I raised my hand to quiet him down. "If you'd known it was Alison you would have done the same thing. And besides, from what I heard from Jimmy, they're not even the same people any more. They're not the Jimmy and Alison that we know. They're not dressed up in fancy-dress costumes. It seems like their bodies have changed and their minds have changed along with them. Jimmy wouldn't answer any of the questions I asked him, and he kept mumbling on about how I wouldn't understand him or what he was doing."

Dan looked at me sagely. "It's possible they're both suffering from severe psychological shock, isn't it? If you or I went through a physical change as drastic and hideous as the one that they've been through—?"

"I don't think that's the problem," I said. "It

seems to me like they've been through a fundamental change of basic attitudes and interests. There was no hysteria, no illogicality. Whatever Jimmy said, it was sane and sequential. The only difference was, it was all about the greatness of the ancient world, and the day that's been promised for thousands and thousands of years."

Dan frowned. "The greatness of the ancient world? Whenever was Jimmy Bodine interested in the greatness of the ancient world?"

"That's the whole point I'm making. Jimmy Bodine was *never* interested in the greatness of the ancient world, nor in predictions or promises or superstitions. He was simple, and straightforward, and pragmatic. Whatever kind of a creature he's changed into, he's mentally different as well as physically different. But it doesn't seem to me like he's traumatized. Look at the way he kept me busy while Alison circled around in back of me. He's acting with cunning, and he's acting with some kind of purpose. Just don't ask me what that purpose is, or what he thinks he's trying to achieve, because I don't know."

Shelley, on the back seat, began to lick himself furiously. For a while we sat in the wagon in silence, and there was only the sound of the rain and the rasping of Shelley's tongue.

Eventually, Dan said: "So what are we going to do? Alert Carter? They're obviously homicidal, whatever their purpose is."

I nodded. "I think we're going to have to."

I started up the engine, and switched on the windshield wipers. But just as I was about the pull away, there was a loud knocking noise at the back of the wagon, and I turned around in my seat in surprise, thinking I must have caught my rear bumper on something.

To my horror, the whole of the rear window of the wagon burst apart in a snowstorm of flying glass, and through the back a giant black-and-green claw raked its way across the pipes and the tools and the junk, clattering and banging at the metal sides of the car.

Dan yelled: "It's them! Get the hell out of here!"

I slammed my foot on the gas, and the rear wheels whinnied and slid on the wet cinder driveway. As the Country Squire gripped and pulled away, the claw seized the rear drop-down door, and wrenched it clear off its hinges, with a jarring, scraping sound that sent adrenalin charging through my arteries. I drove the car wildly up the drive towards the road, praying to whatever saints looked after the sea that the creatures couldn't run too fast. But as we bucked and bounced over the last hump I saw the dark, bulky silhouette of the second one, and I saw another grotesque claw raised to strike us.

I couldn't avoid the creature in time. The tires spat gravel and cinder as I tried to swerve, but the massive claw smashed into the windshield, and we were both sprayed with jagged fragments of glass. Dan cried out: "Jesus, My face!" But I was too worried about the creature's claw, which snatched at the front door pillar and tugged at it as we drove past.

My foot pressed the gas pedal down to the floor, and the engine screamed. The claw could only hold on to the door pillar for a moment, but it twisted it right out of shape, and my own side window cracked and dropped out. The tip of the claw rattled against the side of the wagon as we gave one last burst of power and made the road.

I swerved around on howling tires, steadied the wagon with pipes and wrenches dropping out of the ripped-open tail in a clanging shower, and then I headed towards New Milford and Carter Wilkes' office as fast as the train and the wind and the smashed windshield would allow me.

Dan said almost nothing on the way, except: "I'm bleeding. My damn face. I'm bleeding."

# 5

Carter's office was already in pandemonium when we arrived. There were six or seven deputies' cars parked outside with their beacons flashing, and once we'd left my battered Country Squire in the front lot of the hardware store across the street, and pushed our way through the smeary glass swing doors into the lobby, we were greeted by incessantly jangling telephones, policemen rushing around with concentrated faces and clipboards, and the glaring floods of the local TV crew.

I went up to the front desk, where a harassed young policewoman was trying to cope with a haywire switchboard. Dan followed a little way behind me, still holding a bloodstained handkerchief to his cheek. As it turned out, he hadn't been too badly slashed, but the creature's attack had given him a pretty severe shock.

"I have to see the Sheriff," I told the policewoman. "My name's Mason Perkins. He knows who I am."

The girl looked at me as if I was crazy. "The Sheriff can't see *anyone* right now. No one at all."

"Will you just give him my name and tell him it's desperately urgent?"

The girl disconnected one call and connected another. "Mister, I'm sorry," she said, "but all hell's going on here right now, and Sheriff Wilkes has got more than his hands full."

I looked around. The lobby was thick with smoke from the cigarettes of the waiting newsmen, and the chatter and shouting was almost deafening. The TV people kept switching their lights on and off and framing make-believe shots with their fingers, and the telephones rang in unholy choirs, persistent but unanswered.

"What's going on here?" I asked the policewoman. "Some kind of red alert?"

"I'm sorry, I'm not at liberty to tell you. But as soon as Sheriff Wilkes gets free, I'll try to let him know you're here."

I turned away from the desk in frustration. But then I saw my old drinking buddy Jack Ballo from the New Milford paper, standing slouched against the doorframe with a cigarette dangling from his lips and his little green Tyrolean hat perched on the back of his head. I told Dan: "Wait here one minute," and I pushed my way through the crowds of deputies and reporters until I made it across the lobby. Jack saw me coming, and raised his hand in a slight salute.

"How are you doing?" he asked me, as I squeezed past the paunch of a fat deputy with a Bill Haley haircut.

"I'm doing fine," I told him. "At least, I think I

am. What the hell's going on down here?"

"Haven't you heard? A very nasty homicide out at Washington Depot. A young girl was just about torn to pieces."

"Anyone I know?"

Jack took his notebook out of his sagging coat pocket and flipped through it. "I doubt it. She came from a new family, only moved in about two or three weeks ago. The Steadmans."

"Any clues?" I asked him.

He shook his head. "It sounds like the work of some kind of maniac. And when I say maniac, I mean maniac. Her neck was broken and the flesh was ripped right off her. Most of her internal organs were removed, and the black plastic bag squad are still looking for them. Heart, liver, lungs. All AWOL."

My mouth felt parched, as if I'd been smoking all day without taking a single drink. I could feel my left eye twitching with tiredness and nervous exhaustion.

"What about suspects?" I said. "Did Carter give you any ideas?"

Jack raised an eyebrow. "I hope you're going to pay me for all this information, preferably in a libatory fashion."

"Listen, Jack, it's real urgent. I think I may know something about it. Will you just tell me?"

"I'll tell you what I know if you tell me what *you* know."

I nodded. "Okay. It's a deal. Now, will you please hurry?"

He consulted his notebook again. "Well," he said, slowly, "it seems like only three people are

missing from the Route 109 area round about
Washington Depot, and those are Jimmy and
Alison Bodine, who are both wanted in connection
with the death of their son yesterday, and a man
called Frederick Karlen, who was staying with his
aunt for a couple of days. His aunt's name is Elsa
Greene, and she says that Frederick was the
nicest, most harmless individual you could ever
have met."

"Did she say if he'd drunk any water?" I asked.

Jack frowned. "Water? What does that have to
do with anything?"

"I don't know yet. But did you ask her if he'd
drunk any?"

Jack looked perplexed. "Not that I remember. I
mean, that isn't exactly the kind of question you
ask people about their missing nephews, is it?"

I pressed my hand to my head for a moment, and
thought hard. Then I said: "Somebody should have
done. Carter should have done, for sure. I just
hope that he did."

Jack said warily: "Are you saying this homicide
could be connected with all this water pollution
we've been having lately?"

"I'm not saying anything."

"Come on, Mason, you made a deal. You're a
plumber, right, so what are you doing around here
anyway, unless there's some link between the
polluted water and the dead girl?"

I looked him straight in the eyes. "Will you
promise you'll keep this under wraps until I say
so?"

"Well, I'm not too sure I can do that."

"Either you do or I won't tell you."

He sighed. "All right. As long as you make sure I don't get scooped. Now, what's happening?"

I chose my words carefully. "There's a possibility—only a possibility—that the water pollution around the Washington area is in some way responsible for what happened to Oliver Bodine, and also what's happened to this girl. There's nothing conclusive. But Dan Kirk's been making tests on the water, and he's found out some pretty odd things."

"What kind of odd things?"

I swallowed. I shouldn't have been telling Jack anything at all. But he was an old friend, and an unstoppable gossip, and right now he could be helpful, especially if Carter Wilkes was going to be too busy to pass on any police information.

"The water contains an unidentified microorganism."

Jack took out his ballpen and jotted a few shorthand outlines in his book.

"Anything else?" he asked me.

I shook my head. "That's all I know. But when Dan's finished up with his tests, I think there should be some pretty hair-raising news."

"Does he know what *kind* of microorganism?" Jack wanted to know.

I shook my head. "He's the scientist, not me. Even if he told me, I wouldn't know what he meant."

"Are you sure he hasn't given you some kind of inkling?"

I glanced across the crowded lobby to where Dan was standing waiting for me, dabbing at his cut cheek.

"Dan's a cautious man," I told Jack. "When he's good and ready to say what the organism is, then I guess he'll tell me; and then I'll tell you. But keep it under your hat until it's certain, will you? If it's wrong, and you print it, you'll wind up with egg on your face and Carter Wilkes will have my guts for sock suspenders."

Jack tucked his notebook away. "All right, Mason. This time I'll trust you. But if anything breaks, I want to know the same millisecond that you know—you got it?"

I gave him a nod, and then I pushed my way back through the jostling reporters and policemen. When Dan saw me coming through, he gave a weak smile and said: "I believe you're just in time. I'm going to pass out."

"Pull yourself together," I told him. "You're strong as an ox. A bald ox, possibly—but a strong one. You know what's happened here? There's been another homicide. A young girl was ripped apart out at Washington Depot. And when I say ripped apart, I mean ripped apart."

Dan stared at me, and blinked. "Ripped apart? Who was it?"

"Nobody we know. A young girl called Steadman. Her family moved into the area two or three weeks ago. Jack said it looked like the work of a maniac. She was torn to pieces and all her insides were missing."

"Jesus," said Dan, and his face went paler than ever. I held on to his arm to steady him.

Even amidst all the shouting and the turmoil and the ringing telephones I couldn't help thinking about those dark and desperate moments in the woods in back of old man Pascoe's place. I couldn't help recalling the hard crustaceous grip of that enormous pincer, and the smaller, sharper claw which had begun to probe against my back and my belly in search of my soft and vulnerable insides.

I couldn't help remembering a sea story that my father had read to me when I was a boy, and conjuring up the vision of a dead pirate whose face had decayed into a pale slush, and inside whose gaping body hundreds of crabs teemed.

I said to Dan: "Are you thinking what I'm thinking?"

He gave me a quick, humourless glance. "That Jimmy or Alison might have killed the girl? Yes, that's exactly what I was thinking."

"Right. In that case, it's urgent we get in to see Carter. Why don't you exert some of your inimitable scientific charm over that police lady at the desk, and I'll nip along the corridor and see if I can interrupt whatever it is that Carter's doing."

Dan pulled a face. "Just at this moment I feel far from charming. Look at this cut."

"Don't be ridiculous," I reassured him. "It gives you elan. You look like Douglas Fairbanks Jr, after a heavy swordfight, that's all."

"Okay," he sighed. "I'll do my best."

We split up; and while Dan leaned over the reception desk and involved the young policewoman in a lengthy and convoluted conversation about nothing much in particular, I elbowed my own way through the crowd in the lobby until I reached the closed swing doors that said *Sheriff's Office, Private* in neat black lettering on frosted glass.

I stood with my back to the doors, and when none of the sheriff's deputies were looking my way, I opened the doors up a little way and slipped inside. I paused for a moment or two once I was through, in case anybody came after me, but nobody did, and so I made my way quickly and quietly along the polished corridor that led to the traffic department, the muster room, and Carter Wilkes' private domain.

The door of the sheriff's office was ajar, and cigarette smoke was drifting out into the corridor like tear-gas. It was obvious that Carter was holding some kind of council of war, because the room was packed with deputies and uniformed officers, and when I peeked around the corner to see what was going on, I could make out maps and plans and heaps of files and statements.

Carter, huge and big-bellied, his armpits stained with sweat, was wearing a small pair of half-glasses and poring over a detail map of Washington Depot and the surrounding hills. He was saying harshly: "I want all of that ground searched systematic. Square by square, no matter whether it's hill or valley. I want to know when you boys have finished your job that there isn't a single leaf or a single candy wrapper that you've left unscrutinized."

The phone on his desk rang, and he picked it up. Everyone in the room waited tensely while he said: "Yeah—yeah. I see. Yeah. Okay. Okay, I got it."

He set the phone down in its cradle, took off his glasses and looked around. "That was the coroner's office. They did a preliminary post-mortem on Susan Steadman's remains. She was attacked with some kind of mechanical device which broke her neck and crushed her lower jaw. They're not too sure of what it was, or how it was used, but they reckon she was subjected to a pressure of something close to a thousand pounds. It was only after she collapsed to the ground that she was disembowelled, and that was done with an extremely blunt instrument. Maybe a shovel. They don't have any ideas at all about how the homicide was committed, and all they can say about time so far is that she probably died a little after twelve this afternoon."

"Any sexual assault?" asked a thin young officer with a long nose.

"No. Her underclothing was intact, and there was no sign of any sexual interference."

"Anything missing?" asked another policeman. "Any money, jewelry, that kind of thing?"

Carter Wilkes cleaned his glasses on a soft piece of cloth, breathing on them to bring up the sparkle. "Susan Steadman was carrying four dollars eighty-five cents in a leather Indian-style purse. She wore a twelve-dollar wristwatch. Neither were taken."

"So, as of now, there's no apparent motive?" put in the first officer.

Carter nodded without looking up. He seemed withdrawn and depressed, much quieter than his usual bluff and abrasive self; but I guess he had plenty to be thoughtful about. Ordinary homicide was serious enough, but homicide like this was twice as tough.

I said, quite clearly: "Sheriff? Could I say something?"

Carter raised his eyes. He didn't seem either surprised or annoyed to see me there. He said: "What is it, Mason? Any news from Dan?"

"I just located Jimmy and Alison Bodine. I saw them only a half-hour ago, at old man Pascoe's place."

There was a murmur of surprise around the room, but Carter raised his hand for quiet. "Did you bring them back with you?" he asked. "Are they safe?"

I shook my head. "They're still out there. Least, that's where we left them. They're not exactly what you'd call *compos mentis*."

"What the hell does that mean? Come in here, will you, and tell me what's been going on."

Two officers made way so that I could squeeze further into the hot, smoky room. I looked around at all the earnest young faces and all the uniforms, and I felt like I was in some kind of low-budget crime movie. I said, embarrassed: "I hope you don't mind me coming along here uninvited like this."

Carter planted a big black-booted foot on the seat of his chair and jammed a toothpick between his front incisors. He didn't like to floss in company. He said bluntly: "Just tell us what's on your mind, Mason, that's all."

I cleared my throat. "Paul Denton found them first. I don't know how he got lost in the first place, or why, but he came across Jimmy and Alison, and they sent him back to go get me. That's why Paul was around at my house."

"You didn't tell me any of this before," growled Carter.

"Well, I know, and I wish I had. But Paul said Jimmy and Alison had insisted on no police. So I guess I played along. I didn't want to frighten them off."

Carter rolled his eyes up into his head. "He didn't want to frighten them off. Isn't that terrific? He goes to see two wanted homicide suspects under suspicion for drowning their own son, and he doesn't tell the cops because he doesn't want to frighten them off."

"Sheriff, listen," I interrupted. "It's worse than that. You know what happened to young Oliver—well, it's happened to them. Only they've gone the whole way."

Nobody else in the office except Carter and me knew what that meant. They turned to each other and pulled a variety of baffled faces, and then turned back to us to see if they could work out what was happening.

Carter squinted at me narrowly. "The whole way? You mean—all over? The whole damn thing?"

"We both saw them. Dan Kirk and me. We met them in the woods at the back of old man Pascoe's barn, and they went for us."

"Went for you? What does that mean?"

I tugged open my necktie and unbuttoned my shirt. The deputies and the officers watched me in fascinated silence. When I pulled my collar wide apart, they could see what the creature that had once been Alison Bodine had done to me. There were two irregular rows of inflamed crimson-and-blue bruises running diagonally across the upper part of my chest, across my neck, and taking in the front of my right shoulder. When I peered down and examined my own body, I almost felt as faint as Dan had looked. I resembled nothing less than the victim of a motorcycle-chain beating.

"The Bodines did *that?*" asked Carter, in awe.

"Not the Bodines plural. Just one of the Bodines, singular. Alison Bodine, if I'm not mistaken."

One of the officers, a short, sandy man with hair cropped as close as a toilet brush, stuck a cigarette in his mouth, lit it, and said: "What kind of weapon did they use on you? Bullwhip? Chain?"

"Neither," I told him. "These marks were made by Alison Bodine's own hand, if that's what anybody could sanely call it."

Another officer said: "Those marks look pretty close to the marks we found on Susan Steadman. Except that hers were a damn sight worse."

"That's what I'm trying to suggest," I said. "I think the Bodines might have been responsible for Susan's death."

Carter suddenly lifted his eyes again. "Jerry, Martino, get about twenty deputies together with guns. Do it quick."

"You think I'm right?" I asked him.

He reached for his hat, which had been resting on the top of his filing cabinet, and banged it firmly on to his head. "I don't know whether you're right or wrong. You may be as damn crazy as always. But if you've seen Jimmy and Alison Bodine, and you've got a good idea they killed Susan Steadman as well as their own son, then I think I have a duty to hightail it out to the Pascoe place and hunt them down, don't you? It's a damn sight better than sitting on my butt looking at maps."

He tightened his gunbelt. "Trenton," he ordered, "I want you to take over the search operations around Washington while I'm gone. Ken—I want you to stay by the radio and link communications. We'll go straight out to where Mason last saw the Bodines first, and then we'll fan out and start tracking. Call Huntley and tell him I want all the dogs he can get."

I rubbed my eyes, smarting from too much cigarette smoke. "You'd be better off with cats if you ask me," I remarked. "Shelley goes nuts whenever he picks up that smell of fish."

The sandy-looking deputy, just as everybody was packing up their papers and their belongings and swallowing their last styrofoam cupfuls of coffee, abruptly piped up: "Excuse me, Sheriff, but I think we may be missing out on something here."

"Missing out?" grunted Carter. "What are you talking about?"

"Well," said the deputy, unabashed. "I picked up the impression from the way that you and Mr. Perkins here were talking that Jimmy and Alison look kind of different from the way they used to. And didn't Mr. Perkins say that the marks on his neck were made by Alison Bodine's *hand?*"

Carter glanced across at me, and I shrugged. This was a danger that was affecting the whole community of New Milford and everywhere around, and we knew that we couldn't keep it confidential for very much longer. Carter paused, and then let out a long patient breath, and set his papers back down on his desk. The room was silent, except for the shuffling of feet and the occasional cough.

"This had to come out sooner or later," he growled. "The reason I kept it under wraps for so long is because I didn't want a ridiculous panic. I didn't want people running around like blue-assed baboons creating all sorts of chaos, saying that the Martians had landed, or anything like that. But now I guess that circumstances have proved me wrong, and everyone around here has a right to know."

He looked up in my direction again, and I gave him an encouraging nod. He licked his lips, and said: "Just for tonight, I don't want anybody outside of the police to know what I'm going to tell you now. Tomorrow, we'll tell the newspapers and the television people. But I'm hoping we can catch our murderers before dawn, and if we can do that we can avert a full-scale crisis."

He paused again, and then said softly: "The truth is that Jimmy and Alison Bodine have undergone a pretty bizarre kind of change in their appearance. Don't ask me why, or how, but I promise you it's true. They've grown hard chitinous shells instead of skins, and from what Mason Perkins here says, they have pincers as well, like crabs or lobsters."

There was a moment of silent disbelief. Then one of the policemen tittered. Somebody said: *"Lobsters?"*

Carter was angry. "You heard," he said, with a rough edge on his voice. "They've got shells and pincers, and if they're attacking people the way they've attacked Mason here, then they're obviously dangerous."

"This is kind of a hard story to swallow," remarked the sandy deputy. "I mean—are you absolutely sure of this, Sheriff, or is it just supposition?"

Carter glared at him. "Williams," he growled, "do you know me to be a gullible man? Do you think, from your experience of working with me, that I'm a sap?"

"No, sir."

"No, sir," mimicked Carter. "And that means that if I tell you Jimmy and Alison Bodine have started to look like lobsters, you can bet your ass they have. You just believe what I say, and do what you're told, and you'll get through this with your butt in one piece. I want you to find them first, and bring them in, and when you've done that we can argue about the way they look."

"Yes, sir," said Williams.

"Sheriff," I put in. "I think there's one more thing we ought to consider."

"What's that?" asked Carter, picking up his papers again.

"Well, it's a few miles from Sherman to Washington Depot, and I was wondering how Jimmy and Alison could have made their way right across country without being seen during the afternoon."

"Meaning what?" demanded Carter, impatient to get out into the night with his guns and his dogs and his deputies.

I looked around the room. The officers and the deputies had obviously had quite enough of hearing from me for one evening, and I hesitated for a second or two before I spoke. Their faces were hard and expectant.

"I mean it could have been this man Karlen who killed the girl," I said quietly. "He was nearer the Washington Depot area, right? And he was a visitor who might not have heard about the ban on drinking well water."

"I asked his aunt if he'd drunk the water," said Carter, in an expressionless voice. "She said he hadn't, as far as she knew."

"As far as she knew? And how far was that?"

"I don't know, Mason. And right now I'd much rather be out there looking for Jimmy and Alison Bodine than wondering if somebody's errant nephew drank the well water."

"But it *could* have been him," I insisted. "It *could* have been Karlen, just as easily as it could have been Jimmy or Alison. In fact, more easily because he was nearer the area. Karlen could have changed into one of these crab people, too."

Carter wiped the sweat from his forehead with the back of his hand. "All right, Mason, I believe you. Karlen could have changed, too. If he has, and if he's still in the vicinity, our people will find him. But right now, I think it's more important to get after Jimmy and Alison, before their trail's gone totally cold."

"All right, fine," I told him. "But go easy. Whatever Jimmy and Alison are like right now, I wouldn't want to see them killed. I think that Alison is probably hurt already. Dan Kirk got me out of that situation with the help of my twelve hundred millimeter pipe wrench, and he said that he heard her shell crunch when he hit her."

Carter nodded. One of his deputies said, under his breath: "This is nuts. I mean, this is completely nuts." But Carter said: "Forget the comments. Let's go find them."

With Carter bustling out in front of them, the policemen left the office and went out to look for Jimmy and Alison Bodine. I stayed where I was, listening to the phones ringing and the doors opening and shutting and the shouted questions of the newspapers when Carter appeared through the swing doors at the end of the corridor with his troop of deputies. Then there was no sound at all but the telephones, and most of those were silent as reporters made outgoing calls to their wire services and their papers. Carter's littered, deserted office smelled of stale cigarette smoke and sweat.

I heard the swing doors creak, and footsteps along the corridor, and Dan Kirk appeared. He stood by the door for the moment, holding his makeshift bandage to his face, and then he said: "What happened? Carter came out like a bat out of hell."

"They've gone looking for Jimmy and Alison."

"You told them?"

"Sure I told them. I had to tell them. They're a danger to their own selves, as well as to everyone else. At least if Carter gets them, they stand a chance."

Dan looked at me carefully. "Do you want them to stand a chance? Don't you think they're better off dead?"

I shrugged. "I don't know. They were friends

once, weren't they? Maybe there's an outside chance they could be brought back to what they once were. Changed back again to human beings. And if that's possible, then I don't want to think that I was responsible for killing them."

"You're not responsible," said Dan. "You're here."

I looked at him wryly. "Damn it, Dan," I told him. "We're all responsible. Didn't you hear about loving thy neighbour as thyself?"

"I never heard about loving thy lobster," Dan said kindly.

I stepped out of Carter's office and closed the door. We walked along the corridor together in silence, and when we pushed our way through the swing door and into the lobby, we found it almost deserted, except for a TV technician taking down his lights, and chilly from the night air.

"They're not lobsters, Dan," I said quietly, "and that's the whole mistake that Carter Wilkes and his deputies will probably make. They're people. They've got shells, and they're violent and they're dangerous, but they're still people. They can talk like people and think like people. Different people, sure, but still people. What we have to find out is what kind of people they are."

Dan said unhappily: "Do you seriously think there's any chance of that?"

I stood on the steps looking across at my battered and broken Country Squire. "No," I said, "but we'll have a damned good try."

I drove back to New Preston at a steady ten miles an hour, with the freezing fall wind blowing in through my shattered windshield and my eyes watering almost as much as when I watched *Miracle on 34th Street*. Shelley hated the unexpected cold, and he secreted himself on the floor in front of the passenger seat, crossly letting the hot air from the heater ruffle up his fur. It was better to be untidy than cold. It was better to be almost anything than cold. I wondered if he'd ever forgive me. Oh well, who gave a shit. He was only a cat, and it was my fault if I forgot that once in a while and treated him like he was human.

It took almost twenty minutes to get back to my rented house at that pace, but finally I turned up the steep road that led to my rocky driveway and my own front door. I dragged a worn-out canvas tent from the garage and slung it over the front of the Country Squire in case it rained during the night, and then I wearily climbed the narrow steps to the porch. Shelley followed me, fluffed up with cold and disdain.

Inside the house, the temperature was almost down to ten degrees. The log fire had burned out again, and the log rack was empty apart from a few beetle-ridden twigs, and that meant a cold journey out to the back yard for more. Disconsolate and somewhat lonesome, I raked the ashes out of the fire and ripped up a few old copies of the *TV Guide* for kindling. Then I unlocked the side door and went out across the dark and chilly yard in search of logs.

I don't know if you've ever been up in Connecticut in the late fall, but it has a real mournful coldness about it, a chilly dampness that makes you want to stay by the fire and keep your Jack

Daniel's bottle close, and do nothing more than watch television, even if it's nothing more up-lifting than *The Gong Show*. It isn't as ball-break-ing as New Hampshire or Vermont, but it's frigid enough for someone who would rather live in Florida in any case; and when I traipsed across the sloping grass of my back yard for those logs that evening, my breath was vapourising and I was shivering like Bob Cratchit the night before Christmas, and I was completely unprepared for the heavy crackling sound in the trees that told me someone or something was walking there.

I stopped, and listened, holding my armful of logs. The crackling came again, quieter, but still unmistakable. It wasn't leaves, blowing through the branches. It wasn't a squirrel, or a stray dog. It was something as big and heavy as a human being, and it was skirting around the trees and bushes that surrounded the house.

My pulse-rate quickened, and I guess my blood-pressure soared up too, if I'd had the time or the inclination to measure it. Keeping my eyes wide open, I started to walk slowly and warily back towards the house, hoping that whatever or who-ever was skulking in the undergrowth wouldn't decide to leap out and block my path to the half-open side door. It was still a good fifty feet away, that door, and the light that streamed out of it was as appetizing and welcoming as a wedge of good Wisconsin cheese.

It seemed to take hours to reach the safety of the house. But I made it, and closed the door behind me, and there was Shelley sitting in front of the unlit hearth, impatient as always. I dumped the

logs on to the fire dogs and told him: "One night
I'm going to make *you* go get the wood. It's too
damned spooky out there for me."

Shelley twitched his ears and didn't answer. I
stacked up the logs, and set a light to the torn-up
*TV Guides*, and it wasn't long before the fire was
crackling up nicely, and I could go into the dining-
room and pour myself a hefty bourbon. I have to
admit that I drank the first one standing right
where I was, by the liquor trolley, and that I
poured myself another three fingers to take back
to the hearthside. But then I don't think anyone
would go blaming me. After my encounter with
Jimmy and Alison Bodine, and after hearing
sinister noises outside in the night, I think that
anyone would have been tempted to seek courage
in the square bottle with the black label.

I sat by the fire for a while, warming myself, and
then I tried to call Rheta. There was no answer
from the laboratory, and no answer from her
home number, so I guessed she must have gone
out with Pigskin Packer again. I felt like busting
Pigskin Packer in the mouth, to tell you the truth.
There wasn't anything I would have liked better
right at that moment than to have Rheta snuggled
up beside me by the hearth, preferably dressed in
something casual, and to have the warming and reassuring prospect of a night in a shared and well-
made bed instead of the lonesome tangle that await-
ed me. I finally took off my red baseball cap,
and took out a cigarillo, but I scrutinized the
white plastic holder pretty close before I lit it.
Maybe Greg McAllister was right about cancer.
Maybe he was right about a lot of things. I made a

note on my mental blotter to go down to Candle-wood Furnishers in the morning and dig out that book on *Legends of Litchfield*.

The front door rattled on its hinges, and I heard a shifting of leaves outside. Maybe I should have switched on the television, so I wouldn't hear noises like that. But somehow I preferred to be frightened by something I could actually hear than by something I couldn't. In any case, tele-vision is supposed to be bad for the soul. The only creatures who can watch it with complete mental immunity are cats.

There was another rustling outside. I tried to ignore it for a minute or two, but then I heard it again. With over-exaggerated casualness, I got up from the sofa and stepped across to the window. I hadn't yet drawn the drapes, but it was dark out there, solid dark, and all I could see was my own tired reflection staring back at me. I raised my glass to myself, and then went back and sat down.

About ten minutes passed. I began to nod off. I was feeling so tired that I could happily have gone to bed. But it was only seven o'clock, and if I went to bed now I would probably spend the rest of the night tossing and turning and staring at the ceil-ing, and if there was one thing I couldn't stand it was lying in bed, totally awake, with nothing better to do than wait for the dawn to rise through the venetian blinds. In any case, the fire was blazing brightly and cheerily now, and the sitting-room was just the place to be.

I nodded, dozed, nodded. I dreamed for a moment that I was swimming in some dark ocean, and that I was trying to find a way through a slimy and complicated reef. I opened my eyes and I was still sitting on my sofa with my feet up, and Shelley was still there, with the firelight flickering across his face.

I dozed again, and dreamed again, and I was swimming through darkness, with deep, powerful strokes. I knew that I was searching for something, that I urgently needed to get out of the ocean and into the crevices and grottoes of the rocks. The sea was dangerous tonight. Cold and alien and dangerous. I looked over my shoulder, straining my eyes through the dim water to see if I was being pursued. All I could see was dark shadowy shapes, and things that could have been trailing weed or eels, or both.

A sharp tap woke me up. My eyes were open before I was fully aware of what was going on. I turned towards the fire, and everything was just as before, but then there was another tap, louder, and I looked at the window. My heart must have dropped right down through the upholstery.

Only half-invisible through the reflections on the glass, there was a waving, mottled claw. And behind the claw, scarcely distinguishable in the darkness, were thin tendrils and things that looked like black staring eyes. It was the claw that was tapping on the glass of the window. It was the claw that wanted my flesh.

There was an ear-splitting crack, and Shelley jumped up and away as if he'd been stepped on. The window shattered from side to side in an explosion of glass, and the huge pincer lunged into the room. I rolled off the sofa towards the dining-room, following my fleeing cat, but I wasn't fast enough for what happened next.

Through the open window, with a torrential, sliding roar, poured a foaming cataract of water. It was so powerful that it drowned the fire in a single spurt of steam, and lifted the television bodily across the floor. I didn't have time to reach the kitchen door before the water gushed into the dining-room, hurling the chairs and the table against the wall, and splashing up against the window. It hit me in the back like an icy-cold locomotive, and sent me colliding against the door-jamb.

Panicking, I tried to stand up again, but I couldn't keep my feet, and the room was so full of water that at first I couldn't reach the surface. I kicked myself up from the floor, swimming hard, and I managed to break out into fresh air about a foot below the ceiling. I gulped and trod water, clinging on to the ceiling light for support, but the gurgling waves were rising fast, and I knew that in a second or two the room would be flooded to the top. I looked frantically around for Shelley, but I couldn't see him anywhere at all. I just hoped he'd managed to dive through the kitchen and out through the cat-flap before the tidal wave had hit us.

With a last strong swirl, the water rose to the ceiling, and I just managed to take one deep breath before I was completely immersed. I plunged downwards, trying to swim towards the window, but I was disoriented now, and it was so dark that I couldn't make out which way the kitchen was and which way the window lay. I had a chilling and vivid memory of my dreams about swimming in the ocean, and I forced myself to dive even deeper towards the floor. There was a powerful, cold current running through the water. Fragments of wood from the fire, table mats, bottles and papers were pouring past me as I swam. I felt the drinks trolley roll over and float away, sending half-empty bottles bobbing and clinking all around me.

My breath was nearly exhausted. My head was thumping as hard as a Thanksgiving hangover, and my ears were filled with water and the terrible echoing bubbling noises of my drowned house. I groped against the wall, but I didn't know which wall it was, and even when I kicked my legs and swam a little way along it, I couldn't find a window or a door.

It was then that I recalled something else about my dreams. *The sensation of being hunted. The sensation of being followed by some vicious predator.* I turned around in the water, pedalling hard to keep myself upright in the current, and even though I couldn't make out very much in the churning darkness, I thought I could see something swimming towards me. A black, threatening bulk which seemed to move far more swiftly and far more certainly under the water than it had on land. With my vision blurring from lack of oxygen, and my lungs about to burst out of my throat, I dogpaddled desperately to one side, thrashing around for a way to escape.

The dark bulk came steadily closer. I could make out a heavy, ill-balanced head, and pincers that were raised above me ready to strike. I gulped, swallowed more water, and kicked out at it as hard as I could with my feet.

It may have been cumbersome on land, but under the water its ungainly strugglings became a fast and buoyant ballet. Its smaller pincer snapped out and caught the cuff of my pants, holding me long enough for the large claw to seize me just below the knee. It was a fierce, relentless grip, as painful as having a car run over your shin and stay there. At that moment I was certain I was going to drown, and be devoured.

The creature began to drag me further downwards, towards the floor. I was almost on the point of filling my lungs with water, and I knew that I didn't stand a chance. Now that it had me tight in its pincers, it was determined to take its time, and it floated downwards with slow and silent deliberation. I couldn't think about anything. They say your whole life flashes in front of your eyes when you're drowning, but I guess that last picture show is the privilege of those who go up and down three times. I was just going under, and that was it.

My back bumped against the floor. I tried to reach out to steady myself, hoping to find a door or wall which would give me enough leverage to kick back at my predatory captor. What I found was the heavy black-iron poker which I used for stoking the fire. I seized it, missed it, then seized it again.

The smaller pincer released its hold on my pants and began to feel its way up the side of my leg. It was hard and spiny and I had already heard what it had done to poor young Susan Steadman. Still, by the time it started to do any damage, I would probably be drowned and past caring.

Blindly, wildly, I grasped the poker in both hands and thrust it up into the monster's belly. It wasn't much of a blow. It didn't even penetrate the shell. But it was enough to make the huge claw release its hold for a fraction of a second, and a fraction of a second was all I needed to give myself a powerful push against the floor and propel myself free.

The monster came after me immediately, and the noise it made under the water was like the terrible cacophony of damned souls. It lunged and lunged again, but I had found the window, and it only took a brief struggle with the catch before I dived in a huge torrent of water out of the dining-room and straight into the back yard.

I rolled over and over, almost screaming for breath. The water splashed out of the window I had left open and flooded the flagstoned barbecue pit and the sunken garden. But I was out of the house, and I was breathing air again, and that was all that mattered. I picked myself up, coughing and panting and spluttering, and I leaned for a few moments against my picnic table, trying to get myself back in one piece again.

It was only when I lifted my head and looked back towards the house that I realized the water had stopped pouring out of the dining-room window. It was still dark inside the house, but I could see that all of the water, or most of it, appeared to have vanished. There was no sound but the dripping of soaked drapes and furnishings, and in the woods nearby, the hoot of a long-eared owl.

I waited a while longer, and then I cautiously walked back across the yard to the window from which I had escaped. I was shivering with cold, and my clothes were sticking to me like wet cement. I peered into the room, and all I could see was sodden rugs, overturned tables, and scattered bottles. There was no sign of the creature that had seized my leg, and no sign of what must have amounted to more than six or seven thousand gallons of water.

The first thing I did then was walk around the house to the garage. I had left my flashlight hanging outside on a hook, and I took it down and switched it on. The lights in the house would probably all be out, and I wanted to see where I was going, where my predatory adversary was hiding himself. Or *it*self. I didn't really know what to call it.

I climbed the steps to the front door. From here, I could see the shattered living-room window. But there was no sign of any way in which the house could have been filled with such a maelstrom of water. There wasn't even a hosepipe. If I hadn't been so damned wet, I would have thought that everything that had happened in the past few minutes had been just one more of those undersea nightmares.

I switched on the flashlight, and then quietly opened the front door. I flicked the beam around the passage, but it was deserted. I paused for a moment, listening, and then I stepped inside on squelching feet, throwing the light this way and that in case the creature tried to come up behind me and surprise me.

The living-room was sodden and stinking. I knew what the smell was, and it almost turned my stomach. Dead, decaying fish. It was going to take weeks of hard work and fifty buckets of Lysol to get the smell out of the house. I shone the flashlight over towards the dining-room, where I had nearly drowned, but there was nothing there except for broken furniture and smashed ornaments. The iron poker, my last desperate hope, lay on the floor.

It didn't take long to check the whole house. There was terrible water damage to the rugs and the furnishings, and every room stank like a fishing-port, but there was no sign of the creature. It must have gotten away pretty quickly as soon as I let all the water out.

I picked up the telephone and poured water out of its insides. It was still working, and I called Dan. He had just arrived home, and he sounded tired.

"Mason? What is it?"

I coughed. I was suddenly feeling shocked, and I could hardly make my lips work. Dan couldn't see it, which was probably just as well, but my eyes were filled with tears.

"Dan," I said unsteadily, "one of the crab creatures was here."

"What happened? Are you okay?"

I coughed again. If the creatures didn't get me, then double pneumonia probably would. "I'm okay," I told him. "I got a soaking, though. They pulled the same trick here they pulled at the Bodines' house. They flooded the whole place with water, and almost drowned me."

"You're kidding."

"Dan, would I kid? They filled up the living-room, the dining room, the kitchen. It happened so quick the water didn't even have time to run away. They must have used thousands and thousands of gallons. It was like a damn great tidal bore."

Dan asked: "Did you see how they did it?"

"Dan," I told him, "I was *under* it. I was hardly in any kind of position to see what was going on."

"Do you want me to get out there?"

"I'd appreciate it. My car's smashed and my bed's soaked, and to tell you the truth I don't par-ticularly relish a night out here in the country with those creatures on the loose."

Dan paused for a moment, and then he said: "Okay. It's nine o'clock now. I'll get there by ten at the latest. You haven't heard from Carter, I sup-pose?"

"Not a word. I don't think he'll have much luck tracking Jimmy and Alison down until morning, though."

"I guess he won't. Okay, Mason. Give me an hour and I'll be there."

"Dan," I said quietly,

"What is it?"

"Thanks, Dan."

He laughed, "Don't even mention it. One day the same thing may happen to me."

I put the phone down, and then picked it up again and tried calling the sheriff's office. The phone rang and rang for two or three minutes without anybody answering it, so I gave up. The best thing I could do now was sort out some dry clothes and an overnight bag.

I was walking across the hallway to my bedroom when I heard a scratching noise. I stopped, and didn't breathe. There was silence for a while, and then I heard the scratching noise again. It was coming from the linen cupboard.

Well, there was only one kind of creature who would automatically take refuge *there*, and it wasn't one of the crustaceous variety. I went to open the cupboard door and there was Shelley, ruffled and perplexed, and not at all sure if he was pleased to see me. He jumped down from his shelf, and stalked around the wet rug, and I guess he felt as wary and frightened as I did.

# 6

Around seven-thirty in the morning, Rheta called at Dan's lodgings with the news that Carter Wilkes and his deputies had been searching for Jimmy and Alison all night and found nothing. There were no footprints in the soft, rain-soaked earth—no human footprints, anyway—and no scent that a police dog could be reasonably expected to follow. At dawn, Carter had called everyone off, and announced to the newspapers that he intended to play a waiting game instead. He warned the people of New Milford and its surrounding hamlets that two or possibly three homicidal lunatics were on the loose and that they should keep their children under supervision and their doors locked after dark.

When Rheta came in, I was sitting with my knees wedged under Dan's dinky-sized kitchen table, eating my way uncomfortably but gratefully through a plate of bacon and sausages and over-easy eggs that his landlady had cooked up for me.

Whatever Dan had said about his landlady up until now, none of it was true. She was a handsome and bustling widow in her early forties with a son who looked like Fonzie, an Irish wolfhound who looked like Norman Mailer after a heavy night, and a neat small weatherboard rooming house just opposite the New Milford Hospital. She was so handsome, in fact, that I wondered whether Dan harboured a secret or even not-so-secret affection for her, and that was why he'd constantly told us she was a keyhole-peeping harridan with steel curlers and an insatiable taste for Tanqueray.

Dan was across on the other side of the room, which meant about two feet away, making coffee. It looked like the weather had cleared up overnight, and there was a haze of sunshine coming through his gingham drapes. He said: "Hi, Rheta. Come on in. You want some Granola?"

"I don't eat in the mornings," said Rheta, taking off her fringed shoulder-bag and hanging it on the back of the chair. "Just give me some coffee, black."

I looked up at her, forking a well-yolked piece of sausage into my mouth. "That's how you keep so trim, huh? Not eating in the mornings?"

"Nor the afternoons."

I stirred four spoonfuls of sugar into my coffee, and sipped it to make sure it was sweet enough. Us plumbers need our energy, you know. Rheta watched me in disgusted fascination, as if I had just kissed a live toad. She was dressed in one of those flowing Indian-type dresses this morning, and boots, which made her look like one of those ladies who eat sunflower seeds and brown rice and weave their own comforter covers, but I didn't mind too much. She still had that sexy educated charisma that appealed to me, and there was still time for Pigskin Packer to fall in front of a school bus.

Drinking her coffee, Rheta told us about Sheriff Wilkes and his unsuccessful search for Jimmy and Alison. In a way, I was strangely relieved that they hadn't been found, because once they were cornered, there was only one way they were going to end up, and that was shot to pieces. Our New Milford vigilantes were too well-conditioned by the science-fiction movies of the 'fifties to try taking an alien-looking monster alive. It was shoot first and try the John Williams music afterwards.

Dan leaned against the kitchen sink and swallowed his coffee in scalding mouthfuls. "Did they look around old man Pascoe's place?" he asked Rheta.

"I guess so. They didn't say anything specific."

"I was wondering if there was any sign of broken shell, where I hit Alison with the pipe-wrench."

Rheta shook her head. "If they found it, they didn't mention it. Mind you, I didn't speak to Carter himself. Pete Abrams was the only deputy there, and you know what *he's* like when it comes to police cooperation. You have to cooperate with us, but we don't have to cooperate with you."

I finished my bacon and put down my fork. "Maybe they didn't find anything. Those shells looked pretty tough."

Dan pulled a face. "Maybe they are. But I'm sure I heard a crunching noise, and I could have sworn

I saw pieces flying."

"You're making me feel sick," said Rheta.

"It's a sick business. Did Abrams say anything else?"

"Just one thing. They're considering opening the Bodines' well, and drilling down to find out where the polluted water's coming from."

"That's the most sensible idea they've had in two days."

Rheta nodded. "They're going to call us when they get permission to start work. They'd like you to go out there and take samples as they drill down."

"What about me?" I asked her.

"They didn't say anything about you."

"I was nearly crushed by one creature and half-drowned by another, and they haven't asked me along? I've got to be the expert."

"You can come along," said Dan. "I'll make you an honorary member of my research department."

"It's nice to know that *someone* cares. Anyway, listen, I have to go sort out my car. Are you going to be round at the laboratory all morning?"

"Sure," said Dan. "I have to finish my tests on that sample we took out of the Bodine well yesterday afternoon."

I reached into my pocket and took out Greg McAllister's letter of authorization to the Candlewood Furnishers. "Okay. While you're testing, I'll go pick up this book on the *Legends of Litchfield*. You never know, it might have some kind of clues in it. Shall we meet for lunch?"

"You ate a breakfast that size and you're talking about lunch?" asked Rheta.

"I have to keep my strength up," I told her. "You never know when someone may call on my manly reserves."

"I wish this town had plain, ordinary plumbers who mended pipes and then went away again," said Rheta, picking up her shoulder-bag.

"You don't mean that."

She paused. The sunlight touched her face, and made her eyes sparkle. "No," she said gently. "I don't."

Dan looked first at me and then at Rheta, and then went back to his coffee.

Candlewood Furnishers was a big, cluttered barn of a building out on Route 202 past the giant-sized figure of a handyman advertising paint and the New Milford MacDonald's. I borrowed Rheta's Volkswagen to drive out there and it was so small and shaky that I felt like some French comedian. But Shelley seemed to enjoy the vibration, and he fell asleep almost straight away. It was a bright, dry day, although the sky was still reflected in puddles and pools, and wet leaves left dark patterns on the sidewalks.

I pulled across the highway and parked outside the leaning wooden sign which read "Candlewood Furnishers: Elegant Homes On A Budget, Colonial Furniture Our Specialty, Removals & Storage, Prop: F. Martin." I climbed out of the Volkswagen and gave the door a good solid bang. Then I walked across the gravelled front lot to the wide display window, behind which the prop: F. Martin had arranged what he obviously considered to be a tasteful display of colonial furniture. I particularly liked the colonial television and the colonial telephone seat. I went along to the door and pushed my way inside. The whole showroom was stacked with furniture in varying degrees of suburban ugliness, and behind the stacks, in a small booth-like office, with his radio playing easy-listening music, sat a grey-haired man with heavy spectacles and a jersey-knit suit in brown plaid.

"Mr. Martin?" I said, as he looked up and spotted me.

He came out into the showroom and extended his hand. "That's me. Frederick Martin. How can I help you?"

"It's nothing too much, I'm afraid. I've brought a letter from Mr. Greg McAllister, out near Washington Depot. He has a book in storage and he'd like me to take a look at it."

Fred Martin scrutinized the letter carefully. Then he said: "Have you any idea how long it would take to find that book?"

"Well, no, but I guess it shouldn't be too difficult, should it?"

"Difficult? Mr Perkins, you don't know the meaning of the word difficult if you think it shouldn't be too difficult."

"I'm sorry. I just assumed—

He clutched his grey hair melodramatically. "Do you know how many square feet of storage space I have in back? Do you know how many families have all their possessions wrapped and parcelled and sealed away here? How many bureaux and how many tables? How many cupboards and chairs and complete sets of china?

How many barometers?"

"Barometers?" I asked him, perplexed.

"Barometers, or books. Thousands of books. More books than the whole of New Milford library. Millions of books. And you want *one* book out of all those millions, and you say it shouldn't be too difficult to find it?"

I didn't know what to say. I felt embarrassed for coming. But Fred Martin read McAllister's letter again, and then said quite calmly: "However, in this particular instance, you're fortunate."

"What do you mean?"

"The book you want is *Legends of Litchfield*, right?"

"That's correct."

Fred Martin took off his spectacles, and examined me with watery blue eyes. "It so happens that I'm something of an amateur student of local legends and mythology. It's my hobby. You can see from the furniture I sell that I've always tried to keep up the colonial traditions in the area. I believe in tradition. Tradition means respect for your roots."

I looked around the showroom. "A colonial telephone table is traditional?" I asked him.

He squinted at me warily. "I know what you're getting at. I know what you're trying to say. But to my way of thinking, even a colonial cocktail bar is better than a black vinyl version of the same thing. Gilt and black vinyl are the curses of American design. Apart from white vinyl, which is one hundred times worse. And mock-onyx. Don't ever talk to me about mock-onyx."

"All right," I agreed, "I'll keep my mouth shut

about mock-onyx. But how about the book? Do you know where it is?"

"Sure. It's on my shelf right here. I noticed it on the McAllister inventory, and I dug it out a couple of years ago. It's a real interesting book, too. Real old. And there's some stories in it you don't usually find in local histories. Come on back. Do you want some coffee?"

"No thanks. But I could sure use the john."

"That's right over there, just past the stained-oak hutch. While you're away, I'll get the book out."

When I returned from the head, which had been traditional enough to have neatly-torn squares of the *New Milford Journal* for paper, instead of that invidious modern soft stuff, I found Fred Martin sitting at his desk in his booth of an office, leafing through the pages of a yellowed, spotted, leather-bound book. His office was a snowdrift of inventories, bills, invoices, accounts, magazines and newspapers, and on the wall was a Playmate calendar for three years ago. He was drinking instant coffee out of a mug that proclaimed he was a Sagittarius.

"Take a seat," he said, indicating a brand-new armchair that was still wrapped up in corrugated cardboard. I checked my watch, and did so. I was just hoping he wouldn't take all morning. I was looking forward to my lunch appointment with Rheta.

"I'm interested in any legends about the wells around New Milford and Washington," I told him. "You know there's been this water-pollution scare in the past week or two. I'd like to find out if there's any trace of a similar problem in New Milford's distant history. Mr. McAllister says his family never drank their own well water, because of a curse. Apparently they thought it would turn their skin into shell. You know, like a lobster. He even told me a rhyme about it."

Fred Martin propped his spectacles on the end of his nose and peered at the old book as if he were some species of intelligent animal. With his white shaggy eyebrows and his long nose and his curled-up mouth, he could in fact have been a literate llama. He sniffed with considerable style, and turned a few more pages.

"This is what you want," he said, handing the book over to me. He pointed to a heading at the top of the page, and then ran his finger with its long chalky fingernail down to the bottom. "Page two hundred twenty-nine."

I held the book carefully. It was cracked and musty and the pages were foxed with brown. Keeping my finger on the page that Fred Martin had shown me, I turned forward to the title page, which announced in chiselled-looking lettering: "A Discours On Ye Legendes & Mythes Of Lichfielde In Connecticut. Includ'g Ye Onlie Detailled Account of Ye Witche Trialles At Kento. Dy Adam Prescott Printed & Bound at Ye Signe Of Ye Unicorn, Danburye, 1784." Opposite the title page was a murky woodcut of a young man whose mouth had the same lumpy look as George Washington on the dollar bill, and probably for the same reason: bad teeth.

"I never saw one of these books before this one," said Fred Martin, "and I don't suppose I'll ever see one again. This is what you could call a rare edition. Worth a few hundred, I shouldn't wonder."

I turned back to the page he had first pointed out. It was printed in very tiny, close-together type, and it was so smudgy that it was almost impossible to read it. But when I'd got used to s's that were printed as f's, and some of the most extraordinary spelling outside of New Milford's grade schools, I began to interpret Mr. Adam Prescott's "discours" on the particular problems we were facing with Washington, polluted wells.

The heading of the chapter read: "Certaine Ancient Stories Concerninge Ye Springes & Ye Welles Of Washington & Kente." There was a long introductory paragraph about the beauties of the area, and the gentility of the people who lived there, and how many houses there were, and where they were situated, but eventually I came to his passage, and I read it with increasing fascination.

"Ye older denisons of Lichfielde would not drink of ye water from their own welles, sayinge many of them that it was unfitte for drinking by reason of its taintinge by beasts which dwelt beneath ye surface of ye hilles whose appearance they wist not of. Alle any one of them would say was that ye *stories* had been passed to them by ye Indianes which had lived in those parttes in centuries gone by, and that ye Indiane elders had warned them of ye beasts even at a time when ye settlres had been fighting against ye tribes. By severalle accounts I obtained from ye older people of Lichfield, 'twould *seem* that ye beasts had once lived beneath ye Oceane many million years before, in that submarine *continent* knowne by popular account as Atlantis, although ye Indianes call'd it by ye olde Mic-Mac word meaninge Land of Ye Beast-Gods. When terrible earthquakes beneath ye Ocean had destroyed ye caves and hunting-places of ye beast-gods, they had penetrated *New England* and other Eastern partes with their laste Seed, that in centuries to come their descendantes shoulde grow beneath ye earth in ye welles and in ye cold-water springes & *again live* in ye bodies of those who dranke ye water. It was said that Atlantis was never a continent above ye waves, but alwayes ye dwellinge-place of ye fearsome beast-gods who swam & hunted over ye underwater mountains & who made their grisly domain in underwater cavernes. When asked to describe ye beast-gods, few of ye Lichfielde denizens would speak out clear, yet some plainlie knew. Josiah Walters, of Boardmans Bridge would onlie say that ye beast-gods had been said by ye Indianes to come from ye Skies, *ye muskun*, & have tentacles like unto squiddes & claws like unto lobsters, & above all to exude ye odor like unto ye rottinge fishes. Ye Indianes call'd ye places where ye beast-gods lay sleepinge Pontanipo, ye *cold-water*, & those who had lived below the Oceane in ye dayes of Atlantis ye Neipfolk, people of ye *deep waters*. Ye beast-gods too were possess'd of great Magick & to have made it to floode seven times seven in New England in ancient times gone by, in order that they may *drown* men and devour ye drowned cadavers. And of those few men & mariners who had surviv'd such floodes, and seen ye beast-gods, they could scarcely speak of their Ordeals, nor did manie outlive their rescue long, for almost all who had *drunk* of Ye waters surrounding ye beast gods became sick with ye *leprosie* unto ye death. & their cadavers were afterward burn'd."

There was one more paragraph, which told in a very circumlocutory way about strange rumbling noises which had been heard under the ground during rainstorms, and about three unaccountable drownings in the 1770s, but that was about all. The rest of the legends concerned fairies and ghosts and visions of various saints. And the trouble was that no matter how descriptive and relevant any of this evidence seemed to be, there was no way that I could check it out. I would have given a month's plumbing contracts to talk to Josiah Walters of Boardman's Bridge, because his account of what the so-called "beast-gods" looked like was the closest corroboration I had found of my own impressions of Jimmy and Alison's condition. Unfortunately, Josiah Walters had probably been dead for one hundred and eighty years, and I doubted if any descendants still survived.

"What do you think of these legends?" I asked Fred Martin, who had been sitting quietly watching me read. "Do you think there's any truth in them?"

Fred Martin scratched his grey wiry hair. "You mean the Atlantis stories? I don't think so. From what I've read in my books, all my books here, it seems like almost every country around the Atlantic Ocean has got iself some kind of legend or tradition about Atlantis, or some place like it, and about monsters and beasts that lived in the sea. But as for truth? I don't think so. They're good stories, sure. Good old scary legends. But that's about the length and the breadth of it."

"Supposing I told you I believed them."

He shrugged. "You can believe them if you want. It's a free country. And believers never did any of the old legends any harm; they helped to keep them alive. So good luck to you."

He stirred his coffee solemnly, and then he said: "All kinds of people used to believe Atlantis was real. I've got a book up there about the Mayans. They believed it. And the Druids, too. *And* the Ancient Greeks. They all had stories about giants and monsters who came out of the sea and ate folks for breakfast. You know something—there are still people in Cornwall, in England who think the magic island of Lyonesse really existed, and that giants lived there. And sailors in Scotland still talk about Shony, who was a sort of a sea-creature who called out that he was drowning, and needed help, and whenver a fisherman went to help him, he dragged him under the sea and ate him up alive. Shony had another name, too, and that was Shelly-coat."

"Shellycoat! Why?"

Fred Martin reached up to his bookshelf, hesitated, and then took down a cheap orange-bound book that had obviously been liberated from a public library. He thumbed a few pages, and then he said: "Here we are. This is Sir Walter Scott, right? This is what he says about Shony. 'He seemed to be decked with marine productions, and in particular with shells whose clattering announced his approach.' "

I shivered. It wasn't too warm in Fred Martin's office. I said hoarsely. "What about the wells? Do you think there's any truth in that?"

"Any truth in what?"

"In the story of the beast-gods living down inside the wells, waiting for the chance to revive themselves?"

Fred Martin frowned. He picked up a chewed-looking pencil and tapped it against the side of his spectacles. "Mr. Perkins," he said, "you have to understand that these stories are only stories. Maybe they had some kind of roots in fact, but that was probably hundreds of years ago, thousands of years ago, even. They're just legends. Tales that folks used to make up to explain things that looked unnatural. They didn't know nothing about science, so if they saw something scary, they had to explain it by magic. I don't really see how there *could* be creatures living down wells, do you? Not if we're talking seriously."

I picked up *Legends of Litchfield* again. "Do you understand what it says here?" I asked him. "It says that when Atlantis collapsed, the beast-gods ensured the survival of their race by infiltrating the natural water system of New England with their seed. I guess in modern terms that could mean fertilized eggs, or spawn, or whatever beast-gods used to reproduce themselves."

Fred Martin coughed nervously. "I suppose it could mean that, yes. But it doesn't actually, say so, does it?"

"It says, 'they had penetrated New England and

other partes with their laste Seed.' What other possible interpretation is there?"

Fred Martin was silent for a moment. He tapped his spectacles a couple of times with his pencil, and then he said: "I guess it could all be fiction. *That's* an interpretation, isn't it?"

"Sure. But most legends have some small grain of fact in them, don't they?"

"I guess so. I don't really know what you're trying to say. If you believe in it, then like I said, you're welcome. You're at liberty to do so. But I've lived in New Milford all my life, and *I* don't believe in it."

I opened the book up again and re-read what Adam Prescott had said about the beast-gods from Atlantis. Then I said: "All right. If I could just borrow this book for a while—?"

"Of course you can. Greg McAllister's given his permission, hasn't he? You go right ahead."

He stood up, as if he was quite anxious for me to leave. "All I can say is, don't credit everything you read in them old books. I've read some pretty queer stories in some of my books, stories that would turn your head round if you believed them. They weren't oct down for believing, these legends. They were oct down because they were curious. So that's just a word of warning."

I got up from the cardboard-covered chair. His office was so small that we were standing face to face with our noses almost touching. I said respectfully: "I'll remember what you said."

I stepped out into the showroom and made my way to the door. As I opened it, Fred Martin called: "Give mv best to Mr. McAllister, won't you?"

"Of course I will."

He gave me a quick, uncertain grin. "Thanks."

I said: "Is there anything else?"

"Well, no. No, that's fine. Except that—well, you don't have any *reason* for believing that stuff, do you? Nothing's happened around here that maybe I should know?"

I paused. I didn't really know what to tell him. But then I said, "If there is I'll give you a call. Okay?"

"Okay," he agreed, but he sounded unconvinced. He watched me through the glass of his showroom window as I walked across to Rheta's Volkswagen, climbed in, and started the engine. He was still standing in his ideal colonial sitting-room as I backed noisily out of his parking lot and signalled that I was turning right, towards New Milford. I gave him a wave, but he didn't wave back. I guess people who don't believe in myths and legends are always a little bit crabbier than the rest of us.

Mrs. Wardell had a message for me when I walked into the laboratory. Dan and Rheta had both gone out, in all kinds of a desperate hurry, and lunch was regrettably but definitely cancelled. Mrs. Wardell's upswept spectacles looked even more upswept than usual, and she was agitated and fidgety. As I tore open the message and read it, she bit at her crimson-painted lips and crossed and uncrossed her legs, trying to resist the temptation to tell me what had happened before I could read it for myself.

The note was in Rheta's rounded, feminine writ-

ing. It said: "Carter has called us out to Gaylordsville. Come as soon as you can. Turn right off
7 towards South Kent, then take the *first* turnoff
past the *first* bridge. Love—Rheta."

Oh well, I thought. At least she signed her urgent
messages with love. I folded up the note, gave Mrs.
Wardell an abstracted smile, and went back downstairs and out into the street. Shelley was sitting
up in the passenger seat of the Volkswagen
waiting for me. I think he'd gotten over the novelty
of driving around in a Beetle, and was restless to
get back to the comfort of the Country Squire. He
closed his eyes and flattened his ears in pained dis-
approval as I slammed the car door shut and
started the rackety engine.

I got stuck behind a huge slow-moving truck for
most of the drive, and so I spent an impatient
fifteen minutes choking on diesel fumes and
reading and re-reading the sign on the back of the
truck which read *Konitz Donuts Taste Like Home*.
At last I reached Gaylordsville, a small neat town-
ship with a quaint old post office and a colonial-
type firehouse, and I made a right around the
curve that led towards South Kent.

I couldn't have missed Dan and Rheta and
Sheriff Wilkes if I'd tried. The roadway was
blocked with two patrol cars, an ambulance, and a
wrecking truck, all with flashing beacons. Two
officers were holding back curious bystanders,
while Carter and three of his deputies and two
medics were gathered by a red Impala which was
resting at an angle in the gulley at the side of the
road. Dan and Rheta were standing a little way
back, and both of them looked pale and strained. I

parked the Volkswagen and walked across.

"What's happened here?" I asked them.

Rheta remained tight-lipped, as if she was trying to keep herself from crying or vomiting or even bursting out into hysterical laughter. But Dan nodded towards the red Impala and said softly: "It's happened again. Maybe it's Jimmy and Alison. Maybe there's another one. Maybe there's even more."

"Someone killed?"

Dan took a deep breath to steady himself. "Yes. Why not ask Carter. He knows the details."

I said to Rheta: "How are you feeling? Do you want to go back to the car, keep Shelley company?"

She shook her head. "I'll be all right. It was a shock, that's all. Give me a minute or two."

"Okay." I left them where they were and approached the little group of policemen and medics. As I came closer, I saw that the metal roof of the Impala was gaping apart, as if someone had ripped it up with the point of a giant can-opener. One of the medics was peering into the car through the driver's window, and his expression was distinctly unhappy.

"Carter," I said, walking up to the sheriff. "How are you doing?"

Sheriff Wilkes looked at me philosophically. "Hi, Mason. About as good as possible, considering the circumstances."

I shaded my eyes against the bright grey daylight. I couldn't be sure, but it looked like every window in the red Impala was painted red to match the colour scheme. Then it abruptly occurred to me that it couldn't be paint. Nobody painted their windows. It must be blood.

I turned to Carter and didn't know what to ask him. Carter kept rubbing his chin with his hand as if he didn't know what to say to me, either.

"Is there somebody in there?" I asked, at last.

"As far as we can make out, a whole family. Father, mother, two little kids."

"Carter—what's happened?"

"I don't know. We're going to tow the whole vehicle straight in to headquarters. They're all dead. Looks like something tore open the roof and went straight in there and tore 'em to pieces."

"Something? Something like *what?* What can do that? What earthly thing can tear open the roof of a car and kill everybody inside?"

Carter lowered his eyes. "I don't know, Mason. Maybe a mechanical trencher."

"Or a crab creature?"

Carter shrugged uncomfortably. "You saw the crab creatures for yourself. You said they were man-sized, right? Whatever did this was four times the size of a man, and that's being conservative. *It tore open the roof,* you get me? It tore open the roof and reached inside and just about tore everybody to pieces."

He was deeply upset. In fact, he was almost on the brink of tears. He took out his khaki handkerchief, opened it out, and blew his nose like a bassoon.

It was then that the rear door of the car swung open, and I glimpsed what was inside. I was horrified and nauseated, but I couldn't make my eyes turn away. Almost immediately, the medic

closed the door again, so that none of the bystanders could see what was going on. But it was
too late, I'd seen it, and I stood on that road as if
the Lord and all his angels had paralysed me for
ever.

I had seen a woman's head with curly blonde
hair hanging back over the front passenger seat,
hanging back so far that her eyes had been staring
at me, upside-down, through the open door. I
hadn't been able to see her body, thank God, but
her head had been suspended by nothing more
than a flat blue gristly piece of torn-open neck.
The back seats had been splattered in blood and
mucus, and I had seen livers and intestines, in all
the dark and gaudy colours of butchery, hanging
from the seat-belt straps. There was a stench of
fresh blood and rotten fish, and I knew damn well
who had done this thing, just as Carter knew.

"Children," said the sheriff, in a muffled voice.
"Two innocent little children, with all their lives
ahead of them."

"Any tracks? Any clues?" I asked him.

"Not so far. We've got the dogs out again. I'll
catch those bastards, I warn you. I don't care if
they're creatures or people or what they are. I'll
catch them, and I'll make damn sure they pay for
doing this."

"It looks like they're bigger, doesn't it?" I asked
him. "Maybe they've been growing."

He nodded. "I don't know how, and right now
I'm not going to ask. The whole damn thing's impossible, from the very beginning, and so what I'm
going to do is believe it, no matter how crazy it
gets, because if I don't believe it then more inno-

cent people like this are going to get themselves ripped to pieces; and I tell you, Mason, I tell you true, I'm not going to let this happen again."

I laid my hand on his arm. "I know, Carter. I know you'll get them."

He gave a deep sniff. "I will, don't you worry about it. We're going drilling this afternoon, too, up at the Bodine place, see what's down the damn well. Do you want to come along?"

"Dan's already invited me."

"Well, you come along. You watch me track those bastards down."

"Okay, sheriff."

I went back to Dan and Rheta. They saw the look on my face and they didn't ask me any more questions about the Impala and what was inside it. Behind me, the towing crew were attaching chains to the wrecked car's rear bumper, and one of them was saying: "We have to put the car in neutral. Will anybody put it in neutral?"

One of the medics opened the front door, quickly leaned in and adjusted the gearshift. He closed the door again and stood there with his face white and sticky blood all over his hand. The towing crew glanced at each other and raised their eyebrows. They must have seen some bad ones, but this was an abattoir on wheels.

I said to Dan: "The crabs have grown larger, much larger. They must have. It looks like one of them pulled open the roof with a pincer and then reached inside."

"We know one thing," said Dan, "they're indisputably carnivorous."

Rheta looked away, but she said quietly: "If

they're large enough to tear open a car, surely the police must find them soon. They can't have gotten very far away."

"I don't know," I told her. "What's the speed of a crab, relative to the speed of a human being?"

"Fast," remarked Dan. "A crab could outrun a racehorse, and over a longer distance, too."

We stood in the silence for a short time, I could almost feel the globe turning under my feet.

"How are the tests going?" I asked, eventually. "Have you checked out the new water sample yet?"

Dan nodded. "I've made a preliminary check. It's full of the same species of organism. Without counting heads, it looks like there's more of them, too."

"What does that mean?"

"How should I know? I don't know what any of this means. I can't even believe that it's real. We've completed our tests on the mouse and all we know is that it drank the water from the Bodine well and changed. We still don't know why, or how."

"Did you hear from Newsom about the post-mortem on Oliver Bodine?" I asked him

"Not officially," put in Rheta. "He didn't want to speak officially until he'd run some virus tests in New York. But off the record he knows about as much as we do, which is almost nothing. He's sure the water caused the metamorphosis, or rather the microorganisms did. But he doesn't know how it happened, and he can't understand the life-cycle at all."

"We we're back at square one," said Dan, glumly. "All we can hope for now is some kind of miraculous discovery when we drill down into the well itself."

I took out a cigarillo and lit it with my hands shielding my lighter against the breeze. I puffed a few times, and then I said: "It looks like I've discovered more than you have, then."

Rheta raised her eyes. "You went to look for that book this morning, didn't you? The book of legends?"

"That's right. It's in the car. And there's a whole page about the wells of Washington, and why people wouldn't drink out of them, and that goes as far back as the eighteenth century, if not further."

The wrecking-truck revved up its engine, and a blast of black diesel smoke stained the sky. With a rattle of chains and a groaning of twisted metal, the red Impala was dragged protesting out of the gulley and up on to the road. Its red-plastered windows gave it a hideous and macabre appearance. We looked the other way as a large grey sheet of plastic was thrown over the top of it and secured with ropes, and we didn't look back again until the truck had dragged it like the corpse of some mutilated animal along the road and out of sight around the curve towards Gaylordsville.

Sheriff Wilkes came over and stood beside us for a while, his beefy hands resting on his hips. There was a toothpick sticking out from between his teeth which he chewed and shifted from one side of his mouth to the other in a constant display of dental dexterity.

He was quiet for a long while, looking down along the road where the Impala had at last disappeared. Then he said: "I don't suppose you guys have any helpful ideas."

"We may have," I told him. "We're not sure."

"New evidence?" asked Carter, interested.

"No. Very old evidence. But it could be good. We're going to look it over right now. We'll tell you what we think when we see you this afternoon at the Bodine house."

"Okay," said Carter. "I'd appreciate it."

At that moment, there was a squawk from the radio in Carter's car. He said: "Hold it, guys," and went over to pick up his microphone. We weren't standing too far away, so we easily overheard the message. Carter gave us an intent and meaningful look as the police radio operator spoke.

*"Headquarters to sheriff and all units. Highway Patrol helicopter on Route 7 approximately four miles north Gaylordsville reports possible suspects crossing the highway and making into the woods east."*

Sheriff Wilkes said gruffly: "Wilkes here. We're responding straight away. Over." Then he turned and yelled to the deputies around him: "The Highway Patrol have sighted the Bodines! Let's get after 'em!"

In a burst of car-door slamming and whooping and warbling sirens, Carter and his deputies backed up their vehicles and screeched out of Gaylordsville. I said to Dan: "Come on, let's follow them. We may have half a chance to help."

"Help who?" asked Rheta, as we clambered into the Volkswagen. "The Sheriff or the Bodines?"

"Whoever needs it most," I said tersely, but that was only because I didn't even know myself.

The Volkswagen rattled into life, and I swung
the wheel around and drove us at top speed northwards, shifting the manual gears like I was
stirring my grandmother's Christmas pudding. On
the straightaway past the town, I just glimpsed the
tail of Carter's car as it sped on ahead of us, but
that was about as near as I got to catching up.
However wonderful the German economic miracle may be, there is no way you can overhaul
a souped-up LTD in a battered beige Beetle. But
still, I did my best.

"That book about Litchfield legends is on the
back seat there," I told Dan. "I slipped an envelope
into the page about Washington and the well
water."

"I've got it," said Dan, and for Rheta's benefit
started to read it out loud. I kept my eyes on the
road and my foot jammed against the gas pedal
and hoped that nothing nasty was going to happen
before we caught up with the police.

It was when he reached the piece about Josiah
Walters of Boardman's Bridge that his voice fal-
tered. *"Ye beast-gods have tentacles like unto
squiddes & claws like unto lobsters, & above all
exude ye odor like unto ye rottinge fishes."*

He sat up straight, his eyes wide. "That's an
exact description of Jim and Alison, the way they
are now," he said, in a hollow voice. "That's exactly what they look like, and exactly what they
smell like. And when was this book written?"

He opened the title-page. "Seventeen eighty-
four. My God."

I glanced back at him. "Fred Martin didn't believe it was true. But it must be. The description's

too close. Whoever this Josiah Walters was, it sounds like he saw some of these creatures for himself, and for real, and maybe a few of his neighbours did, too."

Rheta whispered: "Could these creatures really, truly have come from Atlantis?"

Dan, resting his elbows on the back of my seat, said: "It's not as cranky as it sounds, Atlantis. There's plenty of solid evidence that it really existed. It wasn't a sixth continent in the middle of the Atlantic ocean, but it could have been a chain of islands and reefs that ran down the eastern coast of America. Bermuda is probably one of the only islands that survived when Atlantis sank, but there must have been hundreds of others, and even if what this Adam Prescott says is only *partly* true, there could well have been a race of amphibious creatures who lived around the underwater mountains and reefs."

"What about the skeletons that Currie found in Africa? And the people that whats-his-name, that British doctor, found in India? Where did they come from?"

Dan shrugged. "It's impossible to say without looking at the evidence more closely. But maybe, when Atlantic collapsed, they could have swum eastwards and attempted the same kind of infiltration into the water systems of Africa and India that they've achieved here in Connecticut."

He paused, and then he said: "I know it all sounds nuts. But I heard from White Plains today that those organisms *are* two million years old, and maybe older, and this legend seems to be the only feasible explanation we've had so far. Look at the facts. The water *does* contain ancient organisms, and the organisms *do* have the effect of changing human and animal bone structure. Then we've already seen two proveable cases of thousands of gallons of water being poured into houses from nowhere at all; and we've seen people killed, and torn apart. What's more, if you look through the simplest of anthropological textbooks, you'll find that there's plenty of evidence to show that Atlantis, or something similar, really existed. Now we have this book, with its legend. What other conclusion can we possibly draw, except that it's true?"

Rheta said: "I don't know, Dan. It's too fantastic. It's just too fantastic."

Dan shook his head. "It's only fantastic if you ignore centuries and centuries of solid evidence. I studied some of this stuff at college. Almost every nation in the world has some kind of legend about giants and monsters who lived in the sea. The Mayans believed in Quetzalcoatl, who came out of the sea and bore the earth on his shoulders, and that could be a typical example of what we're talking about. When they say he came out of the sea and bore the earth on his shoulders, maybe they didn't mean that he picked up the world, like Atlas, but that he went underground."

"Maybe they did," I put in, "but this is all supposition."

"Sure it's supposition. But then there's the natives of Ponape, in the Caroline Islands. They worshipped a fish-god who was said to transmute his most adoring admirers into amphibious men, with gills in their throats and tentacles emerging from the sides of their chests."

I peered through the fly-specked windshield, but so far there was no sign of Carter Wilkes or his deputies up ahead.

Dan said: "Whatever you think about these legends, and I'm just as suspicious about them as anybody, this guy Adam Prescott picked the best possible source. The Indians who lived on the eastern seaboard of America had the closest natural contact with the ocean, and an immense understanding of the sea's supernatural powers. Look what Prescott says here—how the Indian wise men went as far as warning the white people about the beast-gods, even though the white people were fighting against them. That's how terrible those beast-gods were. White men may have been killing red men, but there was something around which was greater and more terrible than any human being could possibly have been."

"You're making me shudder," said Rheta.

Dan grunted. "I hope I am. I don't know too much about it, but if what this book here says is right, then Jimmy and Alison have turned into direct descendants of the ancient beast-gods who came from the stars."

"Dan," I protested, "this isn't like you. I thought you were going to give me a cold, hard scientific explanation for all this, and put my mind at rest."

Dan was silent for a moment or two, and then he said: "I can only tell you what I know. Anthropology isn't my subject. But I remember what I was taught at college about language, and stuff like that, and all of this legend fits in. You see what it says here? "Ye beast-gods had been said by

ye Indianes to come from ye skies, *ye muskun.*"
Well, muskun is the old Indian word for the vault
of heaven, the place where the elder gods lived,
along with all the ancient and terrible demons.
Sometimes the gods managed to persuade some
human to summon them down to earth, and when
they did, they ravaged the land and the sea and
they ate human flesh whenever they could get it.

"Did you ever read H. P. Lovecraft? He used to
write about "elder gods," and the worst god of all
was a beast who lived in the sea called Cthulhu.
According to my language teacher, Cthulhu was a
twisting around of the god's real name, which was
Quithe. That's an ancient Celtic word for pit, or
chasm. The Indians called him something like
Ottauquechee, which means waters-of-the-pit."

"So what does all this wonderful revival of college knowledge amount to?" I asked him.

"It amounts to a lot," insisted Dan. "It amounts
to the fact that so many cultures knew about the
beast-gods who came out of the sea and made their
way into the underground water-tables, so many
cultures have names for the creatures, and
legends about where they came from, and what
they're going to do, that there must be some truth
in what this books says, and in what our own de-
ductions have led us to believe. It's all bizarre, and
frightening, and crazy, but it's all true, too."

I wiped the steamed-up windshield with my
handkerchief. "Dan," I said, after a while, "I've
agreed with you all along the line. I think you're a
bright guy, and I agree with you now. What can I
say? I just wish it wasn't happening, but it is."

Rheta murmured: "Amen to that."

We came around a long curve in the road, through a hail of windblown leaves, and jammed on the brakes. Carter's car was pulled across the road with its red light flashing. The deputies' car was further away, and it looked as if it had collided with a roadside tree. Only one deputy was around, my ginger-haired friend from the conference room, and he waved his arm and pointed towards the woods that bordered the highway.

"They saw one of the creatures!" he yelled. "They went that way! Down by the stream!"

I climbed out of the car, and Dan quickly pushed my seat forward and hunched his way out after me. "Those cars are made for gnomes," he said, brushing down his sleeves. "What do we do now? Go after them?"

"Why not?" I said. "We're supposed to be the experts. Rheta—I know you're an expert, too, but you'd better stay here. Look after the car. Make sure nobody steals it."

The deputy called, as we crossed the road and crunched through the dry leaves into the woods: "You make sure Sheriff Wilkes don't shoot you down instead of the creature! You make sure you holler out, now and again, so's he knows it's you!"

I gave him a wave, and then we scrambled into the undergrowth, trying to make as little noise as we could. Actually, amidst all those tall leaves, we must have sounded like we were marching through bowls of wheat flakes. Dan asked: "Can you see them? I don't see them."

"I don't see anything," I told him.

We stopped for a few seconds. We were out of sight of the road now, screened by birch and ash and brambles, and all we could see was shadows around us and the pale gum-coloured sky above our heads.

"They must be way ahead," said Dan. "We would have heard them otherwise."

But we were just about to set off again when we heard a sharp rattle of shots, and a scream of pain that would still wake me out of sleep in years to come.

# 7

We ran slantwise down the hill, kicking up leaves as we went, until we reached the bed of a damp overgrown gulley. The trees and the evergreen bushes were so thick down here that it was almost dark, and there was a musty smell of decaying vegetation and mould. We were panting, and confused, but we didn't stop to talk. Instead, we ran on again, through the tangles of briar, and at last we came to a hollow, almost completely surrounded by thickets, where Sheriff Wilkes and two of his deputies were standing. They looked white-faced and frightened, and Sheriff Wilkes was frantically trying to contact his cars through his pocket radio.

"What's happening? Is anybody hurt?" I asked him.

He shook his radio. "Damn thing. Must have busted when I fell over."

One of the deputies, the long-nosed one called Martino, said: "It got Huntley. We came down

here and the goddamned creature came out of the
bushes and got ahold of his arm, dragged him back
in there. It happened so quick we didn't hardly see
it. Fired a couple of shots, but that didn't seem to
do nothing."

Carter tucked his radio back into his pants
pocket. His eyes were dark and displeased. "I told
you I was going to get that monster, and I will.
Martino, go back to the car, call up headquarters,
and tell them I want grenades, and anti-tank
rockets. They'll have to get them from Colonel
Phelps, and he'll probably want to know what
they're for, but just tell 'em to hedge and stall. I
don't want the National Guard in on this unless
I'm forced to."

"Okay, sir," said Martino, and sprinted off.

Dan said: "Did you see where the creature
went?"

Carter pointed a stubby finger towards the
densest part of the bushes. "Right in there. It got
Huntley by the arm. Snap, just like that. It's so
damned prickly in there we couldn't even follow.
Son-of-a-bitch."

"Did you see what size it was?" asked Dan.

The sheriff nodded. He stretched his arms wide,
as if he was telling a fishing story. "Big. Real big.
One large claw, one smaller claw. But the large
claw was five, six hundred pounds of lobster."

"How about the head or the body? Did you get a
good look?"

"No," said Carter. "It was all too quick. Huntley
was behind us, and all I saw was the claw and the
top of the head. It was kind of curved and bony,
you know? Like a helmet, only green-and-black
and patchy."

Dan looked at me. "It could be either of them, couldn't it? Jimmy or Alison. Or it could even be this man Karlen."

"I don't mind if it's Jimmy or Alison," I said. "At least I could try to talk to them."

Carter Wilkes stared at me as if I'd said something obscene.

"*Talk* to them? What in hell do you mean?"

"Just what I say. I was able to talk to Jimmy before. I didn't get too far, but then I didn't know too much about what was going on."

"And now you do?"

"I know more than I did before. I think I know why they've changed into those crab creatures, and I think I might be able to help them."

Carter rested his hands on his hips, and sighed. "If you don't beat everything. You think you can go in there, right into those goddamned brambles and holly bushes, and chew the fat with some homicidal lobster that just tore five people to shreds in one morning?"

"I can try, can't I?" I asked him.

"I don't even see why you want to," he grumbled.

Dan spoke for both of us. "Carter," he said. "Jimmy and Alison Bodine were a fine, gentle couple, and what's happened was not their fault. The way Mason and I understand it, they're being used by some kind of ancient intelligence that found a way to preserve itself in the wells under their land, and that intelligence has now decided it wants to break out."

"Intelligence? What are you talking about, *intelligence?*"

Dan smoothed his hand over his bald head. "I'm

not exactly sure. But people in these parts have told stories for hundreds of years about beasts who live under the ground, and I'm convinced that they're substantially based in fact. You only have to make a simple analysis of the water from the Bodine well to see that it's completely unique, and that those organisms in it are something extraordinary and special. It wasn't Jimmy's fault that he drank the water, nor Alison's. They didn't know the organisms were there, any more than I did, to begin with. They're innocent victims of whatever it is that's down there under the ground. Just like hostages, if you want it in police language. They're behaving the way they do because they've been taken over by a far stronger influence than us, and they don't have any choice in the matter."

"That's why I'd rather talk than shoot," I said quietly. "They deserve a chance."

Carter grunted. "Don't you think *you* deserve a chance, too? They've already attacked you twice. What do you think's going to happen when you go after that creature in the middle of those bushes? What do you think it's going to do? Shake your hand and call you Charlie?"

"I'll just have to wait and see," I replied. "But if I don't go in there, nobody else will."

"Too damned right," said the other deputy, laconically.

Carter said: "I could forbid it, you know. This is a police situation, and I could tell you to get the hell out and stop interfering."

"But you won't."

"No, I won't. I liked Jimmy and Alison too. And I guess if you believe there's a chance of saving them, I'm conscience bound to go along with it. Not duty bound, mind. But conscience bound. And that's why I'm going to give you just five minutes. You get me? Five minutes and no more, and after five minutes we're going to start lobbing tear gas in there, and then we're going to start shooting."

I gave him a quick, nervous grin. "If that's what you feel you have to do."

"It is. I don't want no more families winding up butchered, just because we're exhibiting a little kindness to crabs."

"Okay," I told him. "I get you."

I borrowed a pair of black leather gloves from Carter's deputy, and I wound Dan's striped woollen scarf around my ears and the lower part of my face. While I was tucking my pants into my socks, deputy Martino came puffing back from the road to say that headquarters had arranged for two cars to come out with reinforcements, rifles, and an anti-tank gun. The anti-tank gun was apparently being closely and aggressively supervised by a Sergeant Kominsky from the National Guard, but that didn't worry Carter. He could outshoot any sergeant alive.

"All right, Mason," said Carter, checking his watch. "You have two minutes as of now. Any trouble, just yell. Or scream, depending on how bad the trouble is."

"You can count on it," I said wryly. I tried not to stop and think what I was actually going to do once I'd penetrated the brambles. One moment of hesitation and anybody with sufficient command of the English language to say "don't go" would have persuaded me to stay on the side-lines and watch the crab creature being blown apart by armour-piercing rockets.

Dan rested both his hands on my shoulders. "Nobody's forcing you," he said, quietly.

"I know. Don't remind me."

"All right, then. Good luck."

Carter came up to me and handed me his .38 Police Special. "You know how to use this thing?"

"Not exactly."

"You've seen Starsky and Hutch?"

"For my sins, yes."

Carter raised one beefy hand and steadied it with the other, pointing his finger to represent the gun. "That's how you do it. Steady, aim, squeeze. Don't panic, and make sure you shoot at something that looks important, like its head or its eyes."

I looked down at the gun in my hand without much confidence. Somehow, shooting at things seemed to be the American answer to every problem there was. Maybe that's why I'd given up psychiatry. All people really wanted to hear was that every problem, from impotence to agoraphobia, could be solved by some kind of psychological shoot-out.

"Five minutes, then," said Carter, and turned away. I gave Dan a quick shrug and began to climb up the side of the hollow towards the brambles and the holly bushes.

Going through those thickets was like walking into a hedge of barbed wire. They ripped at my clothes and lacerated my face, and they had a vicious trick of springing back at me as I tried to push them aside. It seemed to take me whole minutes just to force my way past one thick and prickly holly bush, but Carter and Dan were still in sight, and they gave me the thumbs-up. I waved back, half-heartedly, and pushed deeper into the bushes.

Once I'd penetrated the outer layers of bramble and holly, the going was easier. My forehead was bleeding and one of my gloves was badly ripped, but I was reasonably intact. I stuck the .38 in my belt, because it was proving to be more of a nuisance than a help, and it didn't give me much in the way of psychological strength. If Carter was calling for anti-tank guns, which could blow holes in reinforced steel, it didn't seem very likely that a police-issue peashooter could do much to protect me.

I checked my watch. I must have been gone two minutes, maybe two minutes thirty seconds. I trod as quietly as I could through the dry, curled up leaves, shielding my face from the holly with my upraised arm, and every now and then I stopped to listen.

At first, there was only the crackling of leaves, and the wind blowing with almost inaudible softness through the woods. But then I heard something else. A sound like branches splintering, and a kind of sucking, tearing noise. I sniffed, and that distinctive odour of fish was on the air.

I pushed my way forward, until I reached a screen of brambles and tangled creepers. I went down on hands and knees, and crawled forward ten or twenty feet, hiding myself as deeply as I could among the leaves. The sucking, slavering noise was much louder here, and with infinite care

I raised my head above the level of the under-growth to see what was going on.

The creature was there, only fifteen feet away. I had never seen one in daylight before, and I was horrified. My skin seemed to prickle and shrink with fear, and my most immediate urge was to leap up from my hiding-place and run like hell.

It wasn't really a crab, or a lobster, at all. I think I could have accepted it if it was. But instead it was a massive, hideous, bulky crustacean, with a body the size of a small gasoline tanker. The shell on its back was domed and curved, and grotes-quely mottled. Out from under that shell pro-truded an insect-like head, with waving tendrils and black glistening eyes on constantly-moving stalks. The eyes had grey, wrinkled eyelids, which rolled on and off the eyeballs every few moments like the foreskin of some hideous penis.

The major claw had developed enormously, into a heavy, jagged and vicious-looking vice. Beneath the body shell, there were clusters of spiny legs, bristling with tough black hairs, and crusty ex-crescences that appeared to be dried-up scabs. There was something else, too. Out of the abdomen writhed dozens of squid-like tentacles, soft and pale and squirming, and it was these that were holding the ravaged corpse of deputy Huntley while the crab-creature made its meal.

The sucking noise I had heard was the sound of the creature devouring Huntley's intestines, and bloody coils of them were hanging from its beak-like jaw. The tearing had been the smaller claw, ripping open his remains, separating his ribs, and probing inside for the softest, choicest pieces.

Bile rose up in my throat, and for a while there I thought I was going to have to puke. But I managed to keep it down, even though I was chilled and sweating and shaky, the way I used to be when I was car-sick in the back of my father's Plymouth Cranbrook. I took a deep breath, and pulled out Sheriff Wilkes' .38. It might have been useless against a creature as huge and vicious as this crab, but now I was right up close I realized it was all I had.

I tried to call out: "Jimmy? Alison?" but my mouth was so dry I couldn't manage it. I coughed, and tried again. *"Jimmy! Alison! Is that you?"*

The ghastly creature stopped its feeding and raised its bristly head. Blood dripped from its beak on to the leaves. For a moment, there was utter silence, not even a bird twittering or a leaf spinning from out of a tree.

"Jimmy? It's me, Mason Perkins! I'm right here!"

The creature turned its head towards me. I could have jumped up right then and there and high-tailed it out of the woods in six seconds flat, holly or no holly, but I didn't know how fast that creature could move, and in any case that wasn't what I'd struggled all my way through the undergrowth for. I'd come here to see if Jimmy or Alison could possibly be saved. I'd come here because they used to be human, and maybe they still could be. Don't ask me why. The only motivation I had was that I was human, too.

I stood up slowly. The monster wasn't more than ten feet away, and I almost choked on the hot stench of a torn-open body and the odour of rotten fish. Its jaws slowly masticated a remnant of Huntley's viscera, but its black eyes remained totally motionless, fixed in my direction. Its grey eyelids peeled and unpeeled.

"Jimmy, if that's you, we have to talk," I said, in a shaking voice. I felt as if I was crazy, addressing myself to something that looked like a movie horror poster. A small brown thrasher settled on a nearby branch and inspected us both with obvious interest. The wind rustled through the leaves.

I thought for a few long seconds that the creature wasn't going to answer me. After all, it had grown far more bestial than when I had seen it in back of old man Pascoe's place, and maybe the power of human speech had been overwhelmed altogether. But then I heard a sibilant sound in its throat, a slurred and painful hissing, and I knew that however hideous it looked, however cold-blooded and vicious it was, it still harboured the mind of a human being.

"Mason . . . " it hissed. It moved a little towards me, its spidery legs shifting and its tentacles waving, and I moved a little back.

"Is that you, Jimmy?" I said, loudly. "Is that really you?"

"Not—now—" the creature whispered. "Not—any—more "

"Jimmy, can you understand me? Can you understand what I'm saying? I came here to help you."

"Help—I—need—no—help—"

"It's the sheriff, Jimmy. He's going to bring in anti-tank guns. He's going to kill you. No matter how tough you are. No matter what you've turned yourself into. He's going to come through these woods and he's going to smash you to pieces."

The creature came closer. I stepped back an equal distance. I kept the gun raised, and I could feel the sweat on the palm of my hand against its rubber handgrip.

"Nothing—can—stop—me—I—have—my—duty —to—do—my—tasks—to fulfil—"

"Your *tasks?* Your *duty?* What about your duty to Alison? What about your duty to Oliver, and to all the rest of us?"

The creature paused. Then it hissed: "You—are —all—nothing—this land—will—be—ours now—"

"Jimmy," I said loudly, "if you can still talk, then you've still got something human in you. You have to make an effort. You have to resist. If you go on believing you're human, then maybe you'll stand a chance. But if you don't, then sure as eggs are scrambled they'll kill you."

"You—understand—nothing—"

I stood my ground, even though the creature was moving closer. "Don't I?" I challenged it. "Don't I? Don't I know about Atlantis, and the way your masters impregnated the water table, hoping they could survive? Don't I know about Quetral coatl, and Quithe, and don't I know about Ottauquechee?"

The creature stayed silent for a moment. It was growing darker in the woods. For some odd reason, I was reminded of *Alice Through The Looking Glass,* when the sky grows black with the shadow of a monstrous crow. It felt as weird and unreal as looking-glass land in that damp Connecticut scrub, and yet the stink of death and primeval greed was too strong to make me think it was fantasy. The danger was too near.

Slowly, with a creaking of jointed plates and thick membranes, the crab creature that had once been Jimmy Bodine began to rise on its hind legs. I thought at first that it was going to strike out at me, like a cobra, but it stayed erect, its tentacles wriggling, and its black eyes wide. It stood as tall as the lower branches of the trees, maybe seventeen or eighteen feet, like an automobile turned on to its end.

"Who—spoke—to—you—of Ottauquechee—" it whispered.

"Nobody spoke to me. I read it for myself. I read all about the beasts below the ground, and the gods who came from the stars and ruled Atlantis. I know what you are now, Jimmy, and what you're trying to do, and I'm not going to let it happen. Not to you, because you used to be my friend, and not to Alison. And above all, not to all those innocent people you've been killing."

In front of my eyes, the crab creature seemed to become cloudy. I blinked, and stared at it harder, but it was actually changing. The tentacles became as insubstantial as smoke, and the domed head appeared to roll in on itself. The air all around us vibrated, and I felt as if someone had touched a humming tuning-fork against my skull.

The smoke coiled and writhed, and took on dozens of different, shifting shapes. I thought I saw men of impossible stature, hooded and silent, and I thought I saw creatures that were clothed in hooks and spines. I thought I saw people I knew, but whose faces I couldn't quite remember, fleeting impressions of faces from sad and lonesome dreams. I thought I saw Jimmy Bodine, with a faint smile on his lips. I thought I saw myself.

The voice whispered: "I am everything and everyone. I am the servant of the god of times gone by and times yet to be. My name is everything and my face is everyone. I am preparing for the resurrection of the greatest of those who lived beyond the stars, in those ancient places of exile from which none could return unsummoned. You are right that the watery places were ours when we first returned to this earthly domain. We were forced to flee them when the deeps collapsed, and to seek refuge in the inlets and the rivers, and to leave our seed between the layers of the earth itself."

This was Jimmy's voice, but it was gentle, sinister, much more cultured than Jimmy's voice had ever really been. I stared through the smoke and I saw Jimmy, standing in the wood in his simple farmworking clothes, his face smiling and content. Yet how could it possibly be so? He was a monster, wasn't he? A giant and ferocious crab creature? Or was it all a dream, like the dreams of swimming beneath the sea and taking cold briny water straight into my lungs? Was it all some kind of absurd illusion?

"I am the servant of the god of times gone by and times yet to be," repeated the whispery voice. "I was created to fulfill his needs, to revive him according to the rites that were law in the days when the stars were different than they are today, and when men were the slaves of beasts was Quithe, the demon god whom your Indians called

Ottauquechee, he who dwells in the waters of the pit. And his name beyond the stars is the god of times gone by and times yet to be, and he is my master and yours, and he shall rise from his grave to rule the men of this land once again, even as he did in the mighty days of Atlantis."

Jimmy had stepped closer now, and was standing only a few paces away. I could still hear that irritating humming noise, and sometimes it was difficult to distinguish Jimmy's outline in the gloom. He seemed to waver and fluctuate like a poor television picture, and at times he looked like nothing more than a distant image of his real self. But his smile was still fixed on his face, and he held out his left hand to me in greeting, as if everything that had happened before was just a faded nightmare, as if the crab creatures had never been. His smile said, it's okay, I'm Jimmy again, you don't have to worry. It was all a fantasy, all a dream. We can be friends again.

"Jimmy?" I asked nervously, raising my .38. I knew it was him, but I was still frightened.

"There is nothing to fear," whispered the voice. "The day will soon be here when the great god will rise out of the wells which have been his sleeping-place for so long, and when all men will bow down before him and offer themselves happily as sacrifices. The day will come when the god will once again sit inside the minds of all men, and fires will burn across this continent from shore to shore. The day of the great reckoning with the beast-gods is close. The day that was spoken of by men of learning in ancient times, by the disciples of Sa-to-ga and Ya-go-sath. It was those men who first re-

called Quithe, my master, and founded the underwater continent of Atlantis, and there were centuries when the water people dominated the
ocean, which is the greatest domain of this earth.
They were days of glory and sacrifice, and they
shall return."

Jimmy was only two or three feet away now. He
was gliding towards me in a shimmery, watery
kind of a way, and his eyes seemed as dead as
fumigated blackbeetles. It was then, at that
instant, that I knew that everything was wrong,
that I had made a terrible mistake, and that this
wasn't Jimmy at all, and whatever remained of
Jimmy had been totally overwhelmed by the creature that called itself the servant of Quithe. The
Jimmy who stood in front of me now was nothing
more than a wavering illusion, a projection based
on the memories in Jimmy's mind of what he
looked like in the mirror. *He was back-to-front.* His
hair was parted on the wrong side. His tweed coat
was buttoned on the wrong side. His face had that
strange lopsidedness that other people's mirror-
images always seem to have. He was himself as he
remembered himself, but not as I knew him.

He must have sensed my sudden anxiety,
because his right hand instantly whipped towards
me. I stepped back, and tripped on the brambles,
and fell, and as I fell the hand became a gigantic
pincer, and struck me a heavy, glancing blow on
the side of the head. Dazed, I rolled over in the
leaves, and then I scrambled on to my feet and I
was running. It happened so fast that I didn't have
time to look back, but as I charged through the
holly and the creepers with my arms raised in

front of my eyes, I could hear the creature follow-ing me. I could hear those scuttling feet across the floor of the woods, and the snapping of that giant claw was like a hundred knives scraping on a hun-dred dinner-plates.

I didn't make it. I couldn't. I flew into a network of brambles and I was caught. My clothes were snagged, my face was lashed by thorns, and my gun fell down between a twisting tangle of creepers. I couldn't even break free quickly enough to turn around and face the beast that was coming after me with the single intention of crush-ing my head and ripping my guts out. I remember yelling: "Carter! For Christ's sake!" but that was all.

For one hideous, stomach-lurching moment, I heard the creature's beak squeaking, and the grating sound of its joints and its claws. I closed my eyes tight and waited for that first scrunching squeeze.

It didn't happen. I heard, instead, a brisk fusil-lade of pistol shots, and when I opened my eyes I saw Carter and his two deputies running towards me through the bushes.

"Mason!" yelled Carter. "Mason, you stupid fuck! Your live minutes is up!"

I wrestled myself free from the thorns, ripping the sleeve of my coat and taking the seat out of my pants in a wide triangular rip. But I was away, and running, and all around me there was the flat, crackly sound of pistol fire.

Once I was clear, Carter and his deputies re-treated along with me, and we ran back to the hollow, puffing and coughing like a geriatric jogging marathon. I didn't turn around once. I'd seen enough of the creature that was once Jimmy to last me for now. Maybe I'd seen enough to last me for ever. As soon as we were safe, I sat down on the ground with my head between my knees, and I thanked God that I still had lungs that ached and legs that were scratched and eyes that could burst out in tears for a young man who could never come back to a human existence.

Dan reached into the back pocket of his pants and produced a small silver flask.

"Whisky?" he asked me. "It's only Old Grandad."

I looked up at him. He was almost crying.

"You have hidden depths, Dan," I told him, swigging the bourbon with that particular relish that only a narrow escape can give you.

We waited for twenty minutes in the hollow, with Martino keeping a watch for the crab creature. We smoked, drank, talked, but there was no sign of the beast, and it began to look as if it had made its escape, and vanished into the woods. If you've ever seen the Connecticut woods in fall, you'll know how dense they are, and how goddamned difficult it is to find anyone or anything that doesn't want to be found.

Just after one o'clock, a red Jeep came crashing and crackling through the trees, and three deputies jumped out and announced the arrival of reinforcements, grenades, and the anti-tank launcher. Sheriff Wilkes stalked up to the Jeep and was met by the proprietorial stare of the anti-tank gun's custodian, a fat National Guard sergeant in an equally well-laundered uniform. He wore a forage cap, rimless glasses, and a neat little Rudolf Valentino moustache.

"I suppose you know how to work that thing," said Carter, sarcastically.

The sergeant gave a slow, unperturbed blink. "I've done full training in anti-tank weaponry, sir, as well as Nike missiles and unarmed combat."

"Very good, sergeant," said Carter. "Do you know what you're up against now?"

"Just an exercise, sir. That was what Colonel Phelps told me. Something to do with cooperating with civilian forces in the event of hostile invasion."

The sheriff nodded. "You're almost right. The only difference is, this isn't an exercise. We have a real problem right here, and we're looking to you to sort it out for us."

The sergeant blinked. "Problem, sir?"

I leaned on the side of the Jeep, and said carefully: "Did you ever see one of those science-fiction movies, sergeant? One of those invasion from outer space epics? Where the crab monsters try to take over the world?"

He looked at me, obviously wondering who I was. "I guess so," he said, uncertainly.

"Well, sergeant, that's the problem we have now. We have a hostile alien, a kind of shell-backed monster, lurking around in these woods someplace, and we'd like you to knock it out for us."

The sergeant asked Carter: "Is this gentleman a police officer, sir?"

Carter looked across at me with obvious amusement. "No, sergeant, this gentleman isn't. This gentleman is New Milford's most expensive and least efficient plumbing contractor."

The sergeant didn't appear to have any sense of humour whatever. He said: "I'll need proper authorization, sir, if I have to discharge this weapon."

"I'm taking full responsibility," said Carter. "Now let's get that gun off of that Jeep and get going. Every minute we stand here talking that son-of-a-bitch monster gets farther and farther away."

The sergeant looked from Carter to me, and from me to Dan, and from Dan to deputy Martino. It was only when he was quite sure that none of us were smiling that he slowly eased his bulky body out of the Jeep and reached inside for his anti-tank launcher. The gun was all packed up in khaki canvas and it took him three or four minutes of unfastening studs and assembling sights and barrel sections before he announced he was ready.

"I want to tell you, though," he said to us all, with great solemnity, "this weapon packs one hell of a punch. If it's just some small animal you're after, you're going to wipe it off of the face of the earth with this."

Carter slapped him on the back. "It's not small, I promise you. It's about the size of a small truck, and it's twice as bad-tempered."

"All right, then, you'd better lead on," said the sergeant. "And by the way, my name's Hubert Rosner, in case you're interested."

"Okay, Hubert," said Carter. "My name's Carter Wilkes. You can call me 'sir.'"

We fanned out into a small semi-circle, with Sergeant Rosner in the middle, and we made our way slowly and carefully through the bushes and the holly towards the place where I had last seen the crab creature. Carter found his .38 where I had dropped it, and he handed it back to me with an expression of long-suffering tolerance. I gave him a quick, uneasy smile in return.

The day was very dark now, and our progress through the woods was slow. It took us more than five minutes to reach the spot where Deputy Huntley's bloodied remains lay sprawled out on the leaves; but when we did, I think that Sergeant Rosner was at last convinced that we weren't playing Boy Scouts, and that we were really searching for something dangerous.

"Hot shit," he said, respectfully, taking off his forage cap.

Carter stood silent, his head cocked on one side, listening. At last, he said: "I can hear something. That way. Maybe half a mile through the trees."

Sergeant Rosner couldn't take his eyes off the mangled remains of Deputy Huntley. "You think it's the creature that did this, sir?" he asked, with a noticeable lack of relish.

"I don't know," said Carter, brusquely. "But we won't find out unless we go look, will we?"

"No, sir. I guess we won't."

From here, the terrain climbed up to a woody ridge, and then sloped eastwards and downwards, rocky and irregular, until it reached a small trickling tributary of the Housatonic. We scaled the ridge in silence, broken only by the twittering of birds and the puffs and pants of those among us who hadn't kept our walking exercises up. Carter, despite his weight, stayed well ahead of us, and he was the first to reach the brow of the ridge and stand there looking down towards the river. The sky behind him was dark and troubled, and northwards, in the direction of Ellsworth Hill, lightning flashed and flickered in the clouds. I could have sworn for a moment that I felt a shifting vibration in the ground itself, as if something vast and subterranean was turning over in its sleep.

"There's something down there," called Carter. "Martino—bring me the glasses. We could have him if we're lucky."

"Lucky," I panted, under my breath. "If that's luck, I'd rather stay home and pray for disaster."

We finally made it up to the rocky edge of the ridge, and there below us was the shadowy valley which carried the small foaming river to the west, through zig-zag clefts and rapids, to the broad breast of the Housatonic. Carter was pointing diagonally downwards to a russet clump of ash trees, although I couldn't see anything down there at all, except for bushes and grey slabby rocks and tangled creepers. I knew that this countryside up towards Ken was magical, in its own way, and had a long and mysterious heritage of witchery and strange communions with demons and devils in no human shape, and so I guess in some respects I was prepared to see almost anything. But I was damned if I could make out the crab creature.

"There—there it is!" snapped Carter, "I can see its shell moving!"

I peered down the hillside again, and I thought I

saw a flicker of movement, but no more than that, and I wouldn't have liked to swear in a court of law that it was anything at all, except a few over-excited thrashers, let alone a target for Sergeant Rosner's anti-tank gun.

Carter looked at the ash trees again through his field glasses, and beckoned Sergeant Rosner towards him with an impatient wave of his hand. Sergeant Rosner obediently came forward, toting his gun. Carter said: "You see that, Hubert? You see that damned monster down there?"

Sergeant Rosner borrowed the field glasses and squinted into them for what seemed like half an hour. Then he nodded, and said: "I see what you mean there, sir. I'm not sure what it is. But if you want it hit, and if you'll take the responsibility, then I'll hit it."

"Okay, sergeant, you do that," said Carter. "You just blow the ass off that murderous thing, and you do it now."

We waited around awkwardly while Sergeant Rosner unhurriedly unslung his anti-tank rifle and his knapsack loaded with rockets. He inserted a rocket into the gun's wide open barrel, and then positioned himself flat on the ground, resting his elbow on a fallen branch, and adjusting his telescopic sights with such calm and dull application that Carter had to look the other way in suppressed fury.

Eventually, he hunched himself over the weapon, screwed up one eye, and took aim. Carter stood beside him, biting his fingernails and staring down towards the clump of ash trees as if he could shoot streams of daggers at it out of his eyes, like they do in the cartoons.

"Whenever you're ready," said Carter, and there was more than a touch of caustic in his voice.

"Okay, sir," answered Sergeant Rosner, and fired. There was a flash, and a low-pitched whistle, and then we heard a soft thumping noise, like someone punching a pillow. A small puff of greyish smoke drifted out of the ash grove as if someone had tossed a dirty cauliflower out of it in slow-motion.

Carter looked disappointed. "Did you hit it?" he asked.

"I guess so," said Sergeant Rosner. "You want another one in there?"

"Just to make sure, yes," said Carter.

We stood by while Sergeant Rosner reloaded his gun. He resighted his telescopic lens, fiddled around with his wristwatch, and after what seemed like five minutes of twitching and wriggling and getting himself together he was ready for a second shot. If the Russians ever did decide to invade us, they could march in fifteen divisions while Sergeant Rosner was tidying himself up in preparation to drive them back into the sea.

"Are you ready?" asked Carter. In the distance, the thunder rumbled again, and lightning flickered like snakes' tongues on the rim of the South Kent hills.

"I'm ready, sir," said Hubert Rosner, and applied himself to his weapon again, squinting down the sights. "Whenever you say fire, sir, I'll fire."

Carter Wilkes raised his hand as if he was about

to say "fire," but then something strange happened. I heard that humming again, that same tuning-fork sound that I had heard in the woods when the crab creature had created the illusion of being Jimmy Bodine. It was high-pitched, almost intolerable, and it seemed to make my actual skull vibrate and sing in a monotonous, unlistenable key.

Right in front of our eyes, I swear it, on that windy storm-blown ridge in West Connecticut, Sergeant Rosner began to shimmer and waver, just the way that Jimmy's image had before, when the crab creature had tried to deceive me into believing that Jimmy was really there. And Sergeant Rosner turned towards us, with a look of mystification on his face, but it was too late for any of us to understand what was happening or do anything at all to help him.

His face went blue, and then a hideous aubergine purple. He rolled over on the ground, gargling in his throat and clutching at his clothes as if he was suffocating. Then, with a hideous gushing sound, water belched out of his nose and his mouth in gallons, an unstoppable tide that was literally drowning him in front of our eyes—but drowning him *from the inside out.*

We tried to hold him down as he kicked and struggled for breath, and Carter even attempted artificial respiration. But all that happened was that gallons more water were vomited out of his stomach and his lungs, and his asphyxiation came all the quicker. In a few seconds, he slumped back on the turf, his cheeks blue, and it was plain that he was dead. Water still poured from his nostrils and his half-open mouth and soaked the ground, but the crab-servant of Quithe had done enough.

Carter said gruffly: "He drowned. Right out here. Right on top of a goddamned hill."

I nodded. "This thing we're up against, these creatures, they can do stunts with water you wouldn't even believe."

Carter said: "It's impossible. I saw it, but I don't believe it."

Dan knelt down beside Hubert Rosner's bloated corpse. It looked like something that had been dragged out of the Housatonic. He lifted one of Hubert's eyelids, and then remarked: "It's not really impossible, Carter. It looks to me like a very high-powered version of the old rainmaking spells the Indians used out in Arizona. Any medicine man with sufficiently powerful alpha-waves could set up a small field of electropsychic energy which altered the relative humidity in the atmosphere around him. There was one medicine man who could make it rain on the palm of his hand, and nowhere else, just by concentrating his brain-waves. But this is thousands of times more powerful. Wherever or from *what*ever this psychic energy is coming, we're in trouble."

"It's coming from that crab, ain't it?" said Carter, nervously.

"I don't know," answered Dan. "Probably not. The way the legends of Atlantis tell it, and the way that Jimmy-creature tells it, these crab-people are just servants to the real gods. Back in the old days, when Atlantis was still thriving, the gods must have mutated men to serve them and look after them, which is just what they've done here. That psychic energy was channelled *through* the crab, but it didn't originate in the crab's brain. It was probably transmitted from under the ground, in the wells, where the beast-god is lying."

Carter didn't know what to say. He'd never heard Dan talking this way before. He was a good sheriff, a blunt and practical man, and all this airy-fairy nonsense about beast-gods and psychic energy made him angry and frustrated. But he was shrewd enough to know when his friends and his deputies believed something for real; and he knew that good old bald serious Dan wasn't going to come out with a story like this unless he'd considered it deeply, and tested it empirically. Dan's mind was as chemical as litmus paper, and Carter respected him for it.

Awkwardly, Carter said. "So you think there's something down there? You think there's some kind of monster down in the Bodines' well?"

"The evidence suggests it. I admit that the evidence is slight, and what there is of it is all circumstantial. But yes, I'd say there's something down there."

"So what if we drill down, and see if we can find it?"

Dan shrugged. "I'd say that would be a pretty dangerous thing to do."

"But what if we did?" persisted Carter. "What if we found it, and killed it? Would that knock out all these crab-creatures, too?"

"I don't know. I expect so. There's no evidence either way."

Deputy Martino sniffed loudly, and said: "It sounds to me like it's worth a try. We're not going to catch these monsters this way, not chasing 'em, not if the damned thing can drown us from six hundred feet away."

Carter glanced at both of us. "What do you say? We should start the drilling straight away? I called the county engineers in yesterday, and they should have the rig almost ready."

"I guess you should," said Dan. "But we've seen what's happened to people who get this beast-god's back up. I think the whole operation should be done with a whole lot of caution."

"Well, of course," said Carter. "You think I'd drill down there like some half-assed sewage inspector?"

"I think you should try to find yourself a medium," said Dan. "Somebody who's sensitive to psychic impulses. Then if there's any psychic trouble brewing up, you'll have some chance of getting the hell out before anyone gets hurt."

"A medium? You mean like a spiritualist? Crystal balls, all that stuff?"

"Exactly."

Carter rubbed his chin. "Martino, do we know any mediums? Any fortune-tellers, those kind of people?"

Martino thought for a while, and then he said: "There's old Mrs. Thompson out at Boardman's Bridge. That's the only one I can think of."

I looked at Dan and raised an eyebrow. "Seems like Boardman's Bridge is a good spot for psychics. Remember Josiah Walters, in the Litchfield legend book?"

Dan looked thoughtful. "That's right. Well, she sounds as if she might be all right. Maybe we'll go talk to her first, Carter, and then join you up at the Bodines' place. But I shouldn't start drilling until we arrive, if I were you. We don't want any more drownings, or butcherings. Whatever's down in that well looks like it's getting pretty enthusiastic about showing its superiority over us land-locked mortals."

Martino said unhappily: "Sheriff—the crab's coming back. Look down there, by the woods."

We all turned at once and peered down the rocky slope. We couldn't see anything at first, but then we picked up a jerky, irregular movement just under the shadow of the clump of trees where the crab-creature had been hiding. Carter reached down for the anti-tank gun where Hubert Rosner had dropped it, and quickly checked that it was loaded and ready to fire.

"If I were you, Carter, I'd unload that thing and beat the retreat," murmured Dan, keeping his eyes on the movement under the trees. "It seems like it went for Sergeant Rosner because he was threatening it, and if you do the same you may wind up drowned, too."

Carter licked his lips as if he could do with a stiff drink. "Just one shot ought to do it. Just one shot to the brain."

"If it's completely under the control of the beast-god under the ground then you could shoot it to pieces and you still wouldn't stop it," said Dan.

"Dan's right, Carter," I put in. "Maybe this is one of those times when discretion is the better part of valor. Let's pick up poor old Hubert and get our asses out of here."

Carter paused for a moment, the anti-tank gun raised in his hands. Then he gave us a brief, grudging nod, and we all gathered around Sergeant Rosner's body, took an arm or a leg apiece, and lifted him off the ground. He weighed about as much as a dead hippopotamus, and he was still full of water, and I wasn't at all sure that even the four of us could make it through the woods and back to the road if we had to take him with us. But I don't think any of us wanted to leave him there. We'd seen what the crab-creature had done to those people in the red Impala, and to Deputy Huntley.

Martino glanced over his shoulder as we left the brow of the ridge, and said: "It's moving back this way. Maybe more to the west, but it's definitely moving back this way."

"It's after the body," said Dan. "Either it needs to feed on flesh, or else it's storing it up."

"Storing it up?" asked Carter, screwing his nose up in distaste. "What the hell's it storing it up for?"

"Could be that it's scavenging for its master, scouring the countryside for food to take back down to the well. Think about it. If there is some kind of beast down there, some creature that's reviving itself after hundreds of years in suspended animation, what's it going to need? Nutrition, and plenty of it."

Carter paused to change his grip on Hubert Rosner's ankle. "Nutrition," he repeated bitterly, looking down at the dead sergeant.

As we lurched unsteadily down the slope, I was sure I could hear someone calling my name. The thunder was rumbling in the distance, and the wind was freshening up, and so it was hard to tell. But then I heard it again, much more distinctly, and I suddenly realized who it was.

"Hold on there," I said, stopping. "That's Rheta."

"What's Rheta?" asked Dan.

"Listen. She must have tried to follow us here."

Half-swallowed by the noise of the wind and the trees, we heard *"Mason!"* and then *"—on."* It was unmistakably Rheta's voice, and it was coming from the woods around the west of the ridge from which we had just retreated.

Carter put down Hubert's leg, and we all followed suit and laid the poor dead National Guardsman on the ground.

"If she's over that way," said Martino, "then she's going to run straight into the crab-creature. It was headed in that direction, and it looked like it was going real fast."

"Maybe it sensed her coming," said Dan. "Maybe it heard her before we did."

I didn't say anything. I was up and running. I shouted once. *"Rheta!"* but I wanted to save my breath for scrambling up and across the side of the ridge, and for reaching Rheta before that goddamned crab-creature could. I heard Carter and Dan and the deputies start running behind me, and I just prayed that I had the speed and the strength and that I was heading in the right direction.

It seemed to take for ever to get back to the spine of the ridge again so that I could look along the valley westwards. The sky was much darker now, and a peal of thunder banged over my head like a car crash. I couldn't see anything at first, but then I slowed to a fast walk, and I made out Rheta's blondish hair, and her pale-coloured coat. She was descending the other side of the ridge, about two hundred feet away. She was calling *"Mason! Mason!"* and she couldn't have been a more obvious or attractive piece of crab-bait if she tried. Only sixty feet away from her, camouflaged by the darkness and the bushes, I could see the black-and-green mottled shell of the monster that had once been my friend, with its glistening eyes and its terrible waving pincer, and I knew that I couldn't warn her or reach her in time.

# 8

Carter Wilkes must have been closer behind me than I'd realized. He was an officer of the law, so I guess he felt it his duty to keep himself reasonably fit, although how he managed to run up that slope with a forty-two inch belly and a 20-pound anti-tank gun, I shall never know. I'm just glad that he did. I shouted: *"Rheta! Rheta! This way! Run this way!"* and at the same time Carter went down on to one knee, aimed the gun, and fired.

Rheta turned. There was a swoosshh and a flash, and a burst of orange fire on the edge of the crab-creature's shell. I thought I saw pieces of green-and-black carapace tumbling through the air, although I could have been wrong. I just know that the creature stopped, and angrily waved its claw, and that gave me time enough to go sliding down the slope, shouting for Rheta to run my way. I tripped, slipped, and skated through rocks and bushes, but I reached her, and took her hand, and the next thing I knew we were panting back up the ridge again.

I looked upwards. With their light uniforms outlined against the inky and thunderous sky, Carter and Deputy Martino were crouched with their pistols held in both hands, steadily aiming towards the crab-creature behind us. I chanced a quick look over my shoulder. It was coming after us, and after the momentary distraction of the anti-tank rocket, it was coming fast. I could hear the ground tearing under its spidery legs, and the clatter of its shell on the rocks.

Carter opened fire. Bullets whined and pinged all around us, but the crab-creature didn't hesitate a single step. Rheta gasped: "My God, oh my God, I can't make it!"

Carter shouted: "Faster, Mason, for Christ's sake! It's nearly on you! Faster!"

This time, I didn't dare to look round. I could sense how close it was. I could smell the fetid odour of fish with every gasp of air. I closed my eyes for a second and all I could hear was our scrambling footsteps and our harsh struggling for breath.

Carter pulled: "Mason!" but at the same moment Rheta's ankle gave way, and she dropped face down on to the ground, only ten feet away from the top of the ridge. There was another burst of gunfire, but Carter knew that the crab-creature was too tough for .38 ammunition, and we could hear the bullets moan and ricochet into the woods.

I pulled at Rheta's arm and shouted at her to get up. She tried, cried out in pain, and fell down again, and then the creature's icy breath blew against my face and I realized it had caught up with us.

I turned, and the dark sky was almost blotted out by the darker silhouette of claws and beak and antennae, and the overwhelming shadow of that giant shell. I could see the pale squid-like tentacles wriggling on the creature's under-belly, and for the first time in my life I felt a freezing, paralyzing sensation which could only have been terror. Real, naked, this-is-it terror.

*"Jimmy!"* I shrieked out. *"Jimmy! For God's sake, no! Jimmy!"*

The pincer opened. I could hear the gristly muscles creaking. Beside me, Rheta could do nothing but whimper. The crab-creature was right over us now, and even if I'd tried to roll away sideways it would have caught me. It was right over us and it had a ferocious, unstoppable greed for our lungs and our hearts and our stomachs.

*"Jimmy!"* I yelled out again. *"Jimmy, listen! Jimmy! Jimmy!"*

There was a frozen pause. The crab-creature's eyelids rolled over its eyeballs, and then off them again. Its antennae wavered in the breeze. It was so quiet now that I could hear the slippery, sliding sound the squid-tentacles made as they writhed against each other. Carter, only a few feet away, suppressed a cough.

Then, very slowly, step by step, the crab creature backed away from us. We stayed where we were, not moving, not daring to do anything that might break the spell of what had happened, and we watched as it gradually turned and made its way back down the slope again. Rheta lifted her head at last, and stared across at me as if she couldn't believe that I was real. I raised my hand, cautioning her to stay quiet and still.

The crab-creature was almost in the shadows now. The first drops of rain began to spatter the ground. Carter said, hoarsely: "Look. Look what's happening."

I strained my eyes to see down the slope. The crab-creature was faltering, staggering. It stopped for a moment, and it appeared to have a deep fit of shudders. Then suddenly it sagged to one side, and keeled over on to its back. It was only then that we could see the deep soggy wound in its belly, and the tortured way in which its jointed body was struggling for breath and for survival. Carter's last anti-tank shell must have bounced off the ground and penetrated the creature from underneath. We were lucky that he was such a lousy shot.

I said to Rheta: "Stay here. I have to go take a look."

She smiled briefly. "I don't have much choice. My ankle's out."

I walked cautiously back down the ridge, towards the overturned crab-creature. I stayed a respectful distance away from it, but I was close enough to see that its wound was probably fatal. The shell had entered the soft off white shell just below the tentacles, and had obviously travelled up inside the body before exploding. The stench of burned rotten fish was almost too much to bear; and there was another smell, too. The smell of dead human offals.

I turned away, sick. Behind me, the rain pattered on the dying crab-creature's shell. Carter was standing a little way off with his hat in his hand. I said: "You needn't pay your respects. Whatever that was, it wasn't Jimmy any more."

Carter didn't look at me. "I'm paying my respects to Deputy Huntley, and all those innocent people that monster killed. I said I'd get the bastard, and I did."

"There are still others. At least two, maybe more, if more people have been drinking the water."

Carter jammed his hat back on his head. "It's the big one I'm going after now. It seems to me the only way to get this thing stopped is to root out this beast-god, or whatever it calls itself."

"Quithe, the god of the pit."

"Right."

Dan and one of the deputies were helping Rheta to hobble back down the ridge. They steered her away from Sergeant Rosner's body, and of course we didn't have to carry him now. I took a last look back at the overturned creature that lay on the north side of the ridge, at its whitish jointed abdomen, like a dead boiled crab in a supermarket, and as I looked it seemed to collapse and crumple up. There was a breathy, slopping sound, and its abdomen parted and disgorged, in a black slithery heap, the remains of all those people it had killed and devoured. The rain washed the rocks and the turf a brown, bloody colour, and under the lowering, electrified clouds, the crab dwindled away, as if it had been made of nothing but rice paper and celluloid. It didn't take too long before I recognised Jimmy's body lying there, hunched up in a cleft between two boulders, but I didn't want to go down to look. Maybe he'd helped me, right in those last seconds when I was yelling at him not to kill us, and maybe he hadn't. I wasn't in the mood for thinking about it.

Carter said: "Let's go. We've got ourselves some work to do."

I said, absent-mindedly: "Yes," and followed him back to the woods.

Mrs. Thompson's house was one of those dark, rambling old Connecticut houses that stand away from the road, overhung by pin oaks and poison sumac bushes, its grounds black and muddy but overgrown with unnaturally green grass. It must have been all of two hundred and fifty years old, and it looked to me like an old coaching stage, the way the road curved in front of it. The plumbing was probably all lead, with copper ballcocks and zinc tanks.

It was mid-afternoon by the time we drew up outside in Rheta's Volkswagen. We were both suffering from that odd, abstracted exhaustion that usually follows shock, and there was no question at all that we would have been better off in bed. But Carter was going to start drilling at five o'clock, whether we could persuade Mrs. Thompson to help us or not, and with at least two crab-creatures still at loose in the countryside, and the beast-god flexing its psychic muscles already, we couldn't afford the luxury of rest.

The thundery rain had settled down into a damp, persistent drizzle that hung across the trees like a drowned bride's veil. We climbed out of the car, slammed the doors shut, and walked through the dew-beaded grass to Mrs. Thompson's dank verandah, where a sodden rug hung over the tooth-less front rail, and a rotting rocker with creepers entwined in its carved back rest stood where someone had left it to stand, dozens of years ago. I went up to the bottle-green front door, and knocked at the corroded lion's-head knocker. It was like striking an empty barrel with a coal-hammer.

She surprised us by opening one of the sash-windows that looked out on to the verandah. She was surprisingly young, maybe mid-forties, with black hair that was heavily streaked with grey, and a face that would have looked good on a veteran sergeant from the Marine Corps. All bushy eyebrows, and big nose, and heavy chin. She said: "Did you bring the mattress?"

"Mattress?" I asked her. "What mattress?"

"The mattress you were supposed to bring. The mattress I was having recovered."

"We aren't mattress men, ma'am," I told her.

"You're not?"

"No. I'm a plumber and my friend here's an analytical chemist."

She blinked at us. Then she repeated: "A plumber and an analytical chemist?"

I nodded.

She thought for a moment, and then she said: "I don't remember calling for a plumber and an analytical chemist. What's to plumb? What's to analyze?"

I said hesitantly: "You are Mrs. Hilda Thompson, aren't you?"

"That's right."

"Mrs. Hilda Thompson the clairvoyant?"

"That's right."

"Well, that's what we've come for," I told her. "We have a psychic problem, and we need some help."

There was a minute's silence. A whole minute. The rain fell softly on the tangled gardens, and Mrs. Hilda Thompson looked us up and down as if she were trying to penetrate our psyches and see what we *really* wanted. Eventually, she said: "All right," and withdrew her head from the open window. A moment later, the front door opened.

"You'll have to excuse the mess," she said, leading us through a dark and musty hallway, past a wrought-iron umbrella stand crowded with everything from fishing-poles to golf clubs, but no umbrellas; and past dingy daguerreotypes of stern and whiskery men, with such captions as *Holmwood Buffen, Master Medium, 1880*. At length we arrived in a leaky conservatory where ferns languished for lack of attention, and a black Labrador with a dull coat and crusty eyes lay listlessly under a table of unhealthy geraniums. The whole place stank of decay and week-old Gravy Train. Mrs. Thompson showed us a battered garden table, and we drew up three rusty wrought iron garden chairs, their feet squeaking nastily on the tiled floor.

"When it's raining, I like to feel as if I'm out in it, as if I'm part of nature's climate," smiled Mrs. Thompson, sitting down opposite us. She wore a floor-length dress of dusty black, and a necklace of moonstones. There was dried tomato soup on her left sleeve.

I looked up at the glass roof, cracked and green

with lichen. The rain ran down it in sorrowful ribs, and on top of it was a weather-vane which groaned and shuddered in the wind. I said: "Do you mind if I smoke?" and Mrs. Thompson shook her head no. I offered her a cigarillo as a matter of politeness and she took one. Dan waited for us in silence while we lit up.

Soon, wreathed in smoke, Mrs. Thompson smiled and said: "What can I do for you? I'm afraid it's a long time since anybody called on my clairvoyant talents."

"Do you know any of the old legends of Litchfield and New Milford?" I asked her.

"Some. Why?"

"Well, we're wondering if you've ever heard of a legend that the gods who used to rule Atlantis came ashore when Atlantis sank, and secreted themselves in the natural springs under New England, waiting for the time when they could release themselves again."

There was a pause, and then Mrs. Thompson nodded, very slowly.

"Yes," she said, "I've heard that story."

Dan coughed. "The thing is, Mrs. Thompson, and I know this sounds nuts, but the thing is that we believe it's about to happen. We believe the gods from Atlantis are really down there, under the ground, and we believe they've been making themselves ready to—well, making themselves ready to do whatever it is they do when they come out of the ground."

Mrs. Thompson nodded.

"Yes," she said.

"Just 'yes'?" I asked her.

She turned and stared at me. "That's all I can say. I know the legend, and I'm quite sure that much of it is true. So when you come and tell me that it's happening, that the beast-gods are about to emerge as they promised they would in the days when their kingdom collapsed, what else can I say but 'yes'?"

"How come you know this legend?" I asked her. "I haven't met anyone else around here who's heard of it."

She smiled. "I *should* know it. My family has been psychosensitive for generations. My mother used to tell me that my great-great-great grandfather actually spoke to one of the gods who lived under the ground. He found a way into the tunnels and the caves under the hills, and discovered where the beast-god was concealed."

I blew out smoke. "His name wasn't Josiah Walters, by any chance?"

She smiled. "You must have found a copy of the *Legends of Litchfield*."

"I did. That's how I learned about the story in the first place. But it doesn't say too much about the beast-gods themselves, or what they wanted out of life."

"No," said Mrs. Thompson. "The truth was that everybody thought Josiah Walters was quite mad. He went underground one day and was missing for almost a week. When he came out, he said he'd walked for five miles through caves and tunnels beneath Washington, and swam in subterranean lakes, and that he'd survived by catching strange blind fish that thrived under the ground."

"Did anyone try to check out his story?" asked Dan.

"I don't think so. According to his diaries, he wouldn't reveal where the entrances and the exits to the caves were concealed. He said it was too dangerous for anyone else to go down there, and that if scientists and pot holers disturbed the beast-god, then he would awaken and take his revenge on everybody."

"No wonder they thought he was crazy."

"Oh, they did," said Mrs. Thompson. "He was locked up in an insane asylum in Hartford for three months, but in the end they released him. Unfortunately, most of his diaries were discovered by the local church people and destroyed as works of the devil. I suppose, in a way, they were."

"What do you mean by that?" I asked her.

She gazed out at the green, unkempt garden. "From what little remains of his notes, it seems that Josiah Walters was quite sure that he had found the totally evil being that led ancient people to conjure up the idea of Satan. There was one great beast-god, whose name was Chulthe or Quithe, and he was summoned from the stars centuries ago, and set up his kingdom where men could not reach him, in the drowned mountain ranges of Atlantis."

"Who summoned him?" I wanted to know. "Does Josiah say?"

She said: "You can read it for yourself. If you can wait a few moments I'll go find his diary for you."

I checked my watch. It was ten after four. I said: "Sure. We'd appreciate that."

"And you'd care for a cup of mint tea?"

Dan hesitated, and then said: "Sure. Mint tea

would be delightful."

Minutes passed while Mrs. Thompson went in search of the old diary, and made tea. Neither Dan nor I said a word. We were too tense and too tired, and even though it was only twenty after four by the time Mrs. Thompson came back with a tray, we felt as if ten years had passed, instead of ten minutes. On the tray were three green-and-white porcelain cups, very thin with delicate handles, and a teapot in the unlikely shape of a cabbage. Beside the teapot were a few yellowed pages of old paper, loosely tied together with pink legal ribbon. Mrs. Thompson handed them over.

Together, Dan and I pored over Josiah Walters' slanting, crabbed writing. If I'd had access to a time-machine, I would have gone back two hundred years and given him a Papermate. It took us all of ten more minutes to decipher the first two pages alone, but Mrs. Thompson gave us all the time we needed, sitting back and sipping her tea with the equanimity of a society lady at a genteel local gathering.

The pages were numbered from 54 onwards. Obviously the rest had been destroyed by Walters' superstitious friends. They began: ". . . out of ye welles at last and most happie to breathe ye air, I hidde ye exite out of which I had come, lest others should finde it and attempt a similar expedition, which would be perilusse in ye utmost extreme, having regard to ye nature of ye beasts which lie within. And having further thought on ye beasts, and in particular ye great beast-god Chulthe, which lieth so deep beneath ye crust of ye hilles near Washington, it is now evident that I have met face unto face ye very being itself which unlearned peoples of ancient times came to know as Satan, ye Deville. For even though Chulthe was banished beyond ye stars in ancient times, he was summoned back to this Planette by Aaron whose summons was focussed not by ye Golden Calf, as told in ye Olde Testament, but by ye Golden Beast of a visage so terrible that none could describe it, save as a Calf. And upon this Planette from that day forth Chulthe dwell'd, making his kingdom in the mountains beneath ye Atlantic Ocean, and summoning in his turn lesser beast-gods from ye stars as his miniones. So thatte in ye greatest days of Atlantis, Chulthe reign'd over both beast-gods & humans, manie of whom were strangely transmogrified to serve his purpose. And when Atlantis was swallow'd uppe by ye fires beneath ye Ocean, ye beast-gods retreated and hidde themselves in ye wateringe-places of ye Globe, some in England and some in certain rivers in continents of Africa and India, even beneath ye rock itself, in ye cavernes below New England. Here it is that ye supreme eville being Chulthe dwelles, awaiting a time when he is readie to rise up again and rule ye lesser beast-gods again, & ye humans who dwell by ye seas. And it is ye eville wrought by Chulthe and by his miniones in other partes of ye Globe as they lie beneath ye earth thatte has *in all certaintie* led men to believe in Satan, for Chulthe's ghostlie image, and ye images likewise of his miniones have walk'd abroad, even when their bodies rested beneath the earth. And ye certaintie of this is the words and signs which Chulthe himself gave me in ye subterranean caverns beneath New Milford

and Washington, ye most certaine of which is ye
sign appended here."

There were ten or twelve more pages. I wished I
had time to read them all, because they described
how Josiah Walters tried to defend himself
against the Christian anger of his neighbours, and
how he was committed to the lunatic asylum. But
it was what he said about Quithe or Chulthe which
was most important, and right now, with Carter
waiting to drill into the subsoil of Jimmy Bodine's
farm, there wasn't time for historical details.

I turned the page over. "Where's the sign?" I
asked Mrs. Thompson. "He says here that he's
attached a sign."

"He did. I destroyed it."

"You *destroyed* it? Didn't you have any idea how
important that sign could have been?"

"Of course I did. I'm an extremely sensitive
clairvoyant."

"So what made you do it? That sign could have
been real important. It could have helped us lick
the monster."

Mrs. Thompson set down her cup. Her lips were
firmly clenched together, in a straight, unhappy
line.

"Mrs. Thompson?" I asked her.

She looked up. "I didn't want it in the house,"
she said. "It was unsettling. As long as it was here,
things used to happen."

"What things?" asked Dan.

She lowered her eyes again. "If you're an
analytical chemist, you'd probably call them
psychic phenomena. But they were worse than
that. When I was alone in the house, I used to

glimpse people in other rooms. I used to hear voices. Not friendly, human voices, like you hear when you're holding a seance. But alien voices that talked among themselves, and not to me. I was very frightened. I'm still frightened sometimes. Whatever it was that Josiah Walters discovered, it seems to me that it was the epitome of all evil, and that it will never rest until it has regained its kingdom again."

Dan said gently: "Can you describe the sign you destroyed?"

We waited in silence. The rain dribbled down the roof of the gloomy conservatory, and thunder began to bumble again from the hills of New York State. Mrs. Thompson took a breath, and then traced an invisible outline on the white-painted tabletop with the tip of her finger.

"You've probably seen the sign before. In the old days, they used to call it the evil eye. It's an eye, a cyclopean eye, and even though it's very simply drawn it seems to contain the essence of all the cruelty and iniquity you can imagine. It is Chulthe's symbol, the symbol and sign of his own eye."

She paused, and then she said: "The sign had such terrible connotations in these parts that, over the years, its meaning was quite erased from local memory. If you showed it to people now, they wouldn't have a clue what it was, although it might make some of them uneasy. The strange thing was that one drawing of it appeared in one of those books about ancient gods from outer space, you know the kind of thing I mean. The author had taken the drawing to be a primitive representation of a spaceman."

She smiled. "It wasn't of course. It was a rare and fragmentary drawing of Chulthe. But even though the author didn't know what it was, and nobody around here knew, either, the book sold so badly in the local bookstore that they had to send it back to the publishers. Folks were taking it off the shelf, flicking through it, and putting it straight back again when they came across that eye."

I cleared my throat. "Mrs. Thompson," I said, "it's pretty clear that you have something of a sensitivity to Chulthe's vibrations. I mean, if you saw these ghosts and heard these voices . . .?"

She stared at me hard. "Yes," she said. "I am. Is that any surprise, considering my heritage?"

"No, ma'am. But I was wondering if you'd agree to put your sensitivity to some useful purpose."

Mrs. Thompson didn't answer. All three of us sat around the table in that dismal conservatory while the rain rained and the afternoon began to darken into night. It was five to five. Not long now, and Carter Wilkes was going to give the county engineers the go-ahead to start drilling.

Mrs. Thompson turned away. Dan said: "You know what we're asking, don't you?" and she nodded.

"You want me to be your canary. You want me to test the psychic atmosphere while your people dig down in search of Chulthe."

I said: "Canary's kind of a strong way of putting it, Mrs. Thompson. When they took canaries down the mines, they only considered it was time to leave when the canary keeled over and died."

Mrs. Thompson stared at me. Her eyes were very deep and penetrating. "Don't you think that would happen to me?" she demanded. "Don't you think that Chulthe's psychic power would destroy my mind?"

"Well, I—"

"Even now, you don't know what you're up against, do you?" she said. "You're up against Satan, the supreme being of complete evil. You're up against Quithe, the Celtic god of the terrible pit. You're up against a being so powerful and so totally vicious that his memory has lasted for millions of years. You've seen what's happened already, while he's stirring in his sleep. *Stirring in his sleep*, Mr. Perkins, that's all. Just imagine what he's going to be like when he awakes."

I felt embarrassed. I said: "I'm sorry. I didn't mean to ask you to do anything *that* dangerous."

"No," said Mrs. Thompson, "I don't suppose you did. But if you disturb the great beast-god, then I'm afraid you'll be putting everyone at risk, not just yourselves. Everyone who helps you, or digs for you, or watches while you penetrate his hiding-place."

Dan sat back in his garden chair. "So you won't do it?" he asked her.

She gave a gentle smile. "I didn't say that. All I said was, I don't think you appreciate what you're up against."

"We've seen the crab-creatures that Chulthe sent out to find flesh for him, Mrs. Thompson," I said, soberly. "They weren't exactly tame rabbits, if you know what I mean."

"I do."

There was another difficult silence. Then Dan said: "Okay then, we'd better get back to the drilling site. They were due to start work a couple of minutes ago."

Mrs. Thompson said: "Give me five minutes. I must brush my hair and put on my coat."

"You'll come?" I asked her.

She nodded. "I believe I have to. My family's been tied up with the legend of Chulthe for two hundred years. I suppose one of us had to face up to the beast's presence eventually. It's just my misfortune that it happened to be me."

"We're not forcing you," said Dan.

She reached out and touched his hand. "I know you're not. But I have to when you think about it. It's been my destiny for years. If I don't accept it now, then I'll probably spend the rest of my life quite aimlessly, wondering if I should have tried to tackle the beast or not."

Dan laid his hand over hers. "Thank you," he told her, gently.

While Mrs. Thompson went to make herself ready, Dan and I sat in the conservatory and watched the rain. It was almost dark now, and Dan went across to switch on a brass desk lamp with a shell-shaped shade. Our reflections sat out in the rainy garden, observing us mournfully. I finished my cigarillo and stubbed it out.

A voice said: *"Every hour is numbered."*

We both looked up. There was nobody there. Dan frowned and said: "Was that Mrs. Thompson?"

"I don't know," I said, uneasily. "It didn't sound like her."

I scraped back my chair and stood up. I heard another voice, softer, saying: *"Yes, I remember those days."*

I licked my lips nervously. After all, hadn't Mrs. Thompson just told us about strange people glimpsed in other rooms, and alien voices that talked among themselves? I listened and listened, hoping to catch the shuffle of a foot, a cough, just something that would have betrayed the presence of somebody human and real.

*"The time seems close,"* someone whispered, out in the cluttered hallway. I looked down there, to the sepia window through which the last light of the day was filtering through to the staircase, but there was nobody in sight. One of the coats hanging on the pegs by the umbrella stand might have stirred, but I couldn't be sure.

I turned back to Dan. "They know we're here," I said tensely. "Whatever these voices are, they know we're here."

"They probably know *why* we're here, too," said Dan. "But they're only psychic manifestations of Quithe. They're not real. So don't let them bother you."

As he said that, there was a terrible crashing and smashing in the kitchen. We both ran through the conservatory, turned left through the pantry, and scrambled through the kitchen door to see plates flying off the dresser, pots and pans hurtling through the air, and every loose spice jar and butter-dish and whisk and rolling-pin rattling and shaking on their shelves until they fell on to the floor and broke. The clamour was ear-splitting, and there was nothing we could do to stop it.

Dishes shattered, cutlery jangled, windows cracked, and water gushed out of the faucets and filled up the sink to the brim.

Mrs. Thompson appeared, white-faced, at the opposite door.

"It's the beast!" she said. "The beast is angry with me!"

She stood watching the destruction in despair, until the last spoon clattered to the floor, and the last dish was smashed against the wall.

"He doesn't want me to help you," she said. "He would rather kill me first."

She bent down to collect up the fragments of a broken fruit-dish, but as she did so, I heard the soft moaning of a draught under the door that led to the garden. A sad, persistent moan that seemed to speak of sorrow and loneliness, of lives lost and agonies endured. Mrs. Thompson raised her eyes, and listened for a while. Then she gently put down the pieces of china that she had been collecting, and got to her feet.

"I think it's time we left this house," she said, warily. "I'm beginning to feel that something terrible is going to happen."

"You really believe that Chulthe knows what you're planning to do?"

"Yes. Yes, I'm sure of it. Remember that this house has harbored his spirits and his signs for two centuries at least, and he can probably sense what's happening here quite clearly. Are you ready to leave?"

"Any time you like," I said, and I didn't do anything to disguise my enthusiasm. We went down the corridor towards the front door, and Dan reached out to open it. But his hand touched nothing but a blank wall. The front door had disappeared, and its place was a straightforward wallpapered wall, with a faded daguerreotype on it.

Mrs. Thompson reached for my wrist, and held it uncomfortably tight.

"It may be too late," she murmured, under her breath. "If your friends have started drilling, and have broken through to the tunnels, then it may be too late."

"Let's try the back," Dan suggested, and we retreated along the corridor and out into the conservatory again. The minute we did so, the light failed all over the house, and we were plunged into rainy, impenetrable darkness. We stood still for a moment, until our eyes began to make out the vague shapes of the chairs and the plants, and then we held hands and moved cautiously across the tiled floor to the French windows.

"Can you see anything?" Mrs. Thompson hissed, under her breath.

"Nothing at all so far," I told her.

Dan said: "Quiet. If there's anything outside, I'd rather take it by surprise, instead of the other way around."

"You mean a crab-creature?" I asked him.

He turned away. "Don't ask me. It looks like this Chulthe can conjure up almost anything he feels like."

We went on tip-toes across the conservatory floor. Mrs. Thompson's dry, long-fingernailed hand dug into my wrist so tightly that it hurt, and I held on to the tail of Dan's overcoat. Dan led the

way, and I could see just the palest glimmer of
blue light shining from his bald head like a cres-
cent moon. Almost silently we reached the conservatory doors, and peered out through the rain-
beaded glass into the garden.

"Still no sign of anything," whispered Dan.
"Maybe we can get around the side of the house
without any trouble."

He tried the door-handle. It wouldn't budge. He
tried it again, tugging it harder, but it still
wouldn't move. He turned to Mrs. Thompson and
hissed: "Have you locked this? Is there a key?"

"It shouldn't be locked," Mrs. Thompson
replied. "I only lock it at night, when I go to bed."

I nudged Dan to one side. "Let me try. More of a
plumber's job, this." I took the door-handle in
both hands, and twisted it as hard as I could. It
seemed to be stuck rigid.

"Mrs. Thompson," I said, "it seems like we
might have to break a window."

Mrs. Thompson's eyes looked wide and frightened in the gloom. "Yes. All right. If you have to."

I remembered having seen a cast-iron doorstop
down by the dog's bowl, so I went down on hands
and knees and started to feel around for it. But it
turned out, I wasn't going to need it. For just as I
clumsily put my hand into the dog's dried up
lunch, there was a deep rumbling sound like a
New York subway train, and the plant-pots rattled
and shook in excitement. Three or four panes of
glass in the conservatory ceiling cracked and
shattered, and came showering down on us.

I stood up in time to see, outside the conservatory, looming over us in hideous and wrathful

clouds, a shape that conjured up deep racial terrors that I didn't even know I had. It might have been the gaseous shadow of Quithe, or Chulthe, the beast-god of Atlantis; it might have been the oldest and most evil manifestation from beyond the stars. But to me it was one thing only, and I stood there paralyzed by the horrifying familiarity of it. It was huge beyond description, shimmering and strange, changing from a weird electric blue to dark crimsons and fiery yellows. It hovered as if it was floating on the surface of our subconscious minds, a swimmer in the black ocean of our inherited fear. It had an eye that was the concentration of malice and ferocious intent, and long horns that seemed to wave in the thundery air, as if I was seeing the beast through the rippling heat of a night-watchman's brazier.

It wasn't real. It wasn't actually there, in the beastly flesh. It was nothing more than a powerful and frightening psychic image that its actual, buried self created to terrify us. But it was just what Josiah Walters had said it was. It was Satan. It was all the fears and sins of every religion embodied in one totally grotesque and horrible creature. It was the leering temptation that haunts you when you're cruel or self-serving. It was the goat-like incarnation of lust and greed. It was the master of everything that crawled and crept and slithered.

When God drowned the world that had disobeyed Him, saving none but Noah, this devil had also survived. It was the devil of the oceans, of the strange pressurized deeps where hideous creatures lurk. It was the devil of drowned hopes and dreams, of the only natural medium on earth in which man cannot survive. When I had slept and had nightmares of swimming, it was the evil vibrations of this creature that my dreaming mind had picked up.

Dan said: "Oh, Christ," and he said it sincerely, but even an invocation like that couldn't help us. In a split-second, the conservatory roof burst open, and a thundering torrent of water swept us off our feet. It was icy cold, foaming and turbulent, and I took a huge lungful before I could even understand what was happening. I choked and spluttered, and then a current dragged me down into a dark submarine world of floating plant pots, drifting dog food, and tables that danced by themselves with a curious buoyancy.

I thought I felt someone clutch at my sleeve. It could have been Dan or Mrs. Thompson, or maybe something more frightening. I pushed myself backwards, and my head struck the French windows. For a strange moment I was swimming with my face pressed to the glass, staring out at the rain in the garden. Then the weight of the water must have burst the conservatory apart, because there was a smashing and rending of glass, and I found myself tumbling across the wet grass in a foaming rapid of broken windows and water.

I lay there in the dark garden for what seemed like an hour. I was coughing and choking and I couldn't catch my breath. The rain fell all around, and every now and then I heard a far-away crack of lightning, and a responding roll of thunder. At last, soaking and chilled and shaking all over, I managed to get up on to my feet and look around.

Dan was sitting a few feet away. He was coughing, but he seemed all right. It was Mrs. Thompson I was worried about. I walked back to the splintered and twisted ruins of her old conservatory, with glass splitting and snapping beneath my feet, and I called out: "Mrs. Thompson?"

There was no answer. I stepped over the jagged glass teeth that marked the edge of the conservatory, and called again: "Mrs. Thompson?"

The rain fell in my face, and the wind shook the bushes, but there was still no reply. I trod slowly and cautiously forward, through the wreckage of glass and metal.

I found her, on her back, in the center of the tiled floor. She was lying on a glittering bier of broken glass, and her eyes stared up to heaven as if her soul had already left her, and her eyes were following its distant progress. The bronze weather-vane which had topped the apex of the conservatory roof had dropped straight down and was now imbedded in her chest. She must have died even before the conservatory was flooded. Her blood mingled with the rain-water, and she smelled of death already.

Dan came up and stood beside me. He looked down at Mrs. Thompson and wiped the rain from his forehead.

"It looks like we brought this on her," he said, quietly. "We might just as well have killed her with our own bare hands."

I turned away. "I think she knew the beast-god was going to get her, sooner or later. If that's any consolation."

"Not to her it isn't."

I looked across at him sharply. "Well, what do you want me to do about it? She said it was her destiny."

"You feel as guilty as I do," said Dan.

I shook my head. "No, I don't feel guilty. She was playing with fire a long time before we came along and burned her. She seemed like she knew."

Dan checked his watch. "We'd better get across to the Bodines' house, whatever," he said wearily. "They must have started drilling by now, and if what Mrs. Thompson said was true, they're in for some problems."

I looked down at Mrs. Thompson's body again. She seemed, in an eerie kind of way, to be smiling at me. I found myself smiling back before I reminded myself that she was dead, and that any smiles she gave now were tricks of the light, or the distortion of relaxing muscles.

"Did you see that thing, that creature?" I asked Dan, as we walked through the sumac bushes to the car.

He nodded. "A psychic illusion. It couldn't have harmed us with its own physical strength."

"Did it remind you of anything?"

"What do you mean?"

We reached the car and I opened the door. We looked at each other across the curved, rain slicked roof.

"I mean, did it remind you of anything?"

He shrugged. "I guess it did. I'm not quite sure what."

We climbed into the car and closed the doors. The engine whinnied, whined, and finally burst into life. I ground the gears into first, and away we went.

I said: "Why not try to remember? You know what *I* thought of, when I saw it. You tell me what *you* thought of."

Dan looked out at the rainy woods. "The funniest thing is, I think it reminded me of when I was a boy. I was out in the fields near my home with my sister, and we came across some older boys torturing a dog. They were hanging it upside-down from a tree, things like that, and then they doused it in kerosene and set it alight. I saw that poor dumb animal running around and I could smell its hair and its flesh burning, and in the end it rolled over and died. Well, I don't know why, but that creature we saw tonight reminded me of that."

"You know why, don't you?" I asked him. "You remember what Josiah Walters said? 'It is the evil wrought by Chulthe and his minions that has led men in all certainty to believe in Satan.'"

"I don't understand you," said Dan. "Why should Chulthe remind me of that day when the boys burned the dog?"

"Because it was an evil deed, and because it was the work of the devil, and because Chulthe *is* the devil. What we saw tonight, that image, that was Satan himself."

Dan found a pack of paper tissues in the glove box, and started to dab at his face and his hair to get himself dry.

"That's a little too superstitious for my liking," he said, after a while. "I prefer to think that it was a psycho-electric illusion."

"You can think what you like. It was still Satan. Not in person, not in the flesh, but an image of himself which he projected straight out of his own mind."

Dan shrugged. "You could be right. But I'd prefer to use his real names, Quithe or Chulthe. They're so much less emotive, don't you think?"

I glanced across at him. "We're fighting against the devil, and you're worried about being *emotive?*"

"I just don't want to panic people. Especially the drilling crew."

"They're going to dig up Satan and they shouldn't panic?"

Dan frowned at me. "Listen, Mason, whose side are you on?"

I steered the car left at the New Milford rotary, and we crossed the grey steel bridge over the Housatonic.

"I think I'm on the side of the angels," I told him.

He grunted. "That's good. Let's hope the angels are on your side, too."

The rain had temporarily eased off by the time we reached the Bodine house. The roads were wet, reflecting the headlights of passing cars, but the air was dry and windy and fresh, and up above us the clouds were breaking up so that the stars shone through. From as far away as the hill that overlooked the Bodines' property from a mile west, we could see the shifting shafts of the arc-lights that the county engineers had set up around their wellhead. The lights were intense and blue, and they cast shadows as long as dark giraffes. As we pulled up in the driveway, and climbed out of the Volkswagen we saw the tall scaffolding of the drilling-rig, and from the regular chugging and whining of a diesel engine, we guessed that work had already started. I lit a cigarillo, and then followed Dan around the side of the house.

Sheriff Wilkes was standing a few feet away from the center of operations, talking to Dutton Thrush, the engineering supervisor for Litchfield County, who had driven down from Torrington specially. Thrush was a lean, laconic man, like a root vegetable that had been left to shrivel in the back of a cellar. He wore rimless spectacles, a yellow hard-hat. A Camel hung suspended from his lip at all times, and was never seen to be lit.

Dan and I screwed up our eyes as we inspected the brightly-lit drilling rig. The shaft was rotating slowly as the bit cut through topsoil, and down into the rock. A crew of five engineers, dressed in jeans and overalls and windbreakers, were standing around the rig with their collars turned up, clapping their hands together to keep warm.

"Hallo there, Carter," I said quietly. "How are you, Dutton?"

"Surviving," said Dutton, his Camel waggling precariously.

Carter said: "You talk to the Thompson woman?"

I nodded. "For as long as we could. But Quithe got in there and made sure we didn't use her against him."

"What do you mean?"

"She's dead, Carter. We were round at her house and we got hit by another flood."

Carter Wilkes looked at me carefully out of deep-set, almost piggy eyes. "Dead? Drowned?"

"Crushed. The conservatory was flooded. The walls collapsed, and the weather-vane came right down and on to her chest. There wasn't anything we could do to save her."

"How long ago?" asked Carter.

"We just came from there."

Carter took out his personal radio transmitter and called the deputy who was waiting in his car. "Chaffe, get an ambulance out to Mrs. Thompson's place at Boardman's Bridge. They'll know. Yes. She's dead. Make sure you tell Yealland to get out there and check everything. I want pictures, the whole lot. Yes. I'll call you back in a while."

Dan said: "It was definitely Quithe. We both saw him, or some kind of psychic image of him."

"You mean this monster we're drilling after now?"

Dan nodded. "According to some old papers that Mrs. Thompson showed us, this whole area is riddled with caves and underground lakes, and that's where Quithe has been hiding himself."

Dutton Thrush said: "Quithe? What's this Quithe?"

I blew smoke. "It's kind of a pet-name. It means something like 'terrible beast-god from the chasm.'"

"Are you putting me on?"

I shook my head. "There's something down there, Dutton. Something that looks like hell on earth and can drown you in your own bed just by wishing you would. Now, do you think I'd put you on about something like that?"

# 9

With a frenzied screech, the drill suddenly speeded up, spun madly for a few seconds, and then stopped. Dutton called out: "What goes on?"

One of his crew said: "We've broken through into some kind of cavity here, Mr. Thrush. Maybe a cave or a tunnel. You want to come see for yourself?"

Dutton Thrush gave me an extremely old-fashioned look, and stalked across the wet grass to the well-head. The drilling crew were raising the muddy drill-shaft out of the ground, and it finally came up in a surging rush of discoloured water. Dutton scraped his forefinger down the length of the shaft, and examined the dirt on his hand under the nearest arc-light. Then he said: "Jones, Wockik, get that drill opened up and let's take a look at the core-sample."

I went across and stood beside him. I didn't know whether I was welcome there or not, but I guessed what had happened to Jimmy and Alison

Bodine was as much my business as anybody's, and so I stayed. He knelt down beside the bubbling fountain of yellowy water that was still gushing out of the drillhole, and he seemed at a loss to know what to do next.

"Dutton?" I asked him.

"What is it?"

"Do you think there's a cave down there? Or maybe a tunnel?"

"There could be. I won't be sure until I've checked."

"How about underground lakes, that kind of thing?"

He wiped his nose with the back of his hand. "It's possible. The Litchfield hills were created by tectonic pressures on Precambrian stable shield and occasionally that gives you folded hills with caverns beneath. Or sometimes water erodes the lower stratae, and you get your caves that way."

"Tectonic pressures?" I asked him.

"Sure. Volcanic activity. Rumpling up the flat shields of rock like an unmade bed. Mostly Palaeozoic in this area."

"I didn't know you were such a geology buff."

"I'm not. But when you spend your whole damned life drilling holes in the ground, you get to know the ground you're drilling holes in."

The crew's foreman came up with a lump of wet clay in his hand. "Mr. Thrush? It definitely looks like we've drilled ourselves into some kind of underground cavern here. It could be anything up to seventy, eighty feet in height."

"How far down is it?" asked Thrush.

"A little less than seventy-six feet. That's at the

point where we've pierced the roof of it, anyway. It could be deeper in other areas."

Carter Wilkes said: "Can you drill a wider hole?"

The foreman looked at him. "Sir?"

"You heard," Carter responded, in his usual harsh voice. "Can you drill a wider hole—a hole that a man could get down?"

"Well, sure," said the foreman, uncertainly. "But it depends on what you want. Mr. Thrush here told me this was nothing more than a water-sampling project."

Carter sighed. "It doesn't make any difference to you what it is, does it, so long as you get paid at the end of the month?"

The foreman tilted his hard-hat back on his forehead. He was young, with a thick neck like a bull, and a neatly-clipped moustache. "I don't want any of my crew going down that hole, sir, and that's all there is to it. We haven't had adequate surveys, and we haven't had comprehensive sampling bores, and quite frankly it's too damned dangerous. Nobody goes down unless the safety angle is all checked out."

"I'm not asking you or your men to go down there," said Carter.

The foreman blinked. "I can't take responsibility for anybody who does though, sheriff."

"I'm not asking you to do that, either. I'm just asking you to drill a hole down to that cavern, and to make sure that it's wide enough for a man to climb through."

The foreman looked at Dutton Thrush, expecting him to tell Sheriff Wilkes that what he was

asking was out of the question. But Dutton nodded
and said: "Go ahead," and so the foreman shrugged his shoulders and went back to the rig where
his crew were standing waiting. After a brief dis-
cussion, the diesel engine was started up again,
and the drill was shifted a couple of feet nearer
the house so that they could sink a parallel
shaft. I checked my watch as the drill bit tore into
the grass and then deep into the soil. It was well
past six, and my eyes were so tired that I felt as if
I'd been rubbing them with salt and sand. I would
have sold my shoes for a Jack Daniel's, a log fire,
and a soft bed.

It took another hour to go through seventy-six
feet of soft soil and assorted densities of rock. A
few minutes after seven, as a deputy arrived with
a large flask of coffee from the police commissary
in New Milford, the diesel engine was shut off
again, and the foreman of the drilling crew announced that we were almost through.

"The ground's real soft here, because of the
water leakage that's been going on," he said,
wiping the mud from his hands with an even
muddier handkerchief. It's already collapsed into the cavern in parts, and with a little more
drilling we should be able to open up a hole that's
wide enough. Three or four feet wide, at least."

"Will the sides hold?" asked Carter.

"I guess," said the foreman. "But whoever goes
down there had better be prepared for a few slides
of mud on top of the head."

Carter smiled across at me like an unctuous big
brother. "How do you feel about it, Mason?"

"*Me?* You want *me* to go down there?"

"Well, you and Dan together, maybe, and a deputy to help you out. Come on, Mason, you know more about these creatures than anybody. Didn't that crab-creature stop and turn away when you called it by name?"

I couldn't believe what I was hearing. The last goddamned thing in the world that I wanted to do was crawl down some muddy hole in the ground and come face-to-face with the monster that had come through centuries of fear and superstition to be known as the Devil. What I'd seen outside of Mrs. Thompson's conservatory, that flickering and hideous vision of serpentine tentacles and ferocious horns, that had been quite enough for one lifetime. But to face Satan in the flesh— well, that was my cue for discreetly backing out.

"Carter," I said, "I'd love to help you."

"Sure you'd love to help me. Dutton, do you have a hard-hat to spare?"

Dutton nodded. "There's a couple in the back of my Silverado."

"Dutton," I put in, "hold it, Dutton. I'm not going."

Carter pretended to look surprised. "What do you mean, you're not going? This whole goddamned situation has been your baby, right from the very beginning."

"Carter, I'm a plumber."

"I *know* you're a plumber. Don't tell me that you're a plumber. But you're an intellectual too, right? You know about stuff like this. The occult, stuff like this. You know what the hell's going on here, which is more than I do. Of course you've got to go."

"If I go down there, I'm going to get myself killed!" I shouted. "If the goddamned shaft doesn't collapse on top of my head, then that beast-god is going to drown me! And if it doesn't drown me, it's going to eat me! So what do you think I'm going to say to you, but *no*?"

Carter looked at Dutton as if I was a spoiled child who was going to have to be persuaded to do what was best for him. But Dan said: "Mason's right. You can't expect us to go down there without any kind of protection. It's certain death."

"I'd send a deputy, too."

"How about coming down yourself?"

"Me?" said Carter. "I have to stay up here and control everything."

I turned and gave him one of my steadiest, coldest stares. "Carter," I told him, "there's only one way you're going to persuade me to go down that shaft, and that's if you come along, too."

Carter looked uncomfortable. He lifted his head to the sky, and smoothed his double chins with his hand, and breathed in and out like a man who was summoning, not gods, but the greatest of patience. The clouds were clotting again now, like black blood, and we could hear the thunder booming in the distance. A sudden draught of wind blew the fallen leaves into a clattering turmoil.

"Mason," said Carter, "I can't force you to go."

There was another rumble of thunder. I could smell electricity in the air, and something else. The faint but unmistakable odor of fish, as if someone had just opened a can of sardines.

"I'm *not* going, Carter," I told the sheriff, flatly. "I'm not even a deputy, so you can't force me."

Carter sighed some more, and rubbed his chin some more, and huffed and wuffed. "You're right," he said, in a forced voice. "You're absolutely right. I can't force you to go nowhere."

"As long as you realize it."

He turned his back on me, and when he spoke again, it was in a controlled, though muffled, tone.

"If I said that I *would* come, though, what would you say then?"

I looked across at Dan. "Are you willing to go if Carter goes?" I asked him.

He shrugged. "I guess so. I don't have very much to lose. No family, anything like that. And I'd be fascinated to see what this Chulthe looks like."

I felt as if I'd been pushed into checkmate in chess. If Dan was going to go down after this beast-god, and if Carter was prepared to go, too, then it didn't look as if I had much in the way of alternatives. I *could* have refused, sure. I could have stayed behind and thanked the Lord for my life and my career in plumbing, but I knew as well as Carter knew that if Chulthe managed to rise again from under the ground, then there wasn't going to be much in the way of life or careers for anyone. Chulthe, or Quithe, was a powerful and hideous beast who would slaughter or mutate any human being for the sake of his own self-preservation, and he was probably stronger now, after centuries of concealment, than he had ever been before.

Abruptly, a curtain of heavy rain washed across the grass of the Bodines' yard. The brilliant arc-lights sparkled in rainbows of watery color, and the engineers started up their diesel engine again in case they had to pump water out of their excavation.

"All right," I said reluctantly. "Get me a hardhat, and tell me I'm the bravest American since Audie Murphy, and I'll come."

Carter nodded to Dutton Thrush, who went off to his wagon to find us some lids. Dan and Carter and I stood in the rain looking at each other warily, each one of us wondering if the other two were only going down in the cavern because they didn't want to be called chicken, or because they really weren't afraid of what might be down there.

Carter said: "Martino, did you bring that anti-tank gun?"

"I surely did, sheriff."

"Well, bring it around here, and make sure it's loaded."

"Yes, sir."

Dan said: "It's a pity we lost Mrs. Thompson. As far as the psychic side of this goes, we're fumbling around in the dark. Quithe could kill us without any warning, at any time, and we wouldn't even know he was there."

Carter checked his watch. "There's no time to find anybody else. We'll just have to trust our own noses."

"I know one nose that I do trust," I put in.

"Whose nose is that?"

"Shelley's."

"Your *cat* Shelley's?"

I dabbed rainwater out of my eyes with my handkerchief. "Is there any other Shelley?"

"I don't know," said Carter. "Shelley Winters?"

I was so nervous about what we were going to

have to do that I couldn't even take a joke. I said, sharply: "You think we should take Shelley Winters down that goddamned seventy-foot hole? Of course I mean my cat Shelley. This devil and all his mutated servants smell of fish, and that smell gets Shelley going like a bored New York matron with seven cherry brandies under her belt."

"Do you want to go get him?" asked Carter.

"He won't like the rain," I warned him.

Carter beckoned over one of his deputies. "Chaffe," he said, with enormously exaggerated patience, "I want you to go to my car and open the trunk. Inside, there's a spare rain-cape. Would you bring it back here as soon as you conceivably can?"

"Okay, sheriff," said Chaffe, and went off around the house.

We waited for a while. The engineering crew dug the drill-hole wider with trenching shovels, but the soil above the cavern was so soft that they didn't have very much trouble. Every now and then, a huge lump of turf would crumble and subside, causing a minor landslide, and by the time Chaffe came back with the cape, the collapses had widened the hole to four or five feet in diameter. We cautiously approached the edge, and an engineer obligingly trained his flashlight downwards into the darkness for us. You couldn't see much except sodden earth, twisted roots, rocks and shadows. Way down at the bottom of the pit, seventy-six feet below us, there was nothing but blackness.

"Must be a pretty sizeable cave down there," said the foreman. "We can't even penetrate it with the arc-lights. Wide, and deep, and smells pretty damned fishy, too."

"That's right," said Carter, brusquely. "Now, how are you going to get us down there?"

"That's simple enough," the foreman told him. "We put one of these canvas belts around you, and then we lower you down from the drilling rig."

"And supposing we want to come up again, in a real hurry?"

The foreman shrugged. "I'm afraid you can't do that, at least not in a hurry. You just have to whistle for the line to come down, and hitch yourself on to it again, and wait while we haul you up, one at a time."

Dan said: "Let's hope we don't have the hounds of hell on our heels when we need to have ourselves brought back to the surface."

Carter wiped rain from the end of his nose. "I'm beginning to wonder how the damn hell you talked me into going along with you to start with."

"Sheriff," I smiled, "this is the kind of valiant deed they give sheriffs citations for."

"Citations my ass. Look, here's your rain-cape."

I took the cape from a soaking and shivering Chaffe, and then I went around the house to the front drive, where I'd parked the Volkswagen. I looked through the rainy window, and I could just see Shelley lying on the front seat, all curled up and cosy and dreaming he was a Kliban mouser. I tapped on the glass, and he stirred, and then I opened the door and let in a draught of cold air and rain, and he stretched and yawned and shook his head so that his face was all ruffled and cross.

"Shelley," I told him, "this is where you pay me

back for three years of free food, warm chairs, and toll-free worming. Here's your rain-cape. Let's go get that devil before he comes out to get us."

I reached in to wrap him up in the cape, and as I did so, I felt the first tremor. It was a dark, shuddering sensation, more like a giant express train passing deep beneath the ground than a regular earthquake. I'd visited Los Angeles often enough to know what a minor shake on the Richter scale felt like; but this was alien, and odd, and it went on for almost half-a-minute. Even the 'quake that destroyed San Francisco in 1906 only lasted for 28 seconds. I raised my head in alarm, and as I did so, I hit my forehead sharply on the car door-frame. I swore, and Shelley looked up at me disdainfully, as if it was all my fault for lowering the temperature and playing around with rain-capes.

"Right, that settles it," I told him. "Let's get going."

He mewled as I plucked him out of the car, bundled him up in the cape and marched around the house with him dangling under my arm. But I wasn't feeling in a sympathetic mood, I was too scared, too excited, and too concerned about my own survival.

I took Shelley across to the dark, forbidding hole in the ground that the engineers had drilled, and I held him over it, so that he could smell the rank fishy odour that was rising from the cavern beneath. His pink nostrils flared, and he wriggled violently, but I wouldn't let him go. The drilling-rig workers stood around me and stared as if I was totally bananas. One of them said, with sardonic solicitude: "You want a hat for the cat?"

I ignored him. "The cat can sense what's down there," I told him. "Which is more than you can."

"Oh yeah? Well, what's down there? What does he say it is?"

Shelley shook his ears. I said, sarcastically: "He says it sounds like a county drilling engineer having an intelligent conversation, but he reckons he must be mistaken."

"Ah, sit on it," said the engineer.

Dutton Thrush came up with our hard-hats. I took off my baseball cap for the first time in days, and replaced it with a bright red bonedome that made me look like Action Man on his day off. Dan came up in a yellow helmet, and Carter wore a violent shade of green. Carter nodded towards the pit and said: "How does Shelley like it?"

The odour of fish was offensively strong now, and we all felt another vibration beneath the ground, a vibration that set the chains and the hooks on the drilling-rig jangling, and made the diesel-engine falter in its stroke. Above our heads, there was a sizzling crack of lightning that branched out of the clouds and went to earth only a couple of miles northward. We were still dazzled as thunder exploded around our ears, and Shelley ducked deeper into his rain-cape in fear.

"It seems like this beast-god's moving, or getting ready to move," said Carter. He was buckling the strap of the anti-tank gun across his chest, while Chaffe hung two rockets from his belt.

"Maybe the crab-creatures brought Quithe enough sustenance to come to life," said Dan. "We killed the Jimmy-creature, but there was still

Alison, and maybe the Karlen guy."

"How would they get down there?" asked
Dutton. His cigarette was so wet that it was transparent, but he still let it hang from his lip. "Don't
tell me *they* drilled a seventy-six foot shaft."

"They didn't have to," I told him. "There are
ways in and out of these caves and tunnels on the
surface. There was some old guy over at Boardman's Bridge in the eighteenth century who found
out about them."

"I never heard of them," said Dutton, suspiciously.

"Well, let's not argue about it," I countered.
"Let's just get down this goddamned shaft, if
we're going, and see what's there."

The rain was noisy and torrential now, and rivu-
lets of muddy water were pouring into the shaft,
bringing down more mudslides and more rocks.
The foreman came up to Dutton Thrush and said:
"If you want to get this stunt on the road, Mr.
Thrush, you'd better do it soon. What with all this
rain and all these tremors, we can't hold the shaft
open for too long."

As if to emphasize his warning, the ground
shook again, and Oliver Bodine's bicycle, which
had been propped against the side of the house in
the shelter of the verandah, fell to the boards with
a crash. We looked around at it nervously, and
then at each other.

"You'd better go first, Mason," said Carter.
"You're the one with the detecting device."

"Carter—" I started to warn him, but two burly
engineers came across with a harness of damp
canvas, and proceeded to buckle it around me

without ceremony or pause whatsoever. The next thing I knew, I was being led forward to the brink of the hole, and a hook was being attached to my waist with a heavy-duty clip. Someone handed me a heavy flashlight.

This close to the hole, there was a scaly coldness about the air that was even more unpleasant than the rain and the wind. Lightning flickered in the clouds again, and there were more theatrical collisions of thunder. They didn't worry me half as much as the stirrings beneath the ground. God may have been moving his furniture around, but it was the devil, turning over in his sleep, who really scared me.

The foreman stuck two fingers in his mouth and gave a loud whistle. The diesel engine whined, and I was raised bodily off the ground by the drilling winch, so that Shelley and I were spinning gently around and around in the rain, watched by everyone else, as if we'd just been hung on a gallows and they'd all come along to see us swing.

"Are you okay?" yelled Carter. "Are you ready to go?"

I cupped my left hand over my ear, and shouted back: "What did you say?" as I slowly spun past him.

"Are you ready to go down?" he yelled again.

I looked down at my feet, suspended over complete fathomless blackness. My stomach was tightened up as tiny as a nervous sea-anemone, and my heart beat seemed to have slowed down to a relentless clop, clop, clop that deafened me to everything that was going on around me. The earth trembled again, and my harness jingled and swayed. I reached out to steady myself, but of course there was nothing there to hold on to. All I could do was spin and sway and feel nauseous.

"Lower me down!" I shouted. Anything was better than hanging around here in the rain. Carter gave the signal, and the diesel engine stuttered, and the winch went sqweek-sqweek-sqweek and began to drop me, by unsteady inches, into the hole.

One moment I was above the surface of the ground. The next I was looking at everybody's shoes, and the wet grass; and the moment after that I was buried in chilly, fetid darkness, on my way down to the devil's caverns. Shelley tried to wriggle himself free as the fishy chill completely enveloped us, but I clutched him tight and flicked him on the nose with my finger to keep him quiet. Being flicked on the nose with my finger was about the only discipline he ever understood.

As we were lowered down the shaft, the noise of the diesel and the sound of the thunder became gradually more muffled. Soon I could hardly hear anything, except my heartbeat, and the distant squeaking of the winch. A few drops of rain still showered down on me, and when I looked up to check how far I'd been lowered, one of them hit me straight in the eye. But most of the dampness down here came from the soil, and from the putre-fying miasma of Quithe.

It seemed to take forever to reach the bottom of the shaft. There were at least three heavy earth tremors on the way down, and stones and mud kept tumbling and sliding down on top of me, bouncing off my hard-hat and my shoulders, and once, off Shelley's back.

I unhooked my flashlight and shone it on the sides of the shaft. We were down into layers of rock now, fragmented at first and gradually more solid. Then, quite abruptly, it looked as if my flashlight had gone out. We had reached the main cavern, and the flashlight beam, instead of falling on to the sides of the shaft, was now glimmering almost uselessly in a wide and gloomy space as big as a medieval cathedral. There was air circulating from somewhere, because I could feel the flow of it against my face, but it smelled appalling. It was like being shut up in a cold larder with a dish of week-old tuna. Shelley bristled and mewled, and if I hadn't held on to him so tight, I think he would have jumped down and gone after that fishy-smelling devil like furred lightning.

The winch took us down and down through the subterranean darkness, until at last my feet touched bottom. From the length of time it had taken us to drop from the end of the shaft to the floor of the cavern, I would have guessed the cavern to measure about thirty or forty feet high. I jerked on the rope to let the drilling crew know I was down, and then I looked up at the faint light that fell down the muddy shaft through which I had just descended. It was more than faint. It was blueish, and distant, and it was the only way I knew of getting out of this place.

I unhooked my harness, tugged the rope again, and gradually the canvas belts and hooks were winched up and out of sight. As they finally disappeared from view, a massive grumbling sound shook the ground, and more fragments of rock clattered into the cave.

Shining my flashlight all around me, I investigated my new surroundings as they say in castaway stories. I felt like a castaway. In fact, I felt worse than a castaway. I was more isolated and afraid than any castaway could have been. At least Robinson Crusoe had sunshine and sand and a parrot on his shoulder. All I had was darkness and fear and a cat who wouldn't keep still.

I stepped forward a little way, peering into the gloom, and something crunched beneath my feet. I stepped back in distaste, and shone my flashlight downwards. I had trodden on a white skeleton, about the size of a pigeon. I shone my torch around some more, and I saw that the floor of the cave was littered with them, hundreds of them, several layers deep. I looked upwards, following the flashlight beam with my eyes, and there they were. Suspended from the ceiling of the cave in such dense and silent clusters that they could have been stalactites were thousands and thousands of albino bats. They must have made this cave their home for centuries, interbreeding themselves colourless and blind, because of the total lack of light, and feeding on whatever insects or animals strayed into the subterranean tunnel system. As they died, they fell, and their skeletons had turned the floor of the cave into a crisp, crunchy boneyard. It wasn't very pleasant to walk on, particularly in sneakers.

I waited where I was, distastefully inspecting the white bats, until I heard the jingle of the winch harness again. I shone the flashlight up towards the dim smudge of light where the drill-shaft had broken through the ceiling of the cave, and down came Carter Wilkes like a heavy spider on a thin web. He gave me a wave as he was lowered down through the cave, and it was only a few moments before his feet had touched the ground and he was unbuckling his harness.

"Watch the floor," I told him, as I stepped over to help him untangle the canvas straps. "This whole damned cave is full of bats. There are bats on the ceiling and bats on the floor, and it wouldn't surprise me if there were bats standing in line outside for any hanging space that comes free."

Carter switched on his powerful heavy-duty lamp, and took a quick look around. The cave looked as if it was about a hundred and fifty feet in length and forty feet at its highest point, which was where the drilling crew had broken through. It tapered at one end, and where it was smallest, there seemed to be a small dark cavity which probably led through into another cave or tunnel. The whole cave was formed out of a fold in the massive grey rocks, and it looked like it was natural, rather than man- or monster-made, but all the same it had a clinging cold stench about it that made us both feel pukish and uneasy.

"Do you think Shelley will give us some idea where this Quithe might be hiding?" asked Carter.

I looked down at the pointed furry face under my arm. "I don't know. He's acting like he's spooked right at the moment."

"Maybe the best thing you can do is let him go, and then we can follow him."

"Oh, yes? And supposing he gets lost? From what Josiah Walters said, these caves go on for ever."

Carter unfastened the holster of his revolver. "If he gets lost I'll buy you another pet out of police funds. A terrapin, maybe."

It was only a few minutes more before Dan appeared, dangling on the end of the rope. He fell heavily on to one knee when he reached the ground, but he protested that he was quite all right, and so we quickly helped him out of his harness and dusted him down.

He looked around the cavern. "This is obviously some upper chamber of a water system," he said, using Carter's flashlight to inspect the grey shields of rock. "I doubt if it's been flooded in centuries. But it was at one time—look."

He shone the beam of the flashlight along a thick banded encrustation of mineral salts that ran around the cave only a few feet beneath the ceiling. The salts sparkled and twinkled in the light, in white and orange and green.

"Magnesium, copper sulphate, some potassium. They were deposited there when the water rose. We'll probably find that the next chamber below this one is flooded."

"Is it possible that Quithe's hiding-place is right underwater?" I asked him.

"That's what I've been wondering," said Dan. "I was trying to work out why he was coming back to life now, at this particular time, and maybe it's because the underground water-level has risen so high this year."

"I don't get you," said Carter. "Why should the water-level make any difference?"

Dan lowered the flashlight. "The way I see it, this Chulthe or Quithe is a water-beast. He can only regain his full strength if he's surrounded by water. Now, when Atlantis collapsed, the water level was probably very high, because of the volcanic activity and the disturbances under the ocean, and so when Quithe penetrated the inland water system in order to perpetuate himself, he probably came to rest at a higher level under the ground than water normally reached.

"The old legends aren't very clear about how he actually penetrated the wells. The Litchfield book says that the beast-gods infiltrated the subterranean water-table with their seed, which presumably were microscopic like human seed. Yet Josiah Walters says he actually came across Quithe in his hiding place, and so by the eighteenth century Quithe must have been fully grown, or at least half-grown.

"What I think could have happened is that Quithe began to grow in these underground caves soon after his earlier manifestation had deposited his fertilized seed here. The caves were probably still flooded, and so Quithe rapidly gained in strength and size. But then, as the disturbances of Atlantis settled, the water level sank, and left Quithe stranded in a cave from which he was too physically large to escape downwards, into lower levels that might still have been filled with water. He lost strength, and he was left in what amounts to suspended animation. He was dried up, as it were, like dried shellfish, and he stayed that way for centuries."

Carter blinked. "You mean he only came to life again after this year's heavy rainfall, when the water rose up into his cave again, and gave him a good soaking?"

"If you want to put it that way, yes. At least, it's a theory. And when the water rose, and he started to grow again, and live again, he ejaculated more seed into the water so that any human or animal who drank it would mutate into one of his servants. They would turn into crabs, which could find food for him on dry land, but which could also bring it back here, and feed it to him under the water."

I stroked Shelley's head. "There's only one thing, Dan. If Quithe is underwater, how do we winkle him out? We don't have aqua-lungs, or harpoon-guns, or whatever you need to go chasing underwater beast-gods with."

The cavern shook with that deep, threatening vibration again. Some pieces of rock fell from the ceiling and clattered, echoing, on to the debris-strewn floor.

"I don't know what we can do," said Dan. "First of all, we have to find him, and then we can make up our minds what we need to do to get rid of him."

I looked down at Shelley. "I see. This is where my faithful bloodpuss comes in."

"I'm afraid oo," said Carter.

I didn't want to let Shelley go, but I guessed neither of us had much choice. I lifted him out from his rain-cape, and set him down among the bats' bones and the broken rocks, and he stood there in the lamplight with his tail stiff and his nose scenting the air, and I really didn't want to lose him, not for anything.

"Go find him, Shelley," whispered Carter. "He's there someplace. You go find him."

Slowly, selectively, Shelley made his way across

the gloom of the cave, heading towards the
narrower end, where the shadowy crevice was.
Carter's flashlight followed him all the way. He
turned once, his eyes shining green, and then he
disappeared into the darkness without a sound.

We crunched as gently as we could over the
bats' bones until we reached the crevice, and we
looked down it with growing uncertainty. It was
only just over four feet high, and it led steeply
downwards into the ground, with an uneven curve
to the left. I glimpsed Shelley's tail as he jumped
carefully over the craggy, jumbled rocks, and then
he was gone.

"Like they say in the *Lassie* movies, it looks like
he wants us to follow him," said Carter.

"Do you think we can actually get down there?"
I asked him. "It looks about as tight as a llama's
ass."

"How do you know how tight a llama's ass is?"
demanded Carter. "Help me get this gun off my
back. There's no way I'm going to crawl through
there with this goddamned drainpipe tied around
me."

While Dan helped Carter unbuckle the anti-tank
gun, I checked around the entrance to the crevice
with my torch. The rock was sparkling with
minerals, and rough. But as I played the beam
over the left side of the entrance, I thought I
glimpsed a mark that wasn't natural. I crouched
down closer to it, and rubbed away the salts that
had encrusted it over the years, and there was the
reassurance we needed that Shelley was leading
us the right way.

Scratched into the rock, unevenly and hurriedly,

were the initials 'J.W., '87', and an arrow pointing the way that Shelley had gone. I turned around and said to Carter: "This is the devil's den, all right. Josiah Walters left his initials here."

Carter, flexing his shoulder muscles now that he was free of the anti-tank gun, came across and peered at the scratchings.

"That's incredible," he said. "Just to think that guy made that mark all of two hundred years ago, and it's as fresh as if he did it this morning."

There was another shudder of seismic disturbance, briefer than before, but more intense, and for a moment I couldn't keep my balance. We heard rocks clattering and earth sliding, and Carter shone his lamp quickly up to the roof of the cavern. The loosely-drilled hole through which we had entered this subterranean world was slowly falling in. We saw the flicker of a beam from one of the arc-lights on the surface, but then there was a heavier slide of soil, and even that was gone.

Carter looked at me. His face, in the upward-shining light of his lamp, was like a grotesque mask of theatrical tragedy.

"Let's hope we don't need to get out of this place in a hurry," he said hoarsely. "It's going to take them all of an hour to clear that shaft again, and that's being optimistic."

"Your brand of optimism I can do without," I told him. "Now, let's get after Shelley before we lose him altogether."

"You go first," said Carter. "After all, he's your cat."

I bent my head and crouched my way into the crevice. Once I was through the entrance, the roof of the tunnel became a few inches higher, but it was still awkward and narrow and stunningly claustrophobic. Stumbling, grunting, and cursing, we made our way downwards over loose and jagged rocks, sometimes tearing our hands on the rough surface, sometimes squeezing between harsh gaps that seemed to have been deliberately designed to allow a human being through, but only just. We were sweating and exhausted after only a few minutes, and still the tunnel descended into the earth, as narrow and oppressive as before.

"There are times in my life," puffed Carter, "when I really regret all those beers."

He pushed his way past a massive and over-bearing slab of rock. In the glaring, unsteady light of our torches, I could just see Dan's pale face as he brought up the rear.

"And those hot dogs," added Carter.

Dan said: "*And* those giant portions of pecan pie with mountains of whipped cream."

We struggled onwards and downwards, deeper and deeper into the dark earth under Connecticut. Sweat was dropping off of our faces, and we were all panting for lack of air. I felt like I had as a small boy, when I had tunnelled under the bed-clothes and lost any sense of which way was up and which way was down, and my world had suddenly turned into nothing but darkness and oppressive weight and panic.

Carter asked me: "How long have we been down here?"

"Fifteen minutes," I said, over my shoulder.

"How far do you think we've come? Two hundred, three hundred feet?"

"Something like that. Maybe not as far. It's difficult to tell when you don't have any landmarks."

Dan called: "Any sign of it widening out yet?"

I shone my flashlight up ahead, but all I could see was slabby, enclosing rocks.

"Not for the next fifty feet," I told him. "You want to take a rest?"

"Let's just get on with it," growled Carter. "I'm beginning to feel like the red pimiento in a stuffed olive."

We climbed down and down, painfully and silently, for the next ten minutes. At times, the roof of the tunnel was so low that we had to crawl on our hands and knees, at a sharp downward angle, and what that cost in cut hands and bruised foreheads was enough to make us all feel like turning around and getting the hell out of there. The only trouble was, the tunnel was so constricting that we couldn't even turn around.

Unexpectedly, though, after we'd shouldered our way between two gritty and uncompromising boulders, the tunnel began to widen. In a minute or two, we were stepping over the rocky floor quite freely, and then our flashlights picked up the iridescent glitter of white stalactites. We came out on to what appeared to be a kind of natural balcony, overlooking a vast, vaulted cavern. All around, the cavern was pillared with crystallised salts, so that it had taken on the appearance of a strange cloistered cathedral, a totally silent place of worship into which the sun had never shone.

Cautiously, we approached the edge of our balcony, and looked downward. There seemed to be nothing but inky, fathomless blackness; but then Carter shone his flashlight downwards and we saw why. Only ten or twelve feet below us, so still that we could see our lights and our faces suspended in it like Halloween lanterns on a dark night, was the surface of an underground lake. This was how far the water had risen from the depths of the earth, and it was out of here that the Bodines had drunk, and been cursed by the evil organisms in Chulthe's seed.

I heard a mewling sound, and I shone my flashlight to one side. Standing on a broken stalagmite that rose from the water at the edge of the lake was Shelley, and he was pawing and sniffing as if what he was hunting was close, but unreachable.

"You see that?" I said to Dan. "That could mean that Chulthe is right down there, right in this lake."

"That goddamned tuna smell sure is strong enough," said Carter, wiping sweat from his forehead with the back of his hairy arm. "It's like a goddamned fish dock down here."

Dan stared down at the water. "It's completely clear," he said quietly. "If we had a powerful enough lamp, we might be able to see right down to the bottom."

"Any volunteers to go back and get one?" asked Carter.

Shelley, on his precarious perch, miaowed and bristled.

Dan said: "Does your cat know something that we don't?"

I shrugged. "It could be just the smell of the fish. I don't know. I wasn't trained in cat psychology."

We spent a few minutes examining the dark and nightmarish vault. Its resemblance to some kind of holy church was uncanny, and there was even that cold dead atmosphere you can feel in neglected French cathedrals, so cold that you can imagine the knights and saints buried under the flagstones to be numb to the bone. As we shone our flashlights along the white stalactite pillars all around the cavern's flooded nave, they were mirrored in the water to form almost perfect Norman arches.

"It's like the devil's own chapel," said Carter. "Did you ever see a cave like this before? It's unreal."

"I think supernatural is probably the right word," put in Dan.

I coughed. "Supernatural or not, we're going to have to do something positive, aren't we? There's no point in going back unless we know that Chulthe's here for sure."

"What do you suggest?" asked Dan.

"I don't know. Maybe we ought to try disturbing him."

Carter frowned. "You want to disturb a beast-god, one hundred fifty feet underground, with only a jack-rabbit's burrow for an escape route?"

"I don't *want* to. But it looks as if we're going to have to."

Carter let out a testy breath. "I wish I'd been able to bring that anti-tank gun down here. I'd like to have the weight of that thing in my hands right now."

I stepped right up to the edge of the balcony and looked at the lake's limpid surface. Then I turned to Dan and asked him: "This is one hundred fifty feet below the surface, right, or thereabouts?"

"I guess so."

I rubbed my cheek thoughtfully. "When you tested the water, didn't you say that the organisms and the soil material in it came from deeper down? Maybe a mile and a half?"

"That's right. That was where Chulthe was probably lying when he first started to revive. These vaults and chambers must go down miles into the rock. All flooded, too. That was where Jimmy Bodine must have gotten his dream of swimming under tons of rock. But now the flooding's risen up as far as here, and Chulthe must have the freedom of the whole water system."

"You mean he could start to pollute water in other places?" asked Carter, bluntly.

"I'm only theorizing, but yes."

Carter unbuttoned his holster. "Well," he said, "I don't know about you two guys, but I've seen enough of ordinary innocent folks being mutated into horrible creatures that go around murdering more ordinary innocent folks. If Mason here says we ought to disturb this Chulthe to get him out, then let's disturb him."

Dan raised his hand and said: "Carter, I shouldn't—"

But Carter was annoyed, and determined. He took out his police revolver and aimed it down at the surface of the lake. He fired twice, and the whole cavern was filled with ear-splitting echoes. Shelley jumped off his stalagmite on to the balcony, and came to stand nervously close to my legs. The echoes gave one last shout and then there was silence again.

The water had hardly been ruffled. But circles of lightly-drawn ripples ran across the surface, and lapped softly at the stalactite pillars, and then ran back again. We all stood watching them, until the last one had faded away.

"Seems like guns don't worry him none," said Carter. "Maybe we ought to try a few rocks."

I said: "Wait a minute. We've all said how much this place looks like a cathedral. Maybe it's intentional. Maybe this place has been specially formed as the devil's place of worship."

"How can you specially form a place like this?" asked Dan, with undisguised scepticism. "Those stalactites take twenty thousand years to reach that size. Twenty thousand years."

"Maybe they do," I told him, "but we're dealing with a beast who can flood a whole second-floor room, and empty it out again, and think nothing of it. We're dealing with a beast who's supposed to be more than two million years old, something from out of the past beyond the past. Something unbelievably ancient and powerful. This is Satan, Dan. Think about it. Couldn't Satan have made himself a place like this?"

"It's remotely possible, I suppose."

"Well, let's say it's remotely possible, then. If it's remotely possible it's also remotely possible that if we desecrate this place, if we do something to invoke God, or the forces of good, then the devil's going to come out of that water to try stopping us."

Carter and Dan looked at each other without much enthusiasm.

"I'm not too sure about that," said Carter. "What do you want us to do—sing *Bringing in the Sheaves?* My hymn-singing voice would desecrate any place you care to mention, but I'm not convinced it would work."

"Let's just say the blessing. Let's just profess a little Christianity here."

Dan sighed. "All right. I guess we could do dumber things."

We bowed our heads and stood in silence for a while. Shelley fretfully clawed at the ground, and kept rubbing up against my leg, but for a few moments I deliberately ignored him. I wanted to keep my mind firmly concentrated on God, and His son Jesus Christ, and the Holy Spirit, and the sign of the crucifix. I wanted to see some kind of brightness in my mind, something that would show up this subterranean cavern for what it was —the dark cathedral of Hell.

I raised my eyes. I said, clearly but not loudly: "In the name of the Father, and of the Son, and of the Holy Ghost, we three profess our belief in goodness and Christian ministry. We renounce the devil and his works. We bless this place in the name of our God and everything we believe to be right. We cast out evil."

There was a deep, subdued rumbling in the ground. It felt like the beginnings of another earthquake. The surface of the lake began to shudder and ripple, and behind us, loose rocks began to fall.

Carter said: "Mason, hold on there."

But it was too late for holding on. If we were going to rouse Quithe out of his flooded caverns, then we were going to have to use any means possible.

"We bless this place," I repeated. "We ask God to sanctify it, and cast out all evil from it. We ask God to make it untenable for Quithe, who is also Chulthe or Satan."

The vibration in the ground was shaking us so much that we could scarcely keep upright. A huge stalactite cracked and dropped from the ceiling of the balcony on which we were standing, and shattered only a few feet away from us. Our ears were deafened by an endless, painful rumbling noise.

Dan shouted: *"The lake! Mason! The lake!"*

I raised my flashlight and shone it into the water. There, humped and glossy with wet, mottled and crustaceous, rose a crab-creature so huge and hideous that I nearly dropped everything and ran. Its claw lifted out of the water with a noise like a car being dragged out of a river, and its beak grated and squeaked. What was worse, there were wet and tattered remnants of clothing trailing from its jaws and its pincers, and an indescribable shred of human meat caught in its antennae.

With his teeth clenched tight, Carter said: "Dan, I want you to do something, and it's an order. Go back up that tunnel and bring down that anti-tank gun. Go quick as you can. Mason and me will try to hold this thing off until you get back."

Dan hesitated, but Carter snapped: "Go! It's the only chance we've got!" and he went. That left Carter and me and Shelley standing on the balcony above the lake, while the crab-creature rose higher and higher out of the water, an infested beast of horny plates and writhing squid-like tentacles; a soulless monster whose only motivation was to rip out our insides and digest them for its terrible master.

# 10

Carter opened his revolver and fed it with two more shells. Then he snapped it shut, cocked it, and stood ready like Gary Cooper facing the outlaws off of the noon train. All I could find myself was a sharp spear of broken stalactite, but I hefted it in my hand, and swung it around my head, and even if it didn't frighten the crab-creature, at least it gave me some sort of confidence. The creature all this time was wallowing closer and closer, its grey eyelids peeling on and off its glittering black eyes, and its pincers were snapping with greedy anticipation. We couldn't see all of its body, but it seemed to have grown half as large again as the Jimmy-creature that Carter had killed on the ridge. It was far more ugly, too, and the crevices of its shell were alive with black parasitic leeches. The stench of fish was nauseating.

Carter said: "I'm going to try for the eyes. I'd like you to crouch down on your hands and knees here, Mason, because I want to use your back to steady my aim."

"Okay, Carter," I said, mechanically. I turned my hardhat around so that the peak was at the back, and knelt down on the rough, rocky ground. Carter hunkered down beside me, and lifted his .38.

"Maybe if we can blind it, we'll stand more of a chance," he said, in a tight, choked-up kind of a voice. His podgy elbows dug into my back as he took careful aim.

"Don't be too long," I told him, "I'm getting the cramp down here."

"You want to have cramp or you want to be a crab's breakfast?" asked Carter. I felt his arm tendons tense, and he fired one shot. I felt as if the shot had gone off inside my head. I waited, without moving, and then Carter said: "Missed, damnit."

He fired another shot. He muttered: "Missed." I could hear the crab-creature's claws scraping against the side of the rock balcony, and as it shook its hideous head, water sprayed across the ground to where I was crouching. It wasn't more than fifteen feet away now, and once it had humped itself up over the balcony's edge, there was only one thing left for us to do, and that was to try to make it back to the tunnel.

"Carter," I said, trying to sound respectful, "don't you think it's time we retired with dignity? That thing's getting awful close."

Carter grunted. He was concentrating on hitting one of the black eyes that wavered on a stalk from the creature's head. He let out a breath, steadied

himself again, and fired. My ears were ringing
from all the shots, and I hardly heard the crab-
creature's grating scream. But I heard Carter
shout: "Hit it! Hit the bastard!" and I looked up to
see the crab standing uncertainly on the brink of
the balcony, one of its black globular eyes shot
into bloody rags.

"Down!" snapped Carter. "It's no use unless I
hit 'em both!"

He steadied himself on my back once more, and
quickly fired off another shot. This time his confidence, and the crab-creature's confusion, paid him
instant dividends. I turned my head in time to see
the other eye blasted off the end of its stalk. Carter
whooped, and said: "Who said I couldn't hit a
mountain at three feet? See that shooting? That's
what I call *shooting!*"

The crab-creature became hesitant, and its huge
claw flailed noisily at the rocks and the stalactites
as it tried to find its bearings. We had to step back
as it half-mounted the balcony, and swung blindly
around trying to find us. But without its eyes it
was far too slow and cumbersome, and all we had
to do was press ourselves back against the wall of
the cavern and its pincer groped uselessly past us.

After a few minutes of searching, the crab-
creature shifted itself back to the lake, and it
settled in the water just a few feet away, almost
submerged. The ribbon-like leeches which had
been feeding in the soft sores between the shields
of its body now attached themselves to the bleeding stalks of its eyes, and in a few moments it
appeared to have replacement eyes of wriggling
black.

"It's a hard life in the devil's auxiliary, ain't it?" said Carter, his mouth pursed in disgust.

"It's pretty hard on our side, too," I replied.

We waited for almost twenty minutes. I smoked a cigarillo and Carter took a couple of nips from a small silver hip-flask. The crab-creature stayed where it was, floating with only the hump of its shell and its mutilated head above the surface of the water. Now and then, the ground shook with sinister vibrations, but there was no sign of Chulthe, the devil himself, and I wasn't going to try raising him again until Dan had come back with the anti-tank gun.

At last we heard a clattering sound from the narrow entrance to the tunnel, and Dan's puffing and panting as he struggled back down. He came squeezing out from between the two rocks which rested at the tunnel's opening, and half-slid, half-stumbled down towards us. He was bushed, and sweating like a penful of pigs.

"What kept you?" said Carter, taking the anti-tank gun and checking it over.

Dan sat on the ground, gasping for breath. "You're kidding, Carter. I went up that tunnel and come back down again so quick you would have thought I was buttered."

Carter handed him his hip-flask, and Dan took a full mouthful. He winced, and swallowed, and said: "What the hell do you call this?"

"Good old confiscated white lightning, that's what," said Carter.

Dan shuddered.

While Carter loaded the anti-tank gun, I walked as near as I dared to the edge of the rock balcony and inspected the wounded crab-creature. It was floating in the water so idly that I wondered for a moment if it was dying. But when I took one more step closer, its huge claw began to rise out of the water towards me, and I knew that it was still keeping watch. I went back to Carter's side, just as he was finished preparing the gun, and I said: "That thing's guarding us for some reason."

Carter nodded. "That's what I've been thinking. And I've been wondering why."

"Maybe it's trying to deter us from reciting any more Christian prayers."

"I doubt it. More likely it's keeping us here until it can rustle up some reinforcements."

Dan pointed out: "We don't actually know if there are any reinforcements. Only Jimmy and Allison Bodine were mutated for sure. We never had any specific reports on the Karlen guy. That thing there could be Alison, and it could be the only crab-creature left."

"That's possible," nodded Carter. "In that case, maybe it's stopping us from exploring this lake, and finding out what's really down here."

I nodded towards the anti-tank gun. "Are you going to use that thing on it?"

"I guess. A shot to the head should finish it."

I looked around for Shelley. With his usual dis dain, he had retreated to a small niche and was sitting there with his eyes closed, ignoring us. "If you're going to start blasting, then I think we'd better back off," I suggested. "You never know how strong the roofs of these caves might be."

"Okay," said Dan, and while Carter prepared himself for a final attack on the crab-creature, he and I retreated as far back as we could, and shielded our ears with our hands.

With his flashlight wedged between the cavern wall and a stalactite, so that its beam lit up the head of the floating crab, Carter took aim at a distance of only twenty feet. The water glittered with reflected light, and Carter's heavy, portly figure was silhouetted against it. I heard him click the safety-catch off, and his shoulders hunched a little as he applied his eye to the sights.

I suppose we should have guessed the crab-creature was far quicker and far more powerful than it seemed to be. Carter may have shot out its eyes, but we forgot that it was a creature whose natural habitat was pitch darkness, down in the flooded caves and chambers beneath Connecticut, and so it could feel its way around, when it wanted to, with the same speed and strength as it could in the daylight.

Carter didn't even get the chance to fire before the crab-creature rose horrendously out of the water in an explosion of spray, and its massive green-and-black claw swung at his head. He yelled once, hoarsely, but then the pincher closed and his skull was crushed with a noise like a breaking walnut. The crab-creature flung him to the ground, and its subsidiary pincer dragged his bloody body downwards, beneath its abdomen where the writhing tentacles entwined themselves around it.

I didn't even think what I was doing. I must have been claustrophobia-crazy from all that time under the ground. But I picked myself up and leaped across the loose rocks that separated our hiding-place from the crab-creature, and I made a frenzied dive for Carter's discarded anti-tank gun. Dan yelled: *"Mason! It's no use!"* but it was too late by then, even though my own mind was clattering out a message like a teleprinter: IT'S NO USE. I tripped, fell, picked myself up again, and there was the gun right under my feet. I reached its webbing strap, lifted it off the ground, tried to couch it over my shoulder and aim it. But then my vision was filled with nothing but black over- whelming shell, and my senses were blotted with a crushing weight that I couldn't understand or resist.

There was a screeching, scraping noise as the crab-creature slid back off the rock-balcony into the water, dragging me with it. It had gripped my left thigh in its claw, too far up inside the gap be- tween its pincers to crush the bone, but fierce enough to make it impossible for me to twist myself free. I shouted: *"Dan!"* but that was all I had time for. In the next instant, I was pulled down into the freezing depths of the underground lake, and I let out almost all of my breath with shock.

The crab-creature dived straight downwards. I felt the cold water penetrating my eardrums, and I knew that I only had enough breath for a few more seconds. I tried to wriggle my leg, but the beast's strength was unyielding, and I couldn't break loose. My face was battered against the rough shell of its head, and its prickly spines, and once I brushed with terror and disgust against one of its leech-enclustered eyes. We sank down and down, and the water grew colder and darker until the last glimmer of Carter's flashlight was swallowed up. In a second or two, I would have to breathe in water, and when I did that, I was dead.

Swimming at a steep angle, the crab-creature pulled me right down to what must have been the bottom of the lake. But once its claws had touched rock, it scuttled sideways until it reached a wide crevice in the lake's door. In my splitting, oxygen-starved brain, I could only think of Dan's words: *"These vaults and chambers must go down miles into the rock. All flooded, too."*

The crab-creature dived downwards again, down through the crevice, down through a rough angled tunnel that scratched and lacerated my hands and my legs. I knew I couldn't hold my breath any longer, and that meant it was all over. My lifeless body would be dragged down through chambers and vaults and tunnels and then devoured in utter darkness, in the most unhallowed place on earth. This was hell, in the most terrible and medieval meaning of the word.

But like a touch on the shoulder from a saint, the anti-tank gun bumped against my hand. I thought I'd let it go, but its webbing strap had gotten caught up in the crab's pincers, and it had come down with us. I seized it ferociously, grappled with it, tried to feel in the cold and the darkness where its trigger was, where its muzzle was. My lungs were bursting, too near the end of their air supply, and my mind was dizzy with carbon dioxide. But I found the strength to thrust the gun up against the crab's body, deep into the mass of wriggling tentacles that still clung on to Carter's body. And I found the will to pull the trigger.

There was an abrupt rush of bubbles as the gun's rocket was discharged. Then there was nothing but tumbling, walloping, wrenching, heaving chaos. The crab-creature rolled heavily over sideways as the rocket penetrated its belly, and my head was slammed against the rocks. In a second, the rocket blew up, and the water surged and expanded, and I was suddenly released. An underwater blizzard of shell fragments and torn-apart claws and shrapnel followed me and surrounded me as I swam desperately upwards, my arms working as hard as a water-boatman, my body long since out of air. I prayed to God that there was a surface above me, and air, and that the crab-creature hadn't pulled me right through into a lower vault that was flooded right up to the roof. I thought of Jimmy Bodine's dream. I thought of drowning. I thought of Atlantis.

*"The thing that always gets me is the feeling that the water is underneath tons and tons of solid rock, so even if I did reach the surface, I couldn't breathe."*

I saw an odd glimmer of light. A wavering green glimmer. And then my head broke the surface of the water, and I was breathing air. I trod water, coughing and gasping, doggy-paddling my way around until I could relax enough to float. The air was so cold that it hurt my lungs, and I was chilled all over, but right at that moment, I didn't mind. The crab-creature was dead, and I was free of it.

At last, I stopped panting and started shivering instead. I looked around me, and saw that I was swimming in another underground lake. The cavern in which this lake lay was quite different from the devil's cathedral cavern. It was curved, like a boomerang, so that from where I was swimming it was only possible to make out one end of it; and its ceiling was high, slanting and formed out of a huge formation of flaking slate-like rock. The strangest thing of all, though, was that there was light, and that I could see at all. It wasn't lamplight. It was too faint and greenish for that. It was a dim uneven fluorescence, like one of those pictures that glows in the dark. It was emanating from the farther end of the cavern, the end which I couldn't see. Taking a deep breath and kicking my legs, I started to swim around the cave towards it, weighted down by my icy, soggy clothes.

I was exhausted by the time the end of the cavern came into sight, but I wasn't so tired that I couldn't pause, and tread water for a while, and stare at the chilling and terrifying scene which met my eyes with shock and disbelief.

At the end of the cavern, there was tier upon tier of stalactites and stalagmites, in magnificent formations, and they were all glowing and pulsating with dim green light. They reached the roof of the cave like an extraordinary pipe organ, and they formed a fluted wall around a wide rock beach. It was what lay on the beach that horrified me most of all. It looked like a vast black maggot, with dry and wrinkled skin, except where its body was partly submerged in the subterranean lake. It had glossy dark brown mandibles, and with these it was rooting amidst a slough of human offals. It must have been ninety or a hundred feet long, and twenty feet high, and its body had the colour and the sickening softness of the worst kind of worm you can find under a stone. It was Quithe, the beast-god of the chasms. It was Chulthe, the obscene master spirit of Atlantis. It was Satan, in his true larval form.

I didn't know what to do. I couldn't tread water any longer, mainly because my feet and legs were so cold. I had to get out of the lake somewhere. And yet the only possible place was on that gory beach where Chulthe was feeding. There *was* an alternative—diving back down into the water and trying to find the tunnel through which the crab-creature had brought me—but I was pretty certain that if I did that I would kill myself. I just didn't have the strength.

I was about to swim across to the other side of the cave to see if there was a ledge on which I could rest, when a familiar voice called: "Mason! Is that you? Mason!"

I looked back at the grisly beach where Chulthe had been wallowing in blood. Somehow, the maggot-beast seemed to have disappeared, and there was nothing there but plain rock. The voice called: "Mason!" again and I realized it was Rheta. But what the hell was Rheta doing down here, in this Godforsaken subterranean cave? The last time I'd seen her, she'd been on her way to New Milford hospital with a sprained ankle.

Yet—she was there. She was standing by the edge of the water in her white laboratory coat. She was waving. There was no question at all that it was Rheta. I called breathlessly: "Rheta!" and started to swim towards the beach.

Rheta tossed back her blonde hair, and started to unbutton her laboratory coat. I was only fifty or sixty feet away now, and I could see that she was smiling at me. I called, in between swimming strokes: "How did you—make it—down here? Is there—another way in?"

She didn't answer. Instead, she pulled off her laboratory coat, and underneath she was wearing flame-red underwear. A red quarter-cup bra that exposed her wide pink nipples. A red garter-belt, holding up sheer red stockings. And a red G-string that barely covered her.

I floundered the last few feet towards the beach. My feet at last touched bottom, and I waded in to Rheta like Captain Webb after his first successful swim across the English Channel. I coughed water out of my lungs, and held out my arms towards her.

She let the bra catch loose, so that her breasts swayed free. She unclipped her garters, and peeled off her stockings. Then she turned and walked coquettishly away from me, across the uneven rock, the thin red elastic of her G-string tight between her bare white bottom.

"Do you want me?" she asked, over her shoulder.

I stopped. Did I want her? Of course I wanted her. But what the hell was she doing here? She couldn't be here. This couldn't be Rheta. But if it wasn't Rheta, what was it? Or who was it?

"Are you coming?" called Rheta. "Come on, lover, we can lie down here, and do everything you ever dreamed of."

I stayed where I was. I was frightened now. Chilled, shaking, and frightened. Where had that black maggot creature gone? Where was all the blood and the offals?

I said firmly: "You're not Rheta. You can't be."

She hesitated. She was staring at me, and for the first time I saw that her eyes weren't Rheta's eyes at all. They were dark, snake-like, malevolent. They were watching me through Rheta's face like the eyes of someone looking through a mask.

She opened her mouth, but instead of speaking, a thick black torrent of puffy, wrinkled flesh poured out of her. At first I thought she was vomiting, but then the black flesh grew to the size of a man, and larger, until it piled up as huge as the maggot-beast that had been feeding on the shore. Rheta's image was swallowed up altogether, until I was faced by Chulthe, in his basic grotesque form, with scissor-like mandibles, and eyes as dull and emotionless as an insect. I stepped back, away from those terrifying jaws, and as I did so I slipped on a stringy, slithery piece of human flesh.

A voice whispered: "I have come across your kind before. Men who have tried to thwart me. Men who have fondly and foolishly believed that they can prevent me from taking my rightful place in the world. Your weakness is below contempt. Your sins are so petty that you can hardly even be tempted to die like a man should."

I kept on retreating. Maybe it wouldn't do me any good, but I wasn't planning on staying around there to decorate Chulthe's personal beach.

I said: "You've been defeated before. You'll be defeated again."

"Not as long as there is foolishness and jealousy and primitive lust. I am the greatest of the gods from beyond the Hyades, remember, and while men still worship evil, I shall continue to survive, and rule, even while I dream in the wells and the caves and wait for the days of Atlantis yet again."

"Atlantis can never rise again."

The maggot-beast moved towards me. It might have been my imagination, but I kept glimpsing different faces that I knew on its insect countenance. I kept seeing Dan, and Carter, and Jimmy Bodine. I saw Alison, but it was an Alison I scarcely recognized, with her mouth drawn back in a feral grimace, and her eyes as red as if they were filled with blood. I saw Rheta again, smiling with blatant lewdness. I saw my mother and my father, and faces of people who were long-forgotten or dead. I saw myself, in moments of weakness, or pain, or regret.

"Atlantis may never rise," whispered the voice. "But the Kingdom of Quithe will rise again. I sense the world around me, after all these centuries of imprisonment. I sense it well. It has nourished the legacies I left it. It has nourished lust and deceit and cruelty. These are the instruments by which I always ruled, and they are well-maintained for when I take up my rule again. Only this time, the world you will see will be by comparison the blackest night, in which pain and pleasure will be the only beacons on a hellish horizon."

I was wading backwards in the underground lake now, up to my knees. The water was freezing, and I knew damned well that I couldn't survive for long if I tried to swim. And there was no chance at all that I could escape Quithe, dive down to the bottom, and make any kind of escape through the tunnel.

There was a thunderous vibration throughout the cavern, and before my eyes the maggot-beast seemed to roll in on itself, like a black parachute being folded, until a tall horned man stood in front of me, dressed in a long shimmery black cloak. He had high cheekbones, and slanting eyes, and skin the colour of dead parchment.

"I am a creature of the seas," he whispered, "but this is the manifestation I always used to walk in the world, in ancient times when darkness was the rule, and light could not penetrate the deserts nor the swamps, nor the strange cities where men and half-men lived. This face and this body have become engraven in your culture, as objects both of loathing and of worship, and it shall walk again, leaving its cloven hoofprint on the path of the night. This is the manifestation they called Satan, although they could never have known that this was one of my bodies in eons gone by, when I was the proud and evil Agnarga on a world so distant that your people have never perceived it. In the name of Agnarga, your people have committed indescribable sins, and offered backwards prayers, and held up inverted and perverted symbols of your greatest religions. Those things shall be as nothing, compared to what Satan shall do now."

The man pulled apart his cloak, to reveal an erect penis the size of a horse's tool, and the colour of aged wood. Its foreskin peeled back, and black ectoplasm billowed out of it, until the maggot-beast had once again taken on its huge and repulsive form.

"The people who creep on the surface of this earth are so ignorant," whispered the beast. "They have suspected my presence for so long. They have so many stories of the days when I was great. But they have never truly believed that I was still waiting for the Day of Iniquity, when the graves shall be opened not for judgment, but for the dead to rise again and shamble upon the earth to prey upon the living. The living have always fed upon the dead; now it is the turn of the corpses and their miserable spirits. They have never suspected that each of their legends has been one more piece in a jigsaw which could have proved my existence. Yes—gods came from out of the stars in the days when your people were little more than animals. We taught them powers and strengths and practices so arcane that your people can only whisper about them now. We mutated men into sea-people, so that they could serve us both on the land and under the waters, where our greatest citadels were. Yet you have forgotten the water-mutants, who terrorized you, or if you have not forgotten them, you think of them as fanciful fiction. Mermaids and mermen, you call them, and weave them into children's stories. We did many other things. We moved stones so vast that your people today believe their ancestors were magical. We laid down networks of psychic lines upon the earth through which we could communicate, and which men still believe have mystic powers. The whole human species was controlled from the underwater mountains of Atlantis, in a forgotten dynasty of indulgence and viciousness and corruption. They were great and terrifying days. They shall return."

Again, the maggot-beast appeared to shift and alter its form, until it stood before me as a huge cyclopean creature of gaseous milky white. It was this manifestation that gave off such an intense odour of rotting fish, and I recognized it straight away. The single eye was the evil-eye symbol of which Mrs. Thompson had spoken before her death. The creature was the actual beast from which some ancient artist had drawn the being now thought by popular scientists to be one of the "gods from outer space."

I dropped to my knees in the cold water. I don't know why. I was exhausted and bruised and defeated, and I couldn't see what I could possibly do to escape, how I could ever stop Chulthe from breaking loose from these subterranean lakes and recreating hell on earth.

I lifted my eyes towards the beast, and it made illusions for me. Out of the air, it drew pictures that lived and murmured and spoke and breathed. I saw men raking their own skin with barbed hooks, and mumbling at the agony of it. I saw men slicing open their own stomachs, and taking out their stomachs and their intestines in their hands. I saw children guzzling blood and wine mixed, and I heard their high, running laughter. Women poured blazing oil over their own heads, and stood with fiery hair, masturbating in frenzy at the pain. Naked girls crouched on all fours before whispering crowds, and were penetrated by apes and dogs. Their cries and whimpers of pleasure seemed to be hideously close, and yet thousands and millions of miles distant.

The illusions faded. The black beast was close to me now, not more than five or six feet away. It gave off an aura of *deadness* which was frightening and sickening, and even its insect eyes looked devoid of any kind of feeling or any kind of life.

"What are you going to do?" I asked it, and my voice echoed and re-echoed over and over and over again. "Are you going to kill me?"

The creature said nothing at first. Its sharp mandibles dripped with a kind of acrid fluid. Then it whispered: "I need your strength. I need your flesh. I have lain in these caves for so long, dry and powerless. When I have your flesh, I shall swim into the last cavern of all, which is the cavern you and your ridiculous friends first entered. That is the cavern which shall be my throne-room, and my unhallowed church, and from that cavern I shall begin to build my new empire."

More tremors rippled the surface of the subterranean lake, and the green fluorescence of the stalactites and stalagmites dimmed. They must have contained crystalline salts which were excited by the maggot-beast's psycho-kinetic energy, and that was why they glowed. I was glad they did, if glad is the right word. At least it was better than being devoured in complete darkness, by a beast I had never seen.

Kneeling in the cold water, I bowed my head and said a prayer to God. God, whatever I've done wrong, however impetuous and stupid and overbearing I've been, no matter how often I've refused to take other people's problems and other people's fears seriously, no matter what I've done, please deliver me from this Satanic creature, please deliver all of us. Amen. Oh, God. Amen.

There was a slight splashing sound on the surface of the lake. I raised my head, and turned around. The maggot-beast lifted its head, too, and I could see its eyes searching the water.

It took a few seconds before I saw what had made the splash. It was a human body, a woman's body, and it was drifting slowly towards us, still impelled by the earth-tremor which must have dislodged it from where it was trapped in the tunnel on the lake's bed. It was Alison Bodine, my dear friend and terrible enemy, whose death had at last released her from the claws and scales and tentacles of the crab-creature mutation. Even if God hadn't rescued me from Satan, He had taken Alison's soul, and left her body as it had been before.

Chulthe's attention was fixed on the corpse. Its mandibles juddered and squeaked, and its black wrinkled body contracted in peristalsis. It was dead human meat, just what the devil wanted. It was torn, maimed flesh, from which it could feed.

Chulthe slithered and rippled into the water with hardly a splash. It swam quickly and uncaringly, a hundred feet of wet black flesh, like a shark or a moray eel. In a second, its mandibles had risen from the water and snatched at Alison's body, and then it was curving around the surface of the lake and making its way back to the shore.

This was going to be the only chance I was ever going to get. I gulped an enormous breath, and I kicked away from the rocky beach with all my remaining strength, which God help me wasn't much. Chulthe, dragging Alison's body on to the shore, didn't even notice that I had gone, and that I was swimming out towards the place where I had first risen from the lake's bottom with desperate, panicky strokes. I swam and I swam and it seemed to take me for ever to cover nothing more than a few feet.

I glanced back over my shoulder. Alison's body was sprawled out on the rocks, and the maggot-beast was dipping its head towards her torn-open entrails. I took another breath and swam harder, telling myself that my feet weren't really chilled, that my hands weren't really numb, and that I was really going to make it. For the first time in my life, I didn't believe myself.

At last, Chulthe and his dead victim disappeared around the curve in the cavern, and I was treading water over the spot where I guessed I had first emerged. I lifted my head from the surface, and I took one, two, three hefty breaths. Then I sucked in a fourth breath, as agonizingly deep as I could, and I dived beneath the lake, and struck out for the bottom.

Cold water leaked up my nose and into my ears. But I kept on swimming downwards, my eyes wide open, searching and searching for the tunnel that led through to the next cavern. The faint green glimmer of light faded away and then I was swimming in total darkness, forcing myself down and down to the bed of the lake.

I reached it sooner than I had expected. But there was solid rock there, rough and uncompromising. No tunnel. I swam slowly around, kicking my legs and flapping my arms to keep myself submerged, and I felt like nothing less than a fully dressed plumber under twenty feet of iced water looking for a hole that I probably wouldn't have the breath to swim through, even if I found it. I began to feel light-headed and silly, and it occurred to me that if I breathed in water, like I had in my dream, I could probably swim just as well.

I found the tunnel without even realising it. I was struggling so hard to keep myself down on the lake bottom that I swam right down into the cavity before I understood what had happened. Suddenly I felt rock all around me, and nothing but water beneath me, and I struck out desperately pulling myself along by seizing the jagged sides of the tunnel and heaving my body forward.

It took forever. My head was bursting again from lack of air. But I knew that I had a chance, and a chance was all I wanted. I struggled on, and on, and then I felt myself rising, felt myself floating buoyantly upwards until the refracted criss-cross beams of flashlights penetrated the water and I rose from the surface with my lungs screaming for air, but safe.

"Mason!" called Dan, and I wiped the water out of my eyes and saw him standing on that natural balcony, with Shelley beside him. Deputy Martino was there, too, and two more police officers, and a short man in white coveralls whom I recognised as Pete Lansky from Litchfield Quarries. I swam the last few strokes towards the balcony, and Dan knelt down and helped me clamber, shivering and dripping, from the lake.

Dan was close to tears. He pressed his hand

against his bald head and said: "I thought I'd lost you there. I really thought I'd lost you. What happened?"

I gave a shivery smile. "Nothing much. I'll tell you later. I just want to get out of here."

Dan said: "We're going to dynamite the cavern. That's what Pete Lansky is doing down here. I went back and sent up a message to have them bring him along."

"You're going to dynamite it?" I asked him. "What the hell good is that going to do? Dan, that thing is right in the next chamber of this water-system, and whatever you do it's going to come swimming through someplace and fix us for good."

Dan shook his head. "I know that. Or at least I guessed it. That's why I called for Pete. You see, this cavern system isn't all flooded. As soon as you disappeared, I went looking for help, but I missed the tunnel entrance on my way back, and I went down another tunnel that leads to a deep cave just alongside this one. The only difference is, this cave was dry, and when I flashed my light down and took a look at it, it was pretty clear that it led down to a whole new system of caves that are all dry, too."

Deputy Martino handed me his coat, and I hung it around my shoulders to keep me warm. All the same, my teeth were chattering like crazy, and I knew that I was going to have to find dry clothes and a stiff bourbon if I didn't want to go down with pneumonia.

"So what?" I asked Dan. "You've found a whole system of dry caves. So what?"

Dan laid his hand on my shoulder. "So we lay a charge just under the surface of the lake here, or rather Pete Lansky does, and we blow a hole clean through to the dry caverns. The water pours from the flooded caverns into the dry caverns, and we drain the whole structure down to a much lower level."

"Leaving Chulthe stranded again?"

"That's right."

I ran my hand through my dripping, freezing hair. "Dan," I told him, "you're worth something after all."

"I always knew you cared," said Dan. "Now pick up this cat of yours, and get back up to the surface. Pete says it won't take more than ten minutes to fuse the charge, and then we're all getting the hell out of here for good."

I paused for a moment. I looked around the pillared cavern, at the dark lake waters into which so many people had been dragged. There wasn't any doubt at all that it was the vestibule of hell, the entrance to an ungodly world where men behaved like beasts, and beasts walked the earth like men. I shuddered, and then one of the officers led me away. Shelley followed behind, disdainful of my offer to pick him up. He didn't like getting wet, you understand.

We squeezed our way back up the tunnel to the cave of albino bats, and there was a harness waiting for me. I buckled myself up, held Shelley firmly under my arm, and then tugged the rope to be hoisted up above the ground.

It was still raining as the drilling rig lifted me out of the hole and up on to the Bodines' back yard again. The drilling crew were hunched under waterproof hats and coats, and the police were all wearing their raincapes. There was an intense smell of fresh air, and the arc-lights glared and sparkled in the wet, and not far away a cluster of police cars and ambulances were waiting, their beacons flashing red and blue in the darkness.

I was helped to the side of the drill-shaft, and unbuckled from my harness. Two medics came across with a stretcher, and asked me how I was feeling. "Sick," I told them, "and tired." One of them, his spectacles beaded with rain, gave me a miniature bottle of Yukon Jack, which I drank in one gulp. I coughed, and sat on the stretcher for a while, letting the rain sift down on to my head.

After a moment or two, I was ready to go to the ambulance. I let them take off my wet clothes, and give me a shot of antibiotics in case any of my lacerations were infected. But I wouldn't let them drive me off to New Milford hospital until Dan and Deputy Martino were out of the hole, and I knew that the charge had gone off.

The medics tried to talk to me, but I was beyond talking. I lay back in the ambulance wrapped in blankets, and all I could think about was that huge wrinkled black maggot, that devil beast called Quithe, or Chulthe, or Satan. That thing that had left its horrifying mark so strongly on human life that, even after thousands of years, its memory had lingered. That thing that brought out man's most sadistic, lustful and self-destructive feelings. The thing of the dark, subterranean caves beneath Connecticut, which was determined to break loose.

It was no wonder that there had been witch-trials in Massachusetts, with Chulthe sleeping in the water systems of New England. It was no wonder that Celtic fishermen had talked of Shelly-coat, the crab-creature which lured seafaring men to their death. None of the stories and myths of evil spirits seemed ridiculous now; none of the far-flung theories about gods from the stars. They had all originated from the beast-god Chulthe who had ruled Atlantis, the beast-god who wanted to rule again now. They were all true.

I closed my eyes and I could see the devil's obscene illusions again. I could see women's thighs slippery with blood. I could see men's agonized faces as they deliberately mutilated themselves. I could see children crushed for the passing pleasure of strange creatures.

Suddenly, a hand touched my face. I opened my eyes. It was Dan. His face was grimy, and he stank of caves and sweat, but he grinned, and said: "We're almost ready. Pete's wiring up the detonator now. Will they let you out of here to watch?"

The medics looked at each other, and pulled pessimistic faces. But I said quietly: "I don't want to watch. Just do a good job, huh? Just empty that water out of those caves."

Pete Lansky appeared, and looked in at the tail of the ambulance. His woollen hat was sparkling with rain. "How do you feel, Mason?" he asked. "You look like you went to hell and back."

"You could say that, Lansky. When are you going to set off the dynamite?"

"I'm off to do it right now. You just tell those

medics to stay right here. You'll hear something like you never heard before."

"Okay, Lansky. You hear that, guys?"

The medics shrugged, and nodded.

We waited four or five minutes. Then we heard a shrill whistle blow, and some of the drill-rig crew came past us in the rain back out of danger. Another whistle blew, twice, and we guessed that this meant Lansky was about to press down the plunger.

Dan stayed by the ambulance. At first, there was nothing. But then we heard a deep, deep rumbling sound, which shook the ground under our foot. The rumbling was followed by a loud groaning rip, as the rock walls which divided the flooded caverns from the dry caverns were breached, and then the ground shook again as millions of gallons of water collapsed through the hole that Lansky's dynamite had blasted open, and cascaded down cave after cave, vault after vault, emptying out the devil's cathedral, and the strange cavern where Chulthe fed and dwelt and dreamed, foaming and splashing through tunnels and galleries and underground chasms.

After a while, there was silence. Dan looked at me, and said, "That's it. It sounds like we've done it."

"Is anybody going to check?"

"Maybe later. But that's the county's responsibility. Let them handle it. If I were you, I'd go right back to being a plumber."

I said to the medics: "Let's go, guys. I don't think there's anything else to wait for."

One of them said: "Your cat's sitting up front. I

hope you realize that animals aren't strictly allowed in medical emergency vehicles."

I closed my eyes. I was very tired. I told them softly: "Shelley's no animal. Shelley's my friend."

Dan closed the ambulance tailgate, and I think I heard the siren begin to whoop as they drove me away to the hospital. I couldn't be sure.

Rheta came to see me the next morning. I was sitting up in bed, reading a dog-eared copy of McCall's, and occasionally looking out at the rain which ran down the hospital windows. I felt stiff and bruised, and a little distant, but I was anxious to get home and sort out my flooded living-room. I was anxious to get back to normal.

Rheta was wearing a plain black wool suit which made her look severe but very sexy. She sat down by my bed, and laid her hand on mine, and gave me a smile that made me feel better than a whole week's course of penicillin and two anti-tetanus jabs.

"How are you feeling?" she asked me.

"Fine, I guess."

"You still haven't told us what really happened."

I dropped my gaze. "Give me some time. We could talk about it over dinner one evening."

She kept on smiling. "Maybe," she said.

"Is Dan okay?" I asked her.

"He's fine. Just fine. Oh, and I talked to my friend at the sheriff's office. They found that man Karlen. You know the one they thought was missing, and had turned into a crab-creature? He was in Philadelphia, seeing some woman. It was all pretty complicated, but he was alive, and well, and he hadn't turned into anything nasty."

"Good," I nodded. I didn't know what else I should say.

Rheta said: "You'll probably want some help fixing up your house again."

I laced my fingers between hers. "I could sure use it."

She looked me straight in the eye. "Well, we'll be glad to help. If you need anybody to wash drapes, or clean rugs, we'll come up next weekend, and give you a hand."

I paused. The television in my room was turned down low, but it was so quiet that I could hear one of the girls in *As The World Turns* say: *"This is it, then? The finish?"*

"We?" I asked Rheta. Carefully.

She smiled. "Kenny Packer. I guess you could say we're engaged."

I kept my fingers interlaced with hers. It would have been childish to break free. It would have seemed like jealousy.

"You're going to marry Pigskin Packer?" I asked her. "I mean, really marry him?"

"Yes," she said, very softly.

I closed my eyes. I could imagine Rheta as the devil had offered her to me, in that flame-red bra which exposed her nipples; in those scarlet stockings and that tiny red G-string. I could see the way the tight elastic came up between the white cheeks of her bottom.

No wonder, I thought. No wonder. No wonder people served the devil, and made deals with him. No wonder people used to worship the beast-gods who lived in the sunken mountains of Atlantis. There are always moments of regret, of frustration, of lust for somebody or something that we can never hope to have.

And as long as men and women are susceptible to greed, and jealousy, and wanton desire, then the dried-up remains of Chulthe, in their caverns under Connecticut, will always be a threat to us. When it thunders hard, and it rains hard, and nights get dark, then Satan could very easily stir again.

I said to Rheta: "Make sure that Shelley's getting his chopped liver, won't you?"

She smiled. "Sure I will. But I know you can trust Dan."

She bent forward and kissed my cheek. She smelled warm and fragrant and I probably wouldn't feel her this close to me again. She whispered: "I'll always be fond of you, Mason. You know that."

After she'd gone, and left me with a couple of Florida oranges and a copy of *Jaws 2*, I muttered under my breath. "Like hell you will."

# IN THE DARK OF THE MOON —
# TERROR AWAITS!

## Stories of the Occult

# GRAHAM MASTERTON

Buy them at your local bookstore or use this handy coupon:
Clip and mail this page with your order.

Publishers Book and Audio Mailing Service
P.O. Box 120159, Staten Island, NY 10312-0004

Please send me the book(s) I have checked above. I am enclosing $_____
(please add $1.25 for the first book, and $.25 for each additional book to
cover postage and handling. Send check or money order only — no CODs.)

Name _____

Address _____

City _____ State/Zip _____

Please allow six weeks for delivery. Prices subject to change without notice.

# NEW VOICES IN HORROR